THE NAULAHKA

RUDYARD KIPLING

The Centenary Edition

Actions and Reactions
Captains Courageous
The Day's Work
Debits and Credits
A Diversity of Creatures
The Jungle Book
The Second Jungle Book
Just So Stories
Kim
Life's Handicap
The Light that Failed
Limits and Renewals
Many Inventions
The Naulahka
Plain Tales from the Hills
Puck of Pook's Hill
Rewards and Fairies
Soldiers Three
Something of Myself
Stalky & Co.
Thy Servant a Dog
Traffics and Discoveries
Wee Willie Winkie

THE
NAULAHKA

A STORY OF
WEST AND EAST

BY

RUDYARD KIPLING

AND

WOLCOTT BALESTIER

MACMILLAN LONDON

ISBN 0 333 32811 6

MACMILLAN LONDON LIMITED
London and Basingstoke

Associated companies in Auckland, Dallas,
Delhi, Dublin, Hong Kong, Johannesburg,
Lagos, Manzini, Melbourne, Nairobi,
New York, Singapore, Tokyo, Washington
and Zaria

First edition 1892
Reprinted 1901, 1912, 1916, 1918, 1922, 1936
Edition de Luxe 1898
Uniform edition 1899
Pocket edition 1908
Bombay edition 1913
Service edition 1915
Sussex edition 1938
Library edition 1950
Centenary edition (n.s.) 1982
Paperback edition 1983

Printed in Hong Kong

THE NAULAHKA:

A STORY OF WEST AND EAST

I

There was a strife 'twixt man and maid—
   Oh that was at the birth o' time !
But what befell 'twixt man and maid,
   Oh that's beyond the grip o' rhyme.
'Twas : 'Sweet, I must not bide wi' you,'
   And : 'Love, I canna bide alone ' ;
B, baith were young, and baith were true,
   A ᚺ baith were hard as the nether stone.

Auchinleck's Ride.

NICHOLAS TARVIN sat in the moonlight on the unrailed bridge that crossed the irrigating ditch above Topaz, dangling his feet over the stream. A brown, sad-eyed little woman sat beside him, staring quietly at the moon. She was tanned with the tan of the girl who does not mind wind and rain and sun, and her eyes were sad with the settled melancholy of eyes that know big mountains, and seas of plain, and care, and life. The women of the West shade such eyes under their hands at sunset in their cabin-doors, scanning those

hills or those grassless, treeless plains for the home-
coming of their men.   A hard life is always hardest
for the woman.

Kate Sheriff had lived with her face to the West
and with her smouldering eyes fixed upon the
wilderness since she could walk.   She had advanced
into the wilderness with the railroad.   Until she
had gone away to school, she had never lived where
the railroad ran both ways.   She had often stayed
long enough at the end of a section with her family
to see the first glimmering streaks of the raw dawn
of civilisation, usually helped out by the electric
light ; but in the new and still newer lands to which
her father's civil engineering orders called them
from year to year there were not even arc lamps.
There was a saloon under a tent, and there was the
section-house, where they lived, and where her
mother had sometimes taken to board the men
employed by her husband.   But it was not these
influences alone that had produced the young woman
of twenty-three who sat near Tarvin, and who had
just told him gently that she liked him, but that
she had a duty elsewhere.

This duty, as she conceived it, was, briefly, to
spend her life in the East in the effort to better the
condition of the women of India.   It had come to
her as an inspiration and a command two years
before, toward the end of her second year at the
St. Louis school, where she went to tie up the loose
ends of the education she had given herself in
lonely camps.

Kate's mission had been laid on her one April
afternoon, warmed and sunned with the first breath

of spring. The green trees, the swelling buds, and the sunlight outside had tempted her from the prospect of a lecture on India by a Hindu woman ; and it was finally because it was a school duty not to be escaped that she listened to Pundita Ramabai's account of the sad case of her sisters at home. It was a heart-breaking story, and the girls, making the offerings begged of them in strange accents, went from it stilled and awed to the measure of their natures, and talked it over in the corridors in whispers, until a nervous giggle broke the tension, and they began chattering again.

Kate made her way from the hall with the fixed, inward-looking eye, the flaming cheek, and air-borne limbs of one on whom the mantle of the Spirit has descended. She went quickly out into the school-garden, away from everybody, and paced the flower-bordered walks, exalted, rich, sure, happy. She had found herself. The flowers knew it, the tender-leaved trees overhead were aware, the shining sky had word. Her head was high ; she wanted to dance, and, much more, she wanted to cry. A pulse in her forehead went beat, beat ; the warm blood sang through her veins ; she stopped every little while to take a deep draught of the good air. In those moments she dedicated herself.

All her life should take breath from this hour ; she vowed it to the service this day revealed to her, as once to the prophets—vowed all her strength and mind and heart. The angel of the Lord had laid a command upon her. She obeyed joyfully.

And now, after two years spent in fitting herself for her calling, she returned to Topaz, a capable

and instructed nurse, on fire for her work in India,
to find that Tarvin wished her to stay at Topaz
and marry him.

'You can call it what you like,' Tarvin told her,
while she gazed at the moon ; 'you can call it duty,
or you can call it woman's sphere, or you can call
it, as that meddling missionary called it at church
to-night, "carrying the light to them that sit in
darkness." I've no doubt you've got a halo to put
to it ; they've taught you names enough for things
in the East. But for me, what I say is, it's a
freeze-out.'

'Don't say that, Nick ! It's a call.'

'You've got a call to stay at home ; and if you
haven't heard of it, I'm a committee to notify you,'
said Tarvin doggedly. He shied a pebble into the
irrigating ditch, and eyed the racing current with
lowering brows.

'Dear Nick, how can you bear to urge any one
who is free to stay at home and shirk after what
we've heard to-night ?'

'Well, by the holy smoke, some one has got to
urge girls to stand by the old machine, these days !
You girls are no good at all under the new
regulations until you desert. It's the road to
honour.'

'Desert !' gasped Kate. She turned her eyes
on him.

'Well, what do you call it ? That's what the
little girl I used to know on Section 10 of the N.
P. and Y. would have called it. O Kate dear, put
yourself back in the old days ; remember yourself
then, remember what we used to be to each other,

and see if you don't see it that way. You've got a
father and mother, haven't you? You can't say it's
the square thing to give them up. And you've
got a man sitting beside you on this bridge who
loves you for all he's worth—loves you, you dear
old thing, for keeps. You used to like him a
little bit too. Eh?'

He slid his arm about her as he spoke, and for
a moment she let it rest there.

'Does that mean nothing to you either? Don't
you seem to see a call here, too, Kate?'

He forced her to turn her face to him, and
gazed wistfully into her eyes for a moment. They
were brown, and the moonlight deepened their sober
depths.

'Do you think you have a claim?' she asked,
after a moment.

'I'll think almost anything to keep you. But
no; I haven't any claim—or none at least that you
are not free to jump. But we all have a claim;
hang it, the situation has a claim. If you don't
stay, you go back on it. That's what I mean.'

'You don't take a serious view of things, Nick,'
she said, putting down his arm.

Tarvin didn't see the connection; but he said
good-humouredly, 'Oh yes, I do! There's no
serious view of life I won't take in fun to please
you.'

'You see,—you're not in earnest.'

'There's one thing I'm in earnest about,' he
whispered in her ear.

'Is there?' She turned away her head.

'I can't live without you.' He leaned toward

her, and added in a lower voice : 'Another thing, Kate—I won't.'

Kate compressed her lips. She had her own will. They sat on the bridge beating out their difference until they heard the kitchen clock in a cabin on the other side of the ditch strike eleven. The stream came down out of the mountains that loomed above them ; they were half-a-mile from the town. The stillness and the loneliness closed on Tarvin with a physical grip as Kate got up and said decisively that she must go home. He knew she meant that she must go to India, and his own will crumpled helplessly for the moment within hers. He asked himself whether this was the will by which he earned his living, the will which at twenty-eight had made him a successful man by Topaz standards, which was taking him to the State Legislature, and which would one day take him much further, unless what ceased to be what. He shook himself scornfully ; but he had to add to himself that after all she was only a girl, if he did love her, before he could stride to her side, as she turned her back on him, and say, 'See here, young woman, you're away off !'

She did not answer, but walked on.

'You're not going to throw your life away on this Indian scheme,' he pursued. 'I won't have it. Your father won't have it. Your mother will kick and scream at it, and I'll be there to encourage her. We have some use for your life, if you haven't. You don't know the size of your contract. The land isn't fit for rats ; it's the Bad Lands—yes, that's just what it is, a great big Bad

Lands—morally, physically, and agriculturally, Bad Lands. It's no place for white men, let alone white women ; there's no climate, no government, no drainage ; and there's cholera, heat, and fighting until you can't rest. You'll find it all in the Sunday papers. You want to stay right where you are, young lady ! '

She stopped a moment in the road they were following back to Topaz and glanced at his face in the moonlight. He took her hand, and, for all his masterfulness, awaited her word with parted lips.

'You're a good man, Nick, but,' she drooped her eyes, 'I'm going to sail on the 31st for Calcutta.'

II

Beware the man who's crossed in love,
 For pent-up steam must find its vent ;
Step back when he is on the move,
 And lend him all the Continent.
                          The Buck and the Saw.

To sail from New York on the 31st she must leave Topaz by the 27th at latest. It was now the 15th. Tarvin made the most of the intervening time. He called on her at her home every evening, and argued it out with her.

Kate listened with the gentlest willingness to be convinced, but with a dread firmness round the corners of her mouth, and with a sad wish to be good to him, if she could, battling in her eyes with a sadder helplessness.

'I'm called!' she cried. 'I'm called. I can't get away from it. I can't help listening. I can't help going.'

And, as she told him, grieving, how the cry of her sisters out of that dim misery, that was yet so distinct, tugged at her heart—how the useless horror and torture of their lives called on her by night and by day, Tarvin could not refuse to respect the solemnly felt need that drew her from him. He could not help begging her in every accent he knew not to hearken to it, but the painful pull of the cry she heard was not a strange or incredible thing to his own generous heart. He only urged hotly that there were other cries, and that there were other people to attend to this one. He, too, had a need, the need for her ; and she another, if she would stop a moment to listen to it. They needed each other ; that was the supreme need. The women in India could wait ; they would go over and look them up later, when the Three C.'s had come to Topaz, and he had made his pile. Meanwhile there was happiness ; meanwhile there was love ! He was ingenious, he was deeply in love, he knew what he wanted, and he found the most persuasive language for making it seem to be what she wanted in disguise. Kate had to strengthen her resolution often in the intervals between his visits. She could not say much in reply. She had no such gift of communicating herself as Tarvin. Hers was the still, deep, voiceless nature that can only feel and act.

She had the kind of pluck and the capacity for silent endurance which goes with such natures, or she must often have faltered and turned back from the resolve which had come upon her in the school-garden that spring day, in the two years that followed it. Her parents were the first obstacle. They refused outright to allow her to study medicine. She had wished to be both physician and nurse, believing that in India she would find use for both callings ; but since she could follow only one, she was content to enrol herself as a student at a New York training-school for nurses, and this her parents suffered in the bewilderment of finding that they had forgotten how to oppose her gently resolute will through the lifelong habit of yielding to it.

Her ideas had made her mother wish, when she explained them to her, that she had let her grow up wild, as she had once seemed certain to do. She was even sorry that the child's father had at last found something to do away from the awful railroad. The railroad now ran two ways from Topaz ; Kate had returned from school to find the track stretching a hundred miles to the westward, and her family still there. This time the boom had overtaken them before they could get away. Her father had bought city lots in the acre form and was too rich to move. He had given up his calling and had gone into politics.

Sheriff's love for his daughter was qualified by his general flatness ; but it was the clinging affection not uncommon with shallow minds, and he had the habit of indulgence toward her which is the portion of an only child. He was accustomed to say that 'what she did was about right,' he guessed, and he was usually content to let it go at that. He was anxious now that his riches should do her some good, and Kate had not the heart to tell him the ways she had found to make them do her good. To her mother she confided all her plan ; to her father she only said that she wished to learn to be a trained nurse. Her mother grieved in secret with the grim, philosophic, almost cheerful hopelessness of women whose lives have taught them always to expect the worst. It was a sore trial to Kate to disappoint her mother ; and it cut her to the heart to know that she could not do what both her father and mother expected of her. Indefinite as the expectation was—it was simply that she should come home and live, and be a young lady, like the rest of the world—she felt its justice and reason, and she did not weep the less for them, because for herself she believed, modestly, that it was ordered otherwise.

This was her first trouble. The dissonance between those holy moments in the garden and the hard prose which was to give them reality and effect, grew deeper as she went on. It was daunting, and sometimes it was heart-sickening ; but she went forward—not always strong, not every moment brave, and only a very little wise, but always forward.

The life at the training-school was a cruel disillusion. She had not expected the path she had set before her to bloom with ease ; but at the end of her first month she could have laughed bitterly at the difference between her consecrating dreams and the fact. The dreams looked to her vocation ; the fact took no account of it. She had hoped to befriend misery, to bring help and healing to pain from the first days of her apprenticeship. What she was actually set to do was to scald babies' milk-cans.

Her further duties in these early days were no more nearly related to the functions of a nurse, and looking about her among the other girls to see how they kept their ideals alight in the midst of work so little connected with their future calling, she perceived that they got on for the most part by not having any. As she advanced, and was trusted first with babies themselves, and later with the actual work of nursing, she was made to feel how her own purpose isolated her. The others were here for business. With one or two exceptions they had apparently taken up nursing as they might have taken up dressmaking. They were here to learn how to make twenty dollars a week, and the sense of this dispirited her even more than the work she was given to do as a preparation for her high calling. The talk of the Arkansas girl, who sat on a table and swung her legs while she discussed her flirtations with the young doctors at the clinics, seemed in itself sometimes a final discouragement. Through all ran the bad food, the scanty sleep, the insufficient hours for recreation, the cruelly long hours assigned for work, the nervous strain of supporting the life from the merely physical point of view.

In addition to the work which she shared with the others, she was taking regular lessons in Hindustani; and she was constantly grateful for the earlier days which had given her robust health and a sound body. Without them she must often have broken down; and soon it began to be a duty not to break down, because it had become possible to help suffering a little. It was this which reconciled her finally to the low and sordid conditions under which the whole affair of her preparation went on.

The repulsive aspects of the nursing itself she

did not mind. On the contrary, she found herself
liking them as she got into the swing of her work ;
and when, at the end of her first year, she was
placed in charge of a ward at the women's hospital,
under another nurse, she began to feel herself
drawing in sight of her purpose, and kindled with
an interest which made even the surgical operations
seem good to her because they helped, and because
they allowed her to help a little.

From this time she went on working strongly
and efficiently toward her end. Above all, she
wanted to be competent—to be wise and thorough.
When the time came when those helpless, walled-
up women should have no knowledge and no
comfort to lean on but hers, she meant that they
should lean on the strength of solid intelligence.
Her trials were many, but it was her consolation
in the midst of them all that her women loved her,
and lived upon her comings and goings. Her
devotion to her purpose carried her forward. She
was presently in full charge, and in that long, bare
ward where she strengthened so many sufferers for
the last parting, where she lived with death and
dealt with it, where she went about softly, soothing
unspeakable pain, learning the note of human
anguish, hearing no sound but the murmur of
suffering or relief, she sounded one night the
depths of her own nature, and received from an
inward monitor the confirmation of her mission.
She consecrated herself to it afresh with a joy
beyond her first joy of discovery.

And now, every night at half-past eight, Tarvin's
hat hung on the hat-rack in the hall-way of her

home. He removed it gloomily at a little after
eleven, spending the interval in talking over her
mission with her persuasively, commandingly, im-
ploringly, indignantly. His indignation was for
her plan, but it would sometimes irrepressibly
transfer itself to Kate. She was capable not only
of defending her plan, but of defending herself
and keeping her temper ; and as this last was an
art beyond Nick, these sessions often came to an
end suddenly, and early in the evening. But the
next night he would come and sit before her in
penitence, and with his elbows on his knees, and
his head supported moodily in his hands, would
entreat her submissively to have some sense. This
never lasted long, and evenings of this kind usually
ended in his trying to pound sense into her by
hammering his chair-arm with a convinced fist.

No tenderness could leave Tarvin without the
need to try to make others believe as he did ; but
it was a good-humoured need, and Kate did not
dislike it. She liked so many things about him,
that often as they sat thus, facing each other, she
let her fancy wander where it had wandered in her
school-girl vacations—in a possible future spent
by his side. She brought her fancy back again
sharply. She had other things to think of now ;
but there must always be something between her
and Tarvin different from her relation to any other
man. They had lived in the same house on the
prairie at the end of the section, and had risen to
take up the same desolate life together morning
after morning. The sun brought the morning
greyly up over the sad grey plain, and at night left

them alone together in the midst of the terrible
spaces of silence. They broke the ice together in
the muddy river near the section-house, and Tarvin
carried her pail back for her. A score of other
men lived under the same roof, but it was Tarvin
who was kind. The others ran to do what she
asked them to do. Tarvin found things to do,
and did them while she slept. There was plenty
to do. Her mother had a family of twenty-five,
twenty of whom were boarders—the men working
in one capacity or another directly under Sheriff.
The hands engaged in the actual work of building
the railroad lived in huge barracks near by, or in
temporary cabins or tents. The Sheriffs had a
house ; that is, they lived in a structure with pro-
jecting eaves, windows that could be raised or
lowered, and a verandah. But this was the sum
of their conveniences, and the mother and daughter
did their work alone with the assistance of two
Swedes, whose muscles were firm but whose cookery
was vague.

Tarvin helped her, and she learned to lean on
him ; she let him help her, and Tarvin loved her
for it. The bond of work shared, of a mutual
dependence, of isolation, drew them to each other ;
and when Kate left the section-house for school
there was a tacit understanding between them.
The essence of such an understanding, of course,
lies in the woman's recognition of it. When she
came back from school for the first holiday, Kate's
manner did not deny her obligation, but did not
confirm the understanding, and Tarvin, restless
and insistent as he was about other things, did not

like to force his claim upon her. It wasn't a
claim he could take into court.

This kind of forbearance was well enough while
he expected to have her always within reach, while
he imagined for her the ordinary future of an
unmarried girl. But when she said she was going
to India she changed the case. He was not
thinking of courtesy or forbearance, or of the
propriety of waiting to be formally accepted as he
talked to her on the bridge, and afterward in the
evenings. He ached with his need for her, and
with the desire to keep her.

But it looked as if she were going—going in
spite of everything he could say, in spite of his
love. He had made her believe in that, if it was
any comfort; and it was real enough to her to
hurt her, which *was* a comfort!

Meanwhile she was costing him much, in one
way and another, and she liked him well enough
to have a conscience about it. But when she
would tell him that he must not waste so much
time and thought on her, he would ask her not to
bother her little head about him : he saw more in
her than he did in real estate or politics just then ;
he knew what he was about.

'I know,' returned Kate. 'But you forget
what a delicate position you put me in. I don't
want to be responsible for your defeat. Your
party will say I planned it.'

Tarvin made a positive and unguarded remark
about his party, to which Kate replied that if he
didn't care she must ; she couldn't have it said,
after the election, that he had neglected his canvass

for her, and that her father had won his seat in consequence.

'Of course,' she added frankly, 'I want father to go to the State legislature, and I don't want you to go, because if you win the election, he can't; but I don't want to help prevent you from getting in.'

'Don't worry about your father getting that seat, young lady!' cried Tarvin. 'If that's all you've got to lie awake about, you can sleep from now until the Three C.'s comes to Topaz. I'm going to Denver myself this fall, and you'd better make your plans to come along. Come! How would it suit you to be the speaker's wife, and live on Capitol Hill?'

Kate liked him well enough to go half credulously with him in his customary assumption that the difference between his having anything he wanted and his not having it, was the difference between his wanting it and his not wanting it.

'Nick!' she exclaimed, deriding but doubtful, 'you won't be speaker!'

'I'd undertake to be governor, if I thought the idea would fetch you. Give me a word of hope, and you'll see what I'd do!'

'No, no!' she said, shaking her head. 'My governors are all Rajahs, and they live a long way from here.'

'But say, India's half the size of the United States. Which State are you going to?'

'Which——?'

'Ward, township, county, section? What's your post-office address?'

'Rhatore, in the province of Gokral Seetarun, Rajputana, India.'

'All that!' he repeated despairingly. There was a horrible definiteness about it; it almost made him believe she was going. He saw her drifting hopelessly out of his life into a land on the nether rim of the world, named out of the *Arabian Nights* and probably populated out of them. 'Nonsense, Kate! You're not going to try to live in any such heathen fairyland. What's it got to do with Topaz, Kate? What's it got to do with home? You can't do it, I tell you. Let them nurse themselves. Leave it to them! Or leave it to me! I'll go over myself, turn some of their pagan jewels into money, and organise a nursing corps on a plan that you shall dictate. Then we'll be married, and I'll take you out to look at my work. I'll make a go of it. Don't say they're poor. That necklace alone would fetch money enough to organise an army of nurses! If your missionary told the truth in his sermon at church the other night, it would pay the national debt. Diamonds the size of hens' eggs, yokes of pearls, coils of sapphires the girth of a man's wrist, and emeralds until you can't rest —and they hang all that around the neck of an idol, or keep it stored in a temple, and call on decent white girls to come out and help nurse them! It's what I call cheek.'

'As if money could help them! It's not that. There's no charity or kindness or pity in money, Nick; the only real help is to give yourself.'

'All right. Then give me too! I'll go

along,' he said, returning to the safer humorous view.

She laughed, but stopped herself suddenly. 'You mustn't come to India, Nick. You won't do that? You won't follow me! You shan't.'

'Well, if I get a place as rajah, I don't say I wouldn't. There might be a dollar in it.'

'Nick! They wouldn't let an American be a rajah.'

It is strange that men to whom life is a joke find comfort in women to whom it is a prayer.

'They might let him *run* a rajah, though,' said Tarvin, undisturbed; 'and it might be the softer snap. Rajahing itself is classed extra hazardous, I think.'

'How?'

'By the accident insurance companies—double premium. None of *my* companies would touch the risk. They might take a vizier, though,' he added meditatively. 'They come from that *Arabian Nights* section, don't they?'

'Well, you are not to come,' she said definitively. 'You must keep away. Remember that.'

Tarvin got up suddenly. 'Oh, good-night! *Good*-night!' he cried.

He shook himself together impatiently, and waved her from him with a parting gesture of rejection and cancellation. She followed him into the passage, where he was gloomily taking his hat from its wonted peg; but he would not even let her help him on with his coat.

No man can successfully conduct a love-affair and a political canvass at the same time. It was perhaps the perception of this fact that had led Sheriff to bend an approving eye on the attentions which his opponent in the coming election had lately been paying his daughter. Tarvin had always been interested in Kate, but not so consecutively and intensely. Sheriff was stumping the district and was seldom at home, but in his irregular appearances at Topaz he smiled stolidly on his rival's occupation. In looking forward to an easy victory over him in the joint debate at Cañon City, however, he had perhaps relied too much on the younger man's absorption. Tarvin's consciousness that he had not been playing his party fair had lately chafed against his pride of success. The result was irritation, and Kate's prophecies and insinuations were pepper on an open wound.

The Cañon City meeting was set down for the night following the conversation just recorded, and Tarvin set foot on the shaky dry goods box platform at the roller skating rink that night, with a raging young intention to make it understood that he was still here—if he *was* in love.

Sheriff had the opening, and Tarvin sat in the background dangling a long, restless leg from one knee. The patchily illumined huddle of auditors below him looked up at a nervous, bony, loose-hung man, with a kind, clever, aggressive eye, and a masterful chin. His nose was prominent, and he had the furrowed forehead and the hair thinned about the temples which come to young men in the West. The alert, acute glance which went roving about the hall, measuring the audience to

which he was to speak, had the look of sufficiency
to the next need, whatever it might be, which,
perhaps, more than anything else, commends men
to other men beyond the Mississippi. He was
dressed in the short sack-coat, which is good
enough for most Western public functions ; but
he had left at Topaz the flannel of everyday wear,
and was clad in the white linen of civilisation.

He was wondering, as he listened to Sheriff,
how a father could have the heart to get off false
views on silver and the tariff to this crowd, while
his daughter was hatching that ghastly business at
home. The true views were so much mixed up
in his own mind with Kate, that when he himself
rose at last to answer Sheriff, he found it hard not
to ask how the deuce a man expected an intelligent
mass meeting to accept the political economy he
was trying to apply to the government of a State,
when he couldn't so much as run his own family ?
Why in the world didn't he stop his daughter
from making such a hash of her life ?—that was
what he wanted to know. What were fathers
for ? He reserved these apt remarks, and
launched instead upon a flood of figures, facts,
and arguments.

Tarvin had precisely the gift by which the
stump orator coils himself into the heart of the
stump auditor : he upbraided, he arraigned ; he
pleaded, insisted, denounced ; he raised his lean,
long arms, and called the gods and the statistics
and the Republican party to witness, and, when he
could make a point that way, he did not scorn to
tell a story. 'Why,' he would cry defiantly, in

that colloquial shout which the political orator uses for his anecdotes, 'that is like a man I used to know back in Wisconsin, who——' It wasn't very much like the man in Wisconsin; and Tarvin had never been in Wisconsin, and didn't know the man; but it was a good story, and when the crowd howled with delight Sheriff gathered himself together a little and tried to smile, and that was what Tarvin wanted.

There were dissentient voices, and the jointness of the debate was sometimes not confined to the platform; but the deep, relishing groans which would often follow applause or laughter, acted as a spur to Tarvin, who had joined the janitor of the rink that afternoon in mixing the dusky brew on the table before him, and who really did not need a spur. Under the inspiration of the mixture in the pitcher, the passionate resolve in his heart, and the groans and hisses, he melted gradually into an ecstasy of conviction which surprised even himself, and he began to feel at last that he had his audience under his hand. Then he gripped them, raised them aloft like a conjuror, patted and stroked them, dropped them to dreadful depths, snatched them back, to show that he could, caught them to his heart, and told them a story. And with that audience hugged to his breast he marched victoriously up and down upon the prostrate body of the Democratic party, chanting its requiem. It was a great time. Everybody rose at the end and said so loudly; they stood on benches and shouted it with a bellow that shook the building. They tossed their caps in the air, and danced on one another, and wanted to carry Tarvin around the hall on their shoulders.

But Tarvin, with a choking at the throat, turned his back on it all, and, fighting his way blindly through the crowd which had gathered on the platform, reached the dressing-room behind the stage. He shut and bolted the door behind him, and flung himself into a chair, mopping his forehead.

'And the man who can do that,' he muttered, 'can't make one tiny little bit of a girl marry him.'

III

Who are the Rulers of Ind ?—to whom shall we bow the
    knee ?
Make thy peace with the women, and men shall make
    thee L. G.

Maxims of Hafiz.

IT was an opinion not concealed in Cañon City
the next morning, that Tarvin had wiped up the
floor with his adversary ; and it was at least
definitely on record, as a result of Tarvin's speech,
that when Sheriff rose half-heartedly to make the
rejoinder set down for him on the programme, he
had been howled back into his seat by a united
public opinion. But Sheriff met Tarvin at the
railway station where they were both to take the
train for Topaz with a fair imitation of a nod and
smile, and certainly showed no inclination to avoid
him on the journey up. If Tarvin had really
done Kate's father the office attributed to him by
the voice of Canon City, Sheriff did not seem to
be greatly disturbed by the fact. But Tarvin
reflected that Sheriff had balancing grounds of
consolation—a reflection which led him to make
the further one that he had made a fool of himself.
He had indeed had the satisfaction of explaining

publicly to the rival candidate which was the better man, and had enjoyed the pleasure of proving to his constituents that he was still a force to be reckoned with, in spite of the mad missionary notion which had built a nest in a certain young woman's head. But how did that bring him nearer Kate? Had it not rather, so far as her father could influence the matter, put him farther away—as far as it had brought his own election near. He believed he would be elected now. But to what? Even the speakership he had dangled before her did not seem so remote in the light of last night's occurrences. But the only speakership that Tarvin cared to be elected to was the speakership of Kate's heart.

He feared he shouldn't be chosen to fill that high office immediately, and as he glanced at the stumpy, sturdy form standing next him on the edge of the track, he knew whom he had to thank. She would never go to India if she had a man for a father like some men he knew. But a smooth, politic, conciliating, selfish, easy-going rich man —what could you expect? Tarvin could have forgiven Sheriff's smoothness if it had been backed by force. But he had his opinion of a man who had become rich by accident in a town like Topaz.

Sheriff presented the spectacle, intolerable to Tarvin, of a man who had become bewilderingly well-to-do through no fault of his own, and who now wandered vaguely about in his good fortune, seeking anxiously to avoid giving offence. In his politics he carried this far; and he was a treasury of delight just at this time to the committees of railroad engineers' balls, Knight Templars, excursions, and twilight coteries, and to the organisers of church bazaars, theatricals, and oyster suppers, who had tickets to sell. He went indiscriminately to the oyster suppers and bazaars of all denominations in Topaz, and made Kate and her mother go with him; and his collection of Baptist dolls, Presbyterian embroidery, and Roman Catholic sofa-pillows and spatter-work, filled his parlour at home.

But his universal good-nature was not so popular as it deserved to be. The twilight coteries took his money but kept their opinion of him; and Tarvin, as the opposing candidate, had shown what he thought of his rival's system of politics by openly declining to buy a single ticket. This feeble-foolish wish to please everybody was, he understood very well, at the root of Sheriff's attitude toward his daughter's mania. Kitty wanted to go so bad, he supposed he'd better let her, was his slouching version of the situation at home. He declared that he had opposed the idea strongly when she had first suggested it, and Tarvin did not doubt that Sheriff, who he knew was fond of her, had really done what he could. His complaint against him was not on the score of disposition but of capacity. He recognised, however, that this was finally a complaint, like all his others, against Kate; for it was Kate's will which made all pleadings vain.

When the train for Topaz arrived at the station, Sheriff and Tarvin got into the drawing-room car together. Tarvin did not yearn to talk to Sheriff on the way to Topaz, but neither did he wish to seem to shirk conversation. Sheriff offered him a cigar in the smoking-room of the Pullman, and when Dave Lewis, the conductor, came through, Tarvin hailed him as an old friend, and made him come back and join them when he had gone his rounds. Tarvin liked Lewis in the way that he liked the thousand other casual acquaintances in the State with whom he was popular ; and his invitation was not altogether a device for avoiding private talk with Sheriff. The conductor told them that he had the president of the Three C.'s on behind in a special car, with his party.

' *No !* ' exclaimed Tarvin, and begged him to introduce him on the spot ; he was precisely the man he wanted to see. The conductor laughed, and said he wasn't a director of the road—not himself; but when he had left them to go about his duties, he came back, after a time, to say that the president had been asking whom he could recommend at Topaz as a fair-minded and public-spirited man, able to discuss in a reasonable spirit the question of the Three C.'s coming to Topaz. The conductor told him that he had two such gentlemen on board his train at that moment ; and the president sent word to them by him that he would be glad to have a little talk with them if they would come back to his car.

For a year the directorate of the Three C.'s had been talking of running their line through Topaz, in the dispassionate and impartial manner of directorates which await encouragement. The board of trade at Topaz had promptly met and

voted the encouragement. It took the shape of
town bonds and gifts of land, and finally of an
undertaking to purchase shares of stock in the
road itself, at an inflated price. This was hand-
some even for a board of trade ; but, under the
prick of town ambition and town pride, Rustler
had done better. Rustler lay fifteen miles from
Topaz, up in the mountains, and by that much
nearer the mines ; and Topaz recognised it as its
rival in other matters than that of the Three C.'s.

The two towns had enjoyed their boom at
about the same time ; then the boom had left
Rustler and had betaken itself to Topaz. This
had cost Rustler a number of citizens, who moved
to the more prosperous place. Some of the
citizens took their houses up bodily, loaded them
on a flat car and sent them over to Topaz as
freight, to the desolation of the remaining inhabitants of Rustler. But Topaz now began in her
turn to feel that she was losing her clutch. A
house or two had been moved back. It was
Rustler this time which was gaining. If the railroad went there, Topaz was lost. If Topaz secured
the railroad, the town was made. The two towns
hated each other as such towns hate in the West—
malignantly, viciously, joyously. If a convulsion
of nature had obliterated one town, the other must
have died from sheer lack of interest in life. If
Topaz could have killed Rustler, or if Rustler
could have killed Topaz, by more enterprise, push,
and go, or by the lightnings of the local press, the
surviving town would have organised a triumphal
procession and a dance of victory. But the de-

struction of the other town by any other than the
heaven-appointed means of schemes, rustle, and a
board of trade, would have been a poignant grief
to the survivor.

The most precious possession of a citizen of the
West is his town pride. It is the flower of that
pride to hate the rival town. Town pride cannot
exist without town jealousy, and it was therefore
fortunate that Topaz and Rustler lay within con-
venient hating distance of each other, for this living
belief of men in the one spot of all the great
Western wilderness on which they have chosen to
pitch their tents, contains within itself the future
and the promise of the West.

Tarvin cherished this sentiment as a religion.
It was nearer to him than anything in the world
but Kate, and sometimes it was even nearer than
Kate. It did duty with him for all the higher
aspirations and ideals which beckon other men.
He wished to succeed, he wished to make a figure,
but his best wish for himself was one with his best
wish for the town. He could not succeed if the
town failed ; and if the town prospered he must
prosper. His ambition for Topaz, his glory in
Topaz, were a patriotism—passionate and personal.
Topaz was his country ; and because it was near
and real, because he could put his hand on it, and,
above all, because he could buy and sell pieces of
it, it was much more recognisably his country than
the United States of America, which was his
country in time of war.

He had been present at the birth of Topaz.
He had known it when his arms could almost

encircle it; he had watched and fondled and caressed it; he had pegged down his heart with the first peg of the survey; and now he knew what was good for it. It wanted the Three C.'s.

The conductor presented Tarvin and Sheriff to the president when he had led them back to his private car, and the president made them both known to his young wife—a blonde of twenty-five, consciously pretty and conspicuously bridal—by whose side Tarvin placed himself with his instant perception. There were apartments in the private car before and beyond the drawing-room into which they had been shown. The whole was a miracle of compactness and convenience; the decoration was of a specious refinement. In the drawing-room was a smother of plushes, in hues of no kindred, a flicker of tortured nickel work, and a flash of mirrors. The studied soberness of the woodwork, in a more modern taste, heightened the high pitch of the rest.

The president of the embryo Colorado and California Central made room for Sheriff in one of the movable wicker chairs by tilting out a heap of illustrated papers, and bent two beady black eyes on him from under a pair of bushy eyebrows. His own bulk filled and overflowed another of the frail chairs. He had the mottled cheeks and the flaccid fulness of chin of a man of fifty who has lived too well. He listened to the animated representations which Sheriff at once began making him with an irresponsive, sullen face, while Tarvin engaged Mrs. Mutrie in a conversation which did not imply the existence of railroads. He knew

all about the marriage of the president of the
Three C.'s, and he found her very willing to let
him use his knowledge flatteringly. He made
her his compliments ; he beguiled her into telling
him about her wedding journey. They were just
at the end of it ; they were to settle in Denver.
She wondered how she should like it. Tarvin told
her how she would like it. He guaranteed Denver ;
he gilded and graced it for her ; he made it the
city of a dream, and peopled it out of an Eastern
fairy tale. Then he praised the stores and the
theatres. He said they beat New York, but she
ought to see their theatre at Topaz. He hoped
they meant to stay over a day or two at Topaz.

Tarvin would not praise Topaz crudely, as he
praised Denver. He contrived to intimate its
unique charm, and when he had managed to make
her see it in fancy as the prettiest, and finest, and
most prosperous town in the West, he left the
subject. But most· of their subjects were more
personal, and while he discussed them with her he
pushed out experimentally in one direction and
another, first for a chord of sympathy, then for
her weak point. He wanted to know how she
could be reached. *That* was the way to reach the
president. He had perceived it as soon as he
entered the car. He knew her history, and had
even known her father, who had once kept the
hotel where he stayed when he went to Omaha.
He asked her about the old house, and the changes
of proprietorship since he had been there. Who
had it now ? He hoped they had kept the head
waiter. And the cook ? It made his mouth water

to think of that cook. She laughed with instant sociability. Her childhood had been passed about the hotel. She had played in the halls and corridors, drummed on the parlour piano, and consumed candy in the office. She knew that cook—knew him personally. He had given her custards to take to bed with her. Oh yes! *He* was still there.

There was an infectious quality in Tarvin's open and friendly manner, in his willingness to be amused, and in his lively willingness to contribute to the current stock of amusement, and there was something endearing in his hearty, manly way, his confident, joyous air, his manner of taking life strongly, and richly, and happily. He had an impartial kindness for the human species. He was own cousin to the race, and own brother to the members of it he knew, when they would let him be.

He and Mrs. Mutrie were shortly on beautiful terms, and she made him come back with her to the bow-window at the end of the car, and point out the show sights of the Grand Cañon of the Arkansas to her. Theirs was the rearmost carriage, and they looked back through the polished sweep of glass, in which the president's car terminated, at the twisting streak of the receding track, and the awful walls of towering rock between which it found its way. They stooped to the floor to catch sight of the massy heights that hung above them, and peered back at the soaring chaos of rock which, having opened to let them through, closed again immitigably as they left it behind. The train went racketing profanely through the tumbled

beauty of this primeval world, miraculously keeping
a foothold on the knife-edge of space, won for it
at the bottom of the cañon from the river on one
side, and from the rock on the other. Mrs.
Mutrie would sometimes lose her balance as the
train swept them around the ceaseless curves, and
only saved herself by snatching at Tarvin. It
ended in his making her take his arm, and then
they stood and rocked together with the motion of
the train, Tarvin steadying their position with
outstretched legs, while they gazed up at the
monster spires and sovereign hills of stone, wavering and dizzying over their heads.

Mrs. Mutrie gave frequent utterance to little
exclamations of wonder and applause, which began
by being the appropriate feminine response to great
expressions of Nature, and ended in an awed
murmur. Her light nature was controlled and
subdued by the spectacle as it might have been
silenced by the presence of death; she used her
little arts and coquetries on Tarvin mechanically
and half-heartedly until they were finally out of
the cañon, when she gave a gasp of relief, and
taking petulant possession of him, made him return
with her to the chairs they had left in the drawing-
room. Sheriff was still pouring the story of the
advantages of Topaz into the unattending ear of
the president, whose eyes were on the window-
pane. Mutrie received her pat on the back and
her whispered confidence with the air of an embarrassed ogre. She flounced into her former seat,
and commanded Tarvin to amuse her; and Tarvin
willingly told her of a prospecting expedition he

had once made into the country above the cañon.
He hadn't found what he was looking for, which
was silver, but he had found some rather uncommon amethysts.

'Oh, you don't mean it! You delightful man!
Amethysts! Real live ones? I didn't know they
found amethysts in Colorado.'

A singular light kindled in her eyes, a light of
passion and longing. Tarvin fastened on the look
instantly. Was *that* her weak point? If it was—
He was full of learning about precious stones.
Were they not part of the natural resources of the
country about Topaz? He could talk precious
stones with her until the cows came home. But
would that bring the Three C.'s to Topaz? A
wild notion of working complimentary bridal re-
solutions and an appropriation for a diamond tiara
through the board of trade danced through his
head, and was dismissed. No public offerings of
that kind would help Topaz. This was a case for
private diplomacy, for subtle and laborious delicacies, for quiet and friendly manipulation, for the
tact of finger-tips—a touch here, a touch there,
and then a grip—a case, in fine, for Nicholas
Tarvin, and for no one else on top of earth. He
saw himself bringing the Three C.'s splendidly,
royally, unexpectedly into Topaz, and fixing it
there by that same Tarvin's unaided strength; he
saw himself the founder of the future of the town
he loved. He saw Rustler in the dust, and the
owner of a certain twenty-acre plot a millionaire.

His fancy dwelt affectionately for a moment on
the twenty-acre plot; the money with which he

had bought it had not come easily, and business in the last analysis was always business. But the plot, and his plan of selling a portion of it to the Three C.'s for a round-house, when the railroad came, and disposing of the rest as town lots by the front foot, were minor chords in the larger harmony. His dream was of Topaz. If promoters, in accord with the high plan of providence, usually came in on the ground floor when their plans went right, that was a fact strictly by the way.

He noticed now, as he glanced at Mrs. Mutrie's hands, that she wore unusual rings. They were not numerous, but the stones were superb. He ventured to admire the huge solitaire she wore on her left hand, and, as they fell into a talk about jewels, she drew it off to let him see it. She said the diamond had a history. Her father had bought it from an actor, a tragedian who had met bad business at Omaha, after playing to empty houses at Denver, Topeka, Kansas City, and St. Jo. The money had paid the fares of the company home to New York, a fact which connected the stone with the only real good it had ever done its various owners. The tragedian had won it from a gambler who had killed his man in a quarrel over it ; the man who had died for it had bought it at a low price from the absconding clerk of a diamond merchant.

'It ought to have been smuggled out of the mines by the man who found it at Kimberley, or somewhere, and sold to an I.D.B.,' she said, 'to make the story complete. Don't you think so, Mr. Tarvin ?'

She asked all her questions with an arch of the eyebrow, and an engaging smile which required the affirmative readily furnished by Tarvin. He would have assented to an hypothesis denying virtue to the discoveries of Galileo and Newton if Mrs. Mutrie had broached it just then. He sat tense and rigid, full of his notion, watching, waiting, like a dog on the scent.

'I look into it sometimes to see if I can't find a picture of the crimes it has seen,' she said. 'They're so nice and shivery, don't you think so, Mr. Tarvin, particularly the murder? But what I like best about it is the stone itself. It *is* a beauty, isn't it? Pa used to say it was the handsomest he'd ever seen, and in a hotel you see lots of good diamonds, you know.' She gazed a moment affectionately into the liquid depths of the brilliant. 'Oh, there's nothing like a beautiful stone—nothing!' she breathed. Her eyes kindled. He heard for the first time in her voice the ring of absolute sincerity and unconsciousness. 'I could look at a perfect jewel forever, and I don't much care what it is, so it *is* perfect. Pa used to know how I loved stones, and he was always trading them with the people who came to the house. Drummers are great fellows for jewellery, you know, but they don't always know a good stone from a bad one. Pa used to make some good trades,' she said, pursing her pretty lips meditatively; 'but he would never take anything but the best, and then he would trade that, if he could, for something better. He would always give two or three stones with the least flaw in them for one real good one. He knew they were the only ones I cared for. Oh, I do love them! They're better than folks. They're always there, and always just so beautiful!'

'I think I know a necklace you'd like, if you care for such things,' said Tarvin quietly.

'Do you?' she beamed. 'Oh, where?'

'A long way from here.'

'Oh—*Tiffany's!*' she exclaimed scornfully. 'I know you!' she added, with resumed art of intonation.

'No. Further.'

'Where?'

'India.'

She stared at him a moment interestedly. 'Tell me what it's like,' she said. Her whole attitude and accent were changed again. There was plainly one subject on which she could be serious. 'Is it really good?'

'It's the best,' said Tarvin, and stopped.

'Well!' she exclaimed. 'Don't tantalise me. What is it made of?'

'Oh, diamonds, pearls, rubies, opals, turquoises, amethysts, sapphires—a rope of them. The rubies are as big as your fist; the diamonds are the size of hens' eggs. It's worth a king's ransom.'

She caught her breath. Then after a long moment, 'Oh!' she sighed; and then, 'Oh!' she murmured again, languorously, wonderingly, longingly. 'And where is it?' she asked briskly, of a sudden.

'Round the neck of an idol in the province of Rajputana. Do you want it?' he asked grimly.

She laughed. 'Yes,' she answered.

'I'll get it for you,' said Tarvin simply.

'*Yes*, you will!' pouted she.

'I will,' repeated Tarvin.

She threw back her gay blonde head, and laughed to the painted Cupids on the ceiling of the car. She always threw back her head when she laughed; it showed her throat.

IV

Your patience, Sirs, the Devil took me up
To the burned mountain over Sicily,
(Fit place for me), and thence I saw my Earth—
Not all Earth's splendour, 'twas beyond my need ;
And that one spot I love—all Earth to me.
And her I love, my Heaven.   What said I ? . . .
My love was safe from all the powers of Hell—
For you—e'en you—acquit her of my guilt.
But Sula, nestling by our sail-specked sea,
My city, child of mine, my heart, my home.
Mine and my pride—evil might visit there !
It was for Sula and her naked ports,
Prey to the galleys of the Algerine ;
Our city Sula, that I drove my price—
For love of Sula and for love of her.
The twain were woven, gold on sackcloth, twined
Past any sundering—till God shall judge
The evil and the good.
                                    The Grand-Master's Defence.

THE president engaged rooms at the hotel beside
the railroad track at Topaz, and stayed over the
next day.   Tarvin and Sheriff took possession of
him, and showed him the town, and what they
called its 'natural resources.'   Tarvin caused the
president to hold rein when he had ridden with
him to a point outside the town, and discoursed,
in the midst of the open plain, and in the face of

the snow-capped mountains, on the reasonableness
and necessity of making Topaz the end of a
division for the new railroad, and putting the
division superintendent, the workshops, and the
round-house here.

In his heart he knew the president to be absolutely opposed to bringing the railroad to Topaz
at all ; but he preferred to assume the minor
point. It was much easier, as a matter of fact,
to show that Topaz ought to be made a junction,
and the end of a division, than it was to show that
it ought to be a station on the Three C.'s. If it
was anything it would have to be a junction ; the
difficulty was to prove that it ought to be anything.

Tarvin knew the whole Topaz situation forward
and back, as he might have known the multiplica-
tion table. He was not president of the board of
trade and the head of a land and improvement
company, organised with a capital of a million
on a cash basis of $2000, for nothing. Tarvin's
company included all the solid men of the town ;
it owned the open plain from Topaz to the foothills, and had laid it out in streets, avenues, and
public parks. One could see the whole thing on
a map hung in the company's office on Connecticut
Avenue, which was furnished in oak, floored with
mosaic, carpeted with Turkish rugs, and draped
with silk. There one could buy town lots at any
point within two miles of the town ; there, in fact,
Tarvin had some town lots to sell. The habit of
having them to sell had taught him the worst and
the best that could be said about the place ; and

he knew to an exactitude all that he could make
a given man believe about it.

He was aware, for example, that Rustler not
only had richer mines in its near neighbourhood
than Topaz, but that it tapped a mining country
behind it of unexplored and fabulous wealth ; and
he knew that the president knew it. He was
equally familiar with other facts—as, for example,
that the mines about Topaz were fairly good,
though nothing remarkable in a region of great
mineral wealth ; and that, although the town lay
in a wide and well-irrigated valley, and in the
midst of an excellent cattle country, these were
limited advantages, and easily matched elsewhere.
In other words, the natural resources of Topaz
constituted no such claim for it as a 'great railroad centre' as he would have liked any one to
suppose who heard him talk.

But he was not talking to himself. His private
word to himself was that Topaz was created to be
a railroad town, and the way to create it was to
make it a railroad town. This proposition, which
could not have been squared to any system of
logic, proceeded on the soundest system of reasoning. As thus : Topaz was not an existence at all ;
Topaz was a hope. Very well ! And when one
wished to make such hopes realities in the West,
what did one do ? Why, get some one else to
believe in them, of course. Topaz was valueless
without the Three C.'s. Then what was its value
to the Three C.'s ? Obviously the value that the
Three C.'s would give it.

Tarvin's pledge to the president amounted to

this : that if he would give them the chance, they would be worthy of it ; and he contended that, in essence, that was all that any town could say. The point for the president to judge was which place would be most likely to be worthy of such an opportunity—Topaz or Rustler—and he claimed there could be no question about that. When you came to size it up, he said, it was the character of the inhabitants that counted. They were dead at Rustler—dead and buried. Everybody knew that : there was no trade, no industry, no life, no energy, no money there. And look at Topaz ! The president could see the character of her citizens at a glance as he walked the streets. They were wide awake down here. They meant business. They believed in their town, and they were ready to put their money on her. The president had only to say what he expected of them. And then he broached to him his plan for getting one of the Denver smelters to establish a huge branch at Topaz; he said that he had an agreement with one of them in his pocket, conditioned solely on the Three C.'s coming their way. The company couldn't make any such arrangement with Rustler ; he knew that. Rustler hadn't the flux, for one thing. The smelter people had come up from Denver at the expense of Topaz, and had proved Topaz's allegation that Rustler couldn't find a proper flux for smelting its ore nearer to her own borders than fifteen miles—in other words, she couldn't find it this side of Topaz.

Tarvin went on to say that what Topaz wanted was an outlet for her products to the Gulf of

Mexico, and the Three C.'s was the road to furnish
it. The president had, perhaps, listened to such
statements before, for the entire and crystalline
impudence of this drew no retort from his stolidity.
He seemed to consider it as he considered the
other representations made to him, without hearing
it. A railroad president, weighing the advantages
of rival towns, could not find it within his concep-
tion of dignity to ask which of the natural products
of Topaz sought relief through the Gulf. But if
Mutrie could have asked such a question, Tarvin
would have answered unblushingly, 'Rustler's.'
He implied this freely in the suggestion which he
made immediately in the form of a concession.
Of course, he said, if the road wanted to tap the
mineral wealth of the country behind Rustler it
would be a simple matter to run a branch road up'
there, and bring down the ore to be smelted at
Topaz. Rustler had a value to the road as a
mining centre ; he didn't pretend to dispute that.
But a mineral road would bring down all the ore
as well as a main line, make the same traffic for
the road, and satisfy all proper claims of Rustler
to consideration, while leaving the junction where
it belonged by virtue of natural position.

He boldly asked the president how he expected
to get up steam and speed for the climb over the
Pass, if he made Rustler the end of the division,
and changed engines there. The place was already
in the mountains ; as a practical railroad-man the
president must know that his engines could get no
start from Rustler. The heavy grade by which
the railroad would have to get out of the place,

beginning in the town itself, prohibited the idea
of making it the end of a division. If his engines,
by good luck, weren't stalled on the grade, what
did he think of the annual expense involved in
driving heavy trains daily at a high mountain from
the vantage-ground of a steep slope? What the
Three C.'s wanted for the end of their division
and their last stop before the climb over the Pass
was a place like Topaz, designed for them by
nature, built in the centre of a plain, which the
railroad could traverse at a level for five miles
before attacking the hills.

This point Tarvin made with the fervour and
relief born of dealing with one solid and irrefrag-
able fact. It was really his best argument, and he
saw that it had reached the president as the latter
took up his reins silently, and led the way back
to town. But another glance at Mutrie's face
told him that he had failed hopelessly in his main
contention. The certainty of this would have
been heart-breaking if he had not expected to fail.
Success lay elsewhere; but before trying that he
had determined to use every other means.

Tarvin's eye rested lovingly on his town as
they turned their horses again toward the cluster
of dwellings scattered irregularly in the midst of
the wide valley. She might be sure that he would
see her through.

Of course the Topaz of his affections melted in
and out of the Topaz of fact, by shadings and
subtleties which no measurement could record.
The relation of the real Topaz to Tarvin's Topaz,
or to the Topaz of any good citizen of the place,

was a matter which no friendly observer could
wish to press. In Tarvin's own case it was impossible to say where actual belief stopped and
willingness to believe went on. What he knew
was that he did believe; and with him the best
possible reason for faith in Topaz would have been
that it needed to be believed in hard. The need
would have been only another reason for liking it.

To the ordered Eastern eye the city would have
seemed a raw, untidy, lonely collection of ragged
wooden buildings sprawling over a level plain.
But this was only another proof that one can see
only what one brings to the seeing. It was not so
that Tarvin saw it; and he would not have thanked
the Easterner who should have taken refuge in
praise of his snow-whitened hills, walling the valley
in a monstrous circle. The Easterner might keep
his idea that Topaz merely blotted a beautiful
picture; to Tarvin the picture was Topaz's scenery,
and the scenery only an incident of Topaz. It was
one of her natural advantages—her own, like her
climate, her altitude, and her board of trade.

He named the big mountains to the president
as they rode; he showed him where their big
irrigating ditch led the water down out of the
heights, and where it was brought along under the
shadow of the foothills before it started across the
plain toward Topaz; he told him the number of
patients in their hospital, decently subduing his
sense of their numerousness, as a testimony to the
prosperity of the town; and as they rode into the
streets he pointed out the opera-house, the post-
office, the public school, and the court-house, with

D

the modesty a mother summons who shows her first-born.

It was at least as much to avoid thinking as to exploit the merits of Topaz that he spared the president nothing. Through all his advocacy another voice had made itself heard, and now, in the sense of momentary failure, the bitterness of another failure caught him with a fresh twinge ; for since his return he had seen Kate, and knew that nothing short of a miracle would prevent her from starting for India within three days. In contempt of the man who was making this possible, and in anger and desperation, he had spoken at last directly to Sheriff, appealing to him by all he held most dear to stop this wickedness. But there are limp rags which no buckram can stiffen ; and Sheriff, willing as he was to oblige, could not take strength into his fibre from the outside, though Tarvin offered him all of his. His talk with Kate, supplemented by this barren interview with her father, had given him a sickening sense of power-lessness from which nothing but a large success in another direction could rescue him. He thirsted for success, and it had done him good to attack the president, even with the foreknowledge that he must fail with him.

He could forget Kate's existence while he fought for Topaz, but he remembered it with a pang as he parted from Mutrie. He had her promise to make one of the party he was taking to the Hot Springs that afternoon ; if it had not been for that he could almost have found it in his heart to let Topaz take care of herself for the remainder of

the president's stay. As it was, he looked forward
to the visit to the Springs as a last opening to hope.
He meant to make a final appeal; he meant to
have it out with Kate, for he could not believe in
defeat, and he could not think that she would go.

The excursion to the Hot Springs was designed
to show the president and Mrs. Mutrie what a
future Topaz must have as a winter resort, if all
other advantages failed her; and they had agreed
to go with the party which Tarvin had hastily got
together. With a view to a little quiet talk with
Kate, he had invited three men besides Sheriff—
Maxim, the postmaster; Heckler, the editor of
the *Topaz Telegram* (both his colleagues on the
board of trade); and a pleasant young Englishman,
named Carmathan. He expected them to do some
of the talking to the president, and to give him
half an hour with Kate, without detriment to
Mutrie's impressions of Topaz. It had occurred
to him that the president might be ready by this
time for a fresh view of the town, and Heckler
was the man to give it to him.

Carmathan had come to Topaz two years before
in his capacity of colonising younger son, to engage
in the cattle business, equipped with a riding-crop,
top-boots, and $2000 in money. He had lost the
money; but he knew now that riding-crops were
not used in punching cattle, and he was at the
moment using this knowledge, together with other
information gathered on the same subject, in the
calling of cow-boy on a neighbouring range. He
was getting $30 a month, and was accepting his
luck with the philosophy which comes to the

adoptive as well as to the native-born citizens of
the West. Kate liked him for the pride and pluck
which did not allow him the easy remedy of writing
home, and for other things ; and for the first half
of their ride to the Hot Springs they rode side
by side, while Tarvin made Mr. and Mrs. Mutrie
look up at the rocky heights between which they
began to pass. He showed them the mines burrow-
ing into the face of the rock far aloft, and explained
the geological formation with the purely practical
learning of a man who buys and sells mines. The
road, which ran alongside the track of the railroad
already going through Topaz, wandered back and
forth over it from time to time, as Tarvin said, at
the exact angle which the Three C.'s would be
choosing later. Once a train laboured past them,
tugging up the heavy grade that led to the town.
The narrowing gorge was the first closing in of
the hills, which, after widening again, gathered in
the great cliffs of the cañon twenty miles below,
to face each other across the chasm. The sweep
of pictured rock above their heads lifted itself into
strange, gnarled crags, or dipped suddenly and
swam on high in straining peaks ; but for the
most part it was sheer wall—blue and brown and
purplish-red umber, ochre, and the soft hues
between.

Tarvin dropped back, and ranged his horse
beside Kate's. Carmathan, with whom he was in
friendly relation, gave place to him instantly, and
rode forward to join the others in advance.

She lifted her speaking eyes as he drew rein
beside her, and begged him silently to save them

both the continuance of a hopeless contest; but
Tarvin's jaw was set, and he would not have
listened to an angel's voice.

'I tire you by talking of this thing, Kate. I
know it. But I've got to talk of it. I've got to
save you.'

'Don't try any more, Nick,' she answered gently.
'Please don't. It's my salvation to go. It is the
one thing I want to do. It seems to me sometimes,
when I think of it, that it was perhaps the thing
I was sent into the world to do. We are all sent
into the world to do something, don't you think
so, Nick, even if it's ever so tiny and humble and
no account? I've got to do it, Nick. Make it
easy for me.'

'I'll be—hammered if I will! I'll make it hard.
That's what I'm here for. Every one else yields
to that vicious little will of yours. Your father
and mother let you do what you like. They don't
begin to know what you are running your precious
head into. I can't replace it. Can you? That
makes me positive. It also makes me ugly.'

Kate laughed.

'It does make you ugly, Nick. But I don't
mind. I think I like it that you should care. If
I could stay at home for any one, I'd do it for
you. Believe that, won't you?'

'Oh, I'll believe, and thank you into the bargain.
But what good will it do me? I don't want belief.
I want you.'

'I know, Nick. I know. But India wants me
more—or not me, but what I can do, and what
women like me can do. There's a cry from Mace-

donia, "Come over and help us!" While I hear
that cry I can find no pleasure in any other good.
I could be your wife, Nick. That's easy. But
with that in my ears I should be in torture every
moment.'

'That's rough on me,' suggested Tarvin, glancing ruefully at the cliffs above them.

'Oh no. It has nothing to do with you.'

'Yes,' returned he, shutting his lips, 'that's
just it.'

She could not help smiling a little again at his
face.

'I will never marry any one else, if it helps you
any to know that, Nick,' she said, with a sudden
tenderness in her voice.

'But you won't marry me?'

'No,' she said quietly, firmly, simply.

He meditated this answer a moment in bitterness. They were riding at a walk, and he let the
reins drop on his pony's neck as he said, 'Oh, well.
Don't matter about me. It isn't all selfishness,
dear. I *do* want you to stay for my own sake, I
want you for my very own, I want you always
beside me, I want you—want you; but it isn't for
that I ask you to stay. It's because I can't think
of you throwing yourself into the dangers and
horrors of that life alone, unprotected, a girl. I
can't think of it and sleep nights. I daren't think
of it. The thing's monstrous. It's hideous. It's
absurd. You won't do it!'

'I must not think of myself,' she answered in a
shaken voice. 'I must think of *them*.'

'But *I* must think of *you*. And you shan't

bribe me, you shan't tempt me, to think of any
one else. You take it all too hard. Dearest girl,'
he entreated, lowering his voice, 'are you in charge
of the misery of the earth? There is misery elsewhere, too, and pain. Can you stop it? You've
got to live with the sound of the suffering of
millions in your ears all your life, whatever you
do. We're all in for that. We can't get away
from it. We pay that price for daring to be
happy for one little second.'

'I know, I know. I'm not trying to save myself. I'm not trying to stifle the sound.'

'No, but you are trying to stop it, and you
can't. It's like trying to scoop up the ocean with
a dipper. You can't do it. But you can spoil
your life in trying; and if you've got a scheme by
which you can come back and have a spoiled life
over again, I know some one who hasn't. O Kate,
I don't ask anything for myself—or, at least, I
only ask everything — but do think of that a
moment sometimes when you are putting your
arms around the earth, and trying to lift it up in
your soft little hands—you are spoiling more lives
than your own. Great Scot, Kate, if you are
looking for some misery to set right, you needn't
go off this road. Begin on me.'

She shook her head sadly. 'I must begin
where I see my duty, Nick. I don't say that I
shall make much impression on the dreadful sum
of human trouble, and I don't say it is for everybody to do what I'm going to try to do; but it's
right for me. I know that, and that's all any of
us can know. Oh, to be sure that people are a

little better—if *only* a little better—because you
have lived,' she exclaimed, the look of exaltation coming into her eyes; 'to know that you
have lessened by the slightest bit the sorrow and
suffering that must go on all the same, would
be good. Even you must feel that, Nick,' she
said, gently laying her hand on his arm as they
rode.

Tarvin compressed his lips. 'Oh yes, I feel it,'
he said desperately.

'But you feel something else. So do I.'

'Then feel it more. Feel it enough to trust
yourself to me. I'll find a future for you. You
shall bless everybody with your goodness. Do
you think I should like you without it? And you
shall begin by blessing me.'

'I can't! I can't!' she cried in distress.

'You can't do anything else. You must come
to me at last. Do you think I could live if I
didn't think that? But I want to save you all
that lies between. I don't want you to be driven
into my arms, little girl. I want you to come—
and come now.'

For answer to this she only bowed her head on
the sleeve of her riding-habit, and began to cry
softly. Nick's fingers closed on the hand with
which she nervously clutched the pommel of her
saddle.

'You can't, dear?'

The brown head was shaken vehemently.
Tarvin ground his teeth.

'All right; don't mind.'

He took her yielding hand into his, speaking

gently, as he would have spoken to a child in distress. In the silent moment that lengthened between them Tarvin gave it up—not Kate, not his love, not his changeless resolve to have her for his own, but just the question of her going to India. She could go if she liked. There would be two of them.

When they reached the Hot Springs he took an immediate opportunity to engage the willing Mrs. Mutrie in talk, and to lead her aside, while Sheriff showed the president the water steaming out of the ground, the baths, and the proposed site of a giant hotel. Kate, willing to hide her red eyes from Mrs. Mutrie's sharp gaze, remained with her father.

When Tarvin had led the president's wife to the side of the stream that went plunging down past the Springs to find a tomb at last in the cañon below, he stopped short in the shelter of a clump of cottonwoods.

'Do you really want that necklace?' he asked her abruptly.

She laughed again, gurglingly, amusedly, this time, with the little air of spectacle which she could not help lending to all she did.

'Want it?' she repeated. 'Of course I want it. I want the moon, too.'

Tarvin laid a silencing hand upon her arm.

'You shall have this,' he said positively.

She ceased laughing, and grew almost pale at his earnestness.

'What do you mean?' she asked quickly.

'It would please you? You would be glad

of it?' he asked. 'What would you do to get it?'

'Go back to Omaha on my hands and knees,' she answered with equal earnestness. 'Crawl to India.'

'All right,' returned Tarvin vigorously. 'That settles it. Listen! I want the Three C.'s to come to Topaz. You want this. Can we trade?'

'But you can never——'

'No matter; I'll attend to my part. Can you do yours?'

'You mean——' she began.

'Yes,' nodded her companion decisively; 'I do. Can you fix it?'

Tarvin, fiercely repressed and controlled, stood before her with clenched teeth, and hands that drove the nails into his palms, awaiting her answer.

She tilted her fair head on one side with deprecation, and regarded him out of the vanishing angle of one eye provocatively, with a lingering, tantalising look of adequacy.

'I guess what I say to Jim goes,' she said at last with a dreamy smile.

'Then it's a bargain?'

'Yes,' she answered.

'Shake hands on it.'

They joined hands. For a moment they stood confronted, penetrating each other's eyes.

'You'll really get it for me?'

'Yes.'

'You won't go back on me?'

'No.'

He pressed her hand so that she gave a little scream.

'Ouch! You hurt.'

'All right,' he said hoarsely, as he dropped her hand. 'It's a trade. I start for India to-morrow.'

V

Now, it is not good for the Christian's health to hustle the
  Aryan brown,
For the Christian riles, and the Aryan smiles, and he weareth
  the Christian down ;
And the end of the fight is a tombstone white, with the name
  of the late deceased,
And the epitaph drear : 'A fool lies here who tried to hustle
  the East.'

Solo from Libretto of Naulahka.

TARVIN stood on the platform of the station at
Rawut Junction watching the dust cloud that
followed the retreating Bombay mail. When it
had disappeared, the heated air above the stone
ballast began its dance again, and he turned blink-
ing to India.

It was amazingly simple to come fourteen
thousand miles. He had lain still in a ship for a
certain time, and then had transferred himself to
stretch at full length, in his shirt-sleeves, on the
leather-padded bunk of the train which had brought
him from Calcutta to Rawut Junction. The journey
was long only as it kept him from sight of Kate,
and kept him filled with thought of her. But was
this what he had come for—the yellow desolation
of a Rajputana desert, and the pinched-off per-

spective of the track? Topaz was cosier when they had got the church, the saloon, the school, and three houses up; the loneliness made him shiver. He saw that they did not mean to do any more of it. It was a desolation which doubled desolateness, because it was left for done. It was final, intended, absolute. The grim solidity of the cut-stone station-house, the solid masonry of the empty platform, the mathematical exactitude of the station name-board looked for no future. No new railroad could help Rawut Junction. It had no ambition. It belonged to the Government. There was no green thing, no curved line, no promise of life that produces, within eyeshot of Rawut Junction. The mauve railroad-creeper on the station had been allowed to die from lack of attention.

Tarvin was saved from the more positive pangs of home-sickness by a little healthy human rage. A single man, fat, brown, clothed in white gauze, and wearing a black velvet cap on his head, stepped out from the building. This stationmaster and permanent population of Rawut Junction accepted Tarvin as a feature of the landscape: he did not look at him. Tarvin began to sympathise with the South in the war of the rebellion.

'When does the next train leave for Rhatore?' he asked.

'There is no train,' returned the man, pausing with precise deliberation between the words. He sent his speech abroad with an air of detachment, irresponsibly, like the phonograph

'No train? Where's your time-table? Where's your railroad guide? Where's your Pathfinder?'

'No train at all of any kind whatever.'

'Then what the devil are you here for?'

'Sir, I am the stationmaster of this station, and it is prohibited using profane language to employees of this company.'

'Oh, are you? Is it? Well, see here, my friend—you stationmaster of the steep-edge of the jumping-off-place, if you want to save your life you will tell me how I get to Rhatore—quick!'

The man was silent.

'Well, what do I do, anyway?' shouted the West.

'What do I know?' answered the East.

Tarvin stared at the brown being in white, beginning at his patent-leather shoes, surmounted by open-work socks, out of which the calf of his leg bulged, and ending with the velvet smoking-cap on his head. The passionless regard of the Oriental, borrowed from the purple hills behind his station, made him wonder for one profane, faithless, and spiritless moment whether Topaz and Kate were worth all they were costing.

'Ticket, please,' said the baboo.

The gloom darkened. This thing was here to take tickets, and would do it though men loved, and fought, and despaired and died at his feet.

'See here,' cried Tarvin, 'you shiny-toed fraud; you agate-eyed pillar of alabaster——' But he did not go on; speech failed in a shout of rage and despair. The desert swallowed all impartially; and the baboo, turning with awful quiet, drifted through the door of the station-house, and locked it behind him.

Tarvin whistled persuasively at the door with uplifted eyebrows, jingling an American quarter against a rupee in his pocket. The window of the ticket-office opened a little way, and the baboo showed an inch of impassive face.

'Speaking now in offeshal capacity, your honour can getting to Rhatore *via* country bullock-cart.'

'Find me the bullock-cart,' said Tarvin.

'Your honour granting commission on transaction?'

'Cert!' It was the tone that conveyed the idea to the head under the smoking-cap.

The window was dropped. Afterward, but not too immediately afterward, a long-drawn howl made itself heard—the howl of a weary warlock invoking a dilatory ghost.

'O Moti! Moti! O-oh!'

'Ah, there, Moti!' murmured Tarvin, as he vaulted over the low stone wall, gripsack in hand, and stepped out through the ticket wicket into Rajputana. His habitual gaiety and confidence had returned with the prospect of motion.

Between himself and a purple circle of hills lay fifteen miles of profitless, rolling ground, jagged with laterite rocks, and studded with unthrifty trees —all given up to drought and dust, and all colourless as the sun-bleached locks of a child of the prairies. Very far away to the right the silver gleam of a salt lake showed, and a formless blue haze of heavier forest. Sombre, desolate, oppressive, withering under a brazen sun, it smote him with its likeness to his own prairies, and with its home-sick unlikeness.

Apparently out of a crack in the earth—in fact, as he presently perceived, out of a spot where two waves of plain folded in upon each other and contained a village—came a pillar of dust, the heart of which was a bullock-cart. The distant whine of the wheels sharpened, as it drew near, to the full-bodied shriek that Tarvin knew when they put the brakes suddenly on a freight coming into Topaz on the down grade. But this was in no sense a freight. The wheels were sections of tree butts—square for the most part. Four unbarked poles bounded the corners of a flat body; the sides were made of netted rope of cocoa-nut fibre. Two bullocks, a little larger than Newfoundlands, smaller than Alderneys, drew a vehicle which might have contained the half of a horse's load.

The cart drew up at the station, and the bullocks, after contemplating Tarvin for a moment, lay down. Tarvin seated himself on his gripsack, rested his shaggy head in his hands, and expended himself in mirth.

'Sail in,' he instructed the baboo; 'make your bargain. I'm in no hurry.'

Then began a scene of declamation and riot, to which a quarrel in a Leadville gambling saloon was a poor matter. The impassiveness of the stationmaster deserted him like a wind-blown garment. He harangued, gesticulated, and cursed; and the driver, naked except for a blue loin-cloth, was nothing behind him. They pointed at Tarvin; they seemed to be arguing over his birth and ancestry; for all he knew they were appraising his weight. When they seemed to be on the brink of an amicable solution, the question re-opened itself, and they went back to the beginning, and re-classified him and the journey.

Tarvin applauded both parties, sicking one on the other impartially for the first ten minutes. Then he besought them to stop, and when they would not he discovered that it was hot, and swore at them.

The driver had for the moment exhausted himself, when the baboo turned suddenly on Tarvin, and, clutching him by the arm, cried, almost shouting, 'All arrange, sir! all arrange! This man *most* uneducated man, sir. You giving me the money, I arrange everything.'

Swift as thought, the driver had caught his other arm, and was imploring him in a strange tongue not to listen to his opponent. As Tarvin stepped back they followed him with uplifted hands of entreaty and representation, the stationmaster forgetting his English, and the driver his respect for the white man. Tarvin, eluding them both, pitched his gripsack into the bullock-cart, bounded in himself, and shouted the one Indian word he knew. It happened, fortunately, to be the word that moves all India, ' *Challo!* ' which, being interpreted, is 'Go on!'

So, leaving strife and desolation behind him, rode out into the desert of Rajputana Nicholas Tarvin of Topaz, Colorado.

E

VI

In the State of Kot-Kumharsen, where the wild dacoits abound,
   And the Thakurs live in castles on the hills,
Where the *bunnia* and *bunjara* in alternate streaks are found,
   And the Rajah cannot liquidate his bills ;
Where the agent Sahib Bahadur shoots the blackbuck for his
      larder,
   From the tonga which he uses as *machân*,
'Twas a white man from the west, came expressly to invest-
   igate the natural wealth of Hindustan.
                              Song from Libretto of Naulahka.

UNDER certain conditions four days can dwarf
eternity. Tarvin had found these circumstances in
the bullock-cart from which he crawled ninety-six
hours after the bullocks had got up from the dust
at Rawut Junction. They stretched behind him—
those hours—in a maddening, creaking, dusty, de-
liberate procession. In an hour the bullock-cart
went two and a half miles. Fortunes had been made
and lost in Topaz—happy Topaz !—while the cart
ploughed its way across a red-hot river-bed, shut
in between two walls of belted sand. New cities
might have risen in the West and fallen to ruins
older than Thebes while, after any of their meals
by the wayside, the driver droned over a water-pipe
something less wieldy than a Gatling-gun. In

these waits and in others—it seemed to him that the journey was chiefly made up of waits—Tarvin saw himself distanced in the race of life by every male citizen of the United States, and groaned with the consciousness that he could never overtake them, or make up this lost time.

Great grey cranes with scarlet heads stalked through the high grass of the swamps in the pockets of the hills. The snipe and the quail hardly troubled themselves to move from beneath the noses of the bullocks, and once in the dawn, lying upon a glistening rock, he saw two young panthers playing together like kittens.

A few miles from Rawut Junction his driver had taken from underneath the cart a sword which he hung around his neck, and sometimes used on the bullocks as a goad. Tarvin saw that every man went armed in this country, as in his own. But three feet of clumsy steel struck him as a poor substitute for the delicate and nimble revolver.

Once he stood up in the cart and hallooed, for he thought he saw the white top of a prairie schooner. But it was only a gigantic cotton-wain, drawn by sixteen bullocks, dipping and plunging across the ridges. Through all, the scorching Indian sun blazed down on him, making him wonder how he had ever dared praise the perpetual sunshine of Colorado. At dawn the rocks glittered like diamonds, and at noonday the sands of the rivers troubled his eyes with a million flashing sparks. At eventide a cold, dry wind would spring up, and the hills lying along the horizon took a hundred colours under the light of the sunset. Then Tarvin realised the meaning of ' the gorgeous East,' for the hills were turned to heaps of ruby and amethyst, while between them the mists in the valleys were opal. He lay in the bullock-cart on his back and stared at the sky, dreaming of the Naulahka, and wondering whether it would match the scenery.

' The clouds know what I'm up to. It's a good omen,' he said to himself.

He cherished the definite and simple plan of buying the Naulahka and paying for it in good money to be raised at Topaz by bonding the town —not, of course, ostensibly for any such purpose. Topaz was good for it, he believed, and if the Maharajah wanted too steep a price when they came to talk business he would form a syndicate.

As the cart swayed from side to side, bumping his head, he wondered where Kate was. She might, under favourable conditions, be in Bombay by this time. That much he knew from careful consideration of her route ; but a girl alone could not pass from hemisphere to hemisphere as swiftly as an unfettered man, spurred by love of herself and of Topaz. Perhaps she was resting for a little time with the Zenana Mission at Bombay. He refused absolutely to admit to himself that she had fallen ill by the way. She was resting, receiving her orders, absorbing a few of the wonders of the strange lands he had contemptuously thrust behind him in his eastward flight ; but in a few days at most she ought to be at Rhatore, whither the bullock-cart was taking him.

He smiled and smacked his lips with pure

enjoyment as he thought of their meeting, and
amused himself with fancies about her fancies
touching his present whereabouts.

He had left Topaz for San Francisco by the
night train over the Pass a little more than twenty-
four hours after his conference with Mrs. Mutrie,
saying good-bye to no one, and telling nobody
where he was going. Kate perhaps wondered at
the fervour of his 'Good evening' when he left
her at her father's house on their return from their
ride to the Hot Springs. But she said nothing,
and Tarvin contrived by an effort to take himself
off without giving himself away. He had made
a quiet sale of a block of town lots the next day
at a sacrifice, to furnish himself with money for
the voyage ; but this was too much in the way of
his ordinary business to excite comment, and he
was finally able to gaze down at the winking lights
of Topaz in the valley from the rear platform of
his train, as it climbed up over the Continental
Divide, with the certainty that the town he was
going to India to bless and boom was not 'on to'
his beneficent scheme. To make sure that the
right story went back to the town, he told the
conductor of the train, in strict confidence, while
he smoked his usual cigar with him, about a little
placer-mining scheme in Alaska which he was going
there to nurse for a while.

The conductor embarrassed him for a moment
by asking what he was going to do about his
election meanwhile ; but Tarvin was ready for him
here too. He said that he had that fixed. He
had to let him into another scheme to show him

how it was fixed, but as he bound him to secrecy again, this didn't matter.

He wondered now, however, whether that scheme had worked, and whether Mrs. Mutrie would keep her promise to cable the result of the election to him at Rhatore. It was amusing to have to trust a woman to let him know whether he was a member of the Colorado legislature or not; but she was the only living person who knew his address, and as the idea had seemed to please her, in common with their whole 'charming conspiracy' (this was what she called it), Tarvin had been content.

When he had become convinced that his eyes would never again be blessed with the sight of a white man, or his ears with the sound of intelligible speech, the cart rolled through a gorge between two hills, and stopped before the counterpart of the station at Rawut Junction. It was a double cube of red sandstone, but—for this Tarvin could have taken it in his arms—it was full of white men. They were undressed excessively; they were lying in the verandah in long chairs, and beside each chair was a well-worn bullock trunk.

Tarvin got himself out of the cart, unfolding his long stiffened legs with difficulty, and unkinking his muscles one by one. He was a mask of dust —dust beyond sand-storms or cyclones. It had obliterated the creases of his clothing and turned his black American four-button cutaway to a pearly white. It had done away with the distinction between the hem of his trousers and the top of his shoes. It dropped off him and rolled up from him as he moved. His fervent 'Thank God!'

was extinguished in a dusty cough. He stepped into the verandah, rubbing his smarting eyes.

'Good evening, gentlemen,' he said. 'Got anything to drink?'

No one rose, but somebody shouted for the servant. A man dressed in thin Tussur silk, yellow and ill-fitting as the shuck on a dried cob, and absolutely colourless as to his face, nodded to him and asked languidly—

'Who are you for?'

'No? Have they got them here too?' said Tarvin to himself, recognising in that brief question the universal shibboleth of the commercial traveller.

He went down the long line and twisted each hand in pure joy and thankfulness before he began to draw comparisons between the East and the West, and to ask himself if these idle, silent lotos-eaters could belong to the profession with which he had swapped stories, commodities, and political opinions this many a year in smoking-cars and hotel offices. Certainly they were debased and spiritless parodies of the alert, aggressive, joyous, brazen animals whom he knew as the drummers of the West. But perhaps—a twinge in his back reminded him—they had all reached this sink of desolation *viâ* country bullock-cart.

He thrust his nose into twelve inches of whisky and soda, and it remained there till there was no more; then he dropped into a vacant chair and surveyed the group again.

'Did some one ask who I was for? I'm for myself, I suppose, as much as any one—travelling for pleasure.'

He had not time to enjoy the absurdity of this, for all five men burst into a shout of laughter, like the laughter of men who have long been estranged from mirth.

'Pleasure!' cried one. 'O Lord! Pleasure! You've come to the wrong place.'

'It's just as well you've come for pleasure. You'd be dead before you did business,' said another.

'You might as well try to get blood out of a stone. I've been here over a fortnight.'

'Great Scot! What for?' asked Tarvin.

'We've all been here over a week,' growled a fourth.

'But what's your lay? What's your racket?'

'Guess you're an American, ain't you?'

'Yes; Topaz, Colorado.' The statement had no effect upon them. He might as well have spoken in Greek. 'But what's the trouble?'

'Why, the King married two wives yesterday. You can hear the gongs going in the city now. He's trying to equip a new regiment of cavalry for the service of the Indian Government, and he's quarrelled with his Political Resident. I've been living at Colonel Nolan's door for three days. He says he can't do anything without authority from the supreme Government. I've tried to catch the King when he goes out pig-shooting. I write every day to the Prime Minister, when I'm not riding around the city on a camel; and here's a bunch of letters from the firm asking why I don't collect.'

At the end of ten minutes Tarvin began to

understand that these washed-out representatives
of half a dozen firms in Calcutta and Bombay were
hopelessly besieging this place on their regular
spring campaign to collect a little on account from
a king who ordered by the ton and paid by the
scruple. He had purchased guns, dressing-cases,
mirrors, mantelpiece ornaments, crochet work, the
iridescent Chrismas-tree glass balls, saddlery, mail-
phaetons, four-in-hands, scent-bottles, surgical
instruments, chandeliers, and chinaware by the
dozen, gross, or score as his royal fancy prompted.
When he lost interest in his purchases he lost
interest in paying for them; and as few things
amused his jaded fancy more than twenty minutes,
it sometimes came to pass that the mere purchase
was sufficient, and the costly packing-cases from
Calcutta were never opened. The ordered peace
of the Indian Empire forbade him to take up arms
against his fellow-sovereigns, the only lasting delight that he or his ancestors had known for
thousands of years ; but there remained a certain
modified interest of war in battling with bill-
collectors. On one side stood the Political Resident
of the State, planted there to teach him good
government, and, above all, economy ; on the
other side—that is to say, at the palace gates—
might generally be found a commercial traveller,
divided between his contempt for an evasive debtor
and his English reverence for a king. Between
these two his Majesty went forth to take his
pleasure in pig-sticking, in racing, in the drilling of
his army, in the ordering of more unnecessaries, and
in the fitful government of his womankind, who

knew considerably more of each commercial
traveller's claims than even the Prime Minister.
Behind these was the Government of India, ex-
plicitly refusing to guarantee payment of the King's
debts, and from time to time sending him, on a
blue velvet cushion, the jewelled insignia of an
imperial order to sweeten the remonstrances of the
Political Resident.

'Well, I hope you make the King pay for it,'
said Tarvin.

'How's that?'

'Why, in my country, when a customer sillies
about like that, promising to meet a man one day
at the hotel and not showing up, and then promising to meet him the next day at the store and not
paying, a drummer says to himself, "Oh, all right!
If you want to pay my board, and my wine, liquor,
and cigar bill, while I wait, don't mind me. I'll
mosey along somehow." And after the second day
he charges up his poker losings to him.'

'Ah, that's interesting. But how does he get
those items into his account?'

'They go into the next bill of goods he sells
him, of course. He makes the prices right for
that.'

'Oh, we can make prices right enough. The
difficulty is to get your money.'

'But I don't see how you fellows have the time
to monkey around here at this rate,' urged Tarvin,
mystified. 'Where I come from a man makes his
trip on schedule time, and when he's a day behind
he'll wire to his customer in the town ahead to
come down to the station and meet him, and he'll

sell him a bill of goods while the train waits. He
could sell him the earth while one of your bullock-
carts went a mile. And as to getting your money,
why don't you get out an attachment on the old
sinner? In your places I'd attach the whole
country on him. I'd attach the palace, I'd attach
his crown. I'd get a judgment against him, and
I'd execute it too—personally, if necessary. I'd
lock the old fellow up and rule Rajputana for him,
if I had to ; but I'd have his money.'

A compassionate smile ran around the group.
'That's because you don't know,' said several at
once. Then they began to explain voluminously.
There was no languor about them now ; they all
spoke together.

The men in the verandah, though they seemed
idle, were no fools, Tarvin perceived after a time.
Lying still as beggars at the gate of greatness was
their method of doing business. It wasted time,
but in the end some sort of payment was sure to
be made, especially, explained the man in the yellow
coat, if you could interest the Prime Minister in
your needs, and through him wake the interests of
the King's women.

A flicker of memory made Tarvin smile faintly,
as he thought of Mrs. Mutrie.

The man in the yellow coat went on, and
Tarvin learned that the head queen was a murderess,
convicted of poisoning her former husband. She
had lain crouching in an iron cage awaiting execu-
tion when the King first saw her, and the King
had demanded whether she would poison him if
he married her, so the tale ran. Assuredly, she

replied, if he treated her as her late husband had treated her. Thereupon the King had married her, partly to please his fancy, mainly through sheer delight in her brutal answer.

This gipsy without lineage held in less than a year King and State under her feet—feet which women of the household sang spitefully were roughened with travel of shameful roads. She had borne the King one son, in whom all her pride and ambition centred, and, after his birth, she had applied herself with renewed energy to the maintenance of mastery in the State. The supreme Government, a thousand miles away, knew that she was a force to be reckoned with, and had no love for her. The white-haired, soft-spoken Political Resident, Colonel Nolan, who lived in the pink house, a bow-shot from the city gates, was often thwarted by her. Her latest victory was peculiarly humiliating to him, for she had discovered that a rock-hewn canal, designed to supply the city with water in summer, would pass through an orange garden under her window, and had used her influence with the Maharajah against it. The Maharajah had thereupon caused it to be taken around by another way at an expense of a quarter of his year's revenue, and in the teeth of the almost tearful remonstrance of the Resident.

Sitabhai, the gipsy, behind her silken curtains, had both heard and seen this interview between the Maharajah and his Political, and had laughed.

Tarvin devoured all this eagerly. It fed his purpose; it was grist to his mill, even if it tumbled his whole plan of attack topsy-turvy. It opened

up a new world for which he had no measures and
standards, and in which he must be frankly and
constantly dependent on the inspiration of the next
moment. He couldn't know too much of this
world before taking his first step toward the
Naulahka, and he was willing to hear all these lazy
fellows would tell him. He began to feel as if he
should have to go back and learn his A B C's over
again. What pleased this strange being they
called King? what appealed to him? what tickled
him? above all, what did he fear?

He was thinking much and rapidly.

But he said, 'No wonder your King is bank-
rupt if he has such a court to look after.'

'He's one of the richest princes in India,'
returned the man in the yellow coat. 'He doesn't
know himself what he has.'

'Why doesn't he pay his debts, then, instead of
keeping you mooning about here?'

'Because he's a native. He'd spend a hundred
thousand pounds on a marriage feast, and delay
payment of a bill for two hundred rupees four
years.'

'You ought to cure him of that,' insisted
Tarvin. 'Send a sheriff after the crown jewels.'

'You don't know Indian princes. They would
pay a bill before they would let the crown jewels
go. They are sacred. They are part of the
government.'

'Ah, I'd give something to see the Luck of the
State!' exclaimed a voice from one of the chairs,
which Tarvin afterward learned belonged to the
agent of a Calcutta firm of jewellers.

'What's that?' he asked, as casually as he knew how, sipping his whisky and soda.

'The Naulahka. Don't you know?'

Tarvin was saved the need of an answer by the man in yellow. 'Pshaw! All that talk about the Naulahka is invented by the priests.'

'I don't think so,' returned the jeweller's agent judicially. 'The King told me when I was last here that he had once shown it to a viceroy. But he is the only foreigner who has ever seen it. The King assured me he didn't know where it was himself.'

'Pooh! Do you believe in carved emeralds two inches square?' asked the other, turning to Tarvin.

'That's only the centre-piece,' said the jeweller; 'and I wouldn't mind wagering that it's a tallow-drop emerald. It isn't that that staggers me. My wonder is how these chaps, who don't care anything for water in a stone, could have taken the trouble to get together half a dozen perfect gems, much less fifty. They say that the necklace was begun when William the Conqueror came over.'

'That gives them a year or two,' said Tarvin. 'I would undertake to get a little jewellery together myself if you gave me eight centuries.'

His face was turned a little away from them as he lay back in his chair. His heart was going quickly. He had been through mining-trades, land-speculations, and cattle-deals in his time. He had known moments when the turn of a hair, the wrinkle of an eyelid, meant ruin to him. But they were not moments into which eight centuries were gathered.

They looked at him with a remote pity in their eyes.

'Five absolutely perfect specimens of the nine precious stones,' began the jeweller; 'the ruby, emerald, sapphire, diamond, opal, cat's-eye, turquoise, amethyst, and——'

'Topaz?' asked Tarvin, with the air of a proprietor.

'No; black diamond—black as night.'

'But how do you know all these things—how do you get on to them?' asked Tarvin curiously.

'Like everything else in a native state— common talk, but difficult to prove. Nobody can as much as guess where that necklace is.'

'Probably under the foundations of some temple in the city,' said the yellow-coated man.

Tarvin, in spite of the careful guard he was keeping over himself, could not help kindling at this. He saw himself digging the city up.

'Where *is* this city?' inquired he.

They pointed across the sun-glare, and showed him a rock girt by a triple line of wall. It was exactly like one of the many ruined cities that Tarvin had passed in the bullock-cart. A rock of a dull and angry red surmounted that rock. Up to the foot of the rock ran the yellow sands of the actual desert—the desert that supports neither tree nor shrub, only the wild ass, and somewhere in its heart, men say, the wild camel.

Tarvin stared through the palpitating haze of heat, and saw that there was neither life nor motion about the city. It was a little after noonday, and his Majesty's subjects were asleep. This solid block of loneliness, then, was the visible end of his journey—the Jericho he had come from Topaz to attack.

And he reflected, 'Now, if a man should come from New York in a bullock-cart to whistle around the Sauguache Range, I wonder what sort of fool I'd call him!'

He rose and stretched his dusty limbs. 'What time does it get cool enough to take in the town?' he asked.

'Do *what* to the town? Better be careful. You might find yourself in difficulties with the Resident,' warned his friendly adviser.

Tarvin could not understand why a stroll through the deadest town he had ever seen should be forbidden. But he held his peace, inasmuch as he was in a strange country, where nothing, save a certain desire for command on the part of the women, was as he had known it. He would take in the town thoroughly. Otherwise he began to fear that its monumental sloth—there was still no sign of life upon the walled rock—would swallow him up, or turn him into a languid Calcutta drummer.

Something must be done at once before his wits were numbed. He inquired the way to the telegraph-office, half doubting, even though he saw the wires, the existence of a telegraph in Rhatore.

'By the way,' one of the men called after him, 'it's worth remembering that any telegram you

send here is handed all round the court and shown
to the King.'

Tarvin thanked him, and thought this *was*
worth remembering, as he trudged on through the
sand toward a desecrated Mohammedan mosque
near the road to the city which was doing duty as
a telegraph-office.

A trooper of the State was lying fast asleep on
the threshold, his horse picketed to a long bamboo
lance driven into the ground. Other sign of life
there was none, save a few doves cooing sleepily
in the darkness under the arch.

Tarvin gazed about him dispiritedly for the
blue and white sign of the Western Union, or its
analogue in this queer land. He saw that the
telegraph wires disappeared through a hole in the
dome of the mosque. There were two or three
low wooden doors under the archway. He opened
one at random, and stepped upon a warm, hairy
body, which sprang up with a grunt. Tarvin had
hardly time to draw back before a young buffalo
calf rushed out. Undisturbed, he opened another
door, disclosing a flight of steps eighteen inches
wide. Up these he travelled with difficulty,
hoping to catch the sound of the ticker. But the
building was as silent as the tomb it had once
been. He opened another door, and stumbled
into a room, the domed ceiling of which was
inlaid with fretted tracery in barbaric colours,
picked out with myriads of tiny fragments of
mirror. The flood of colour and the glare of the
snow-white floor made him blink after the pitchy
darkness of the staircase. Still, the place was

undoubtedly a telegraph-office, for an antiquated instrument was clamped upon a cheap dressing-table. The sunlight streamed through the gash in the dome which had been made to admit the telegraph wires, and which had not been repaired.

Tarvin stood in the sunlight and stared about him. He took off the soft, wide-brimmed Western hat, which he was finding too warm for this climate, and mopped his forehead. As he stood in the sunlight, straight, clean-limbed, and strong, one who lurked in this mysterious spot with designs upon him would have decided that he did not look a wholesome person to attack. He pulled at the long thin moustache which drooped at the corners of his mouth in a curve shaped by the habit of tugging at it in thought, and muttered picturesque remarks in a tongue to which these walls had never echoed. What chance was there of communicating with the United States of America from this abyss of oblivion ? Even the 'damn' that came back to him from the depths of the dome sounded foreign and inexpressive.

A sheeted figure lay on the floor. 'It *takes* a dead man to run this place!' exclaimed Tarvin, discovering the body. 'Hallo, you ! Get up there !'

The figure rose to its feet with grunts, cast away its covering, and disclosed a very sleepy native in a complete suit of dove-coloured satin.

'Ho !' cried he.

'Yes,' returned Tarvin imperturbably.

'You want to see me ? '

'No; I want to send a telegram, if there's any electric fluid in this old tomb.'

'Sir,' said the native affably, 'you have come to right shop. I am telegraph operator and postmaster-general of this State.'

He seated himself in the decayed chair, opened a drawer of the table, and began to search for something.

'What you looking for, young man? Lost your connection with Calcutta?'

'Most gentlemen bring their own forms,' he said, with a distant note of reproach in his bland manner. 'But here is form. Have you got pencil?'

'Oh, see here, don't let me strain this office. Hadn't you better go and lie down again? I'll tap the message off myself. What's your signal for Calcutta?'

'You, sir, not understanding this instrument.'

'*Don't* I? You ought to see me milk the wires at election time.'

'This instrument require most judeecious handling, sir. You write message. I send. That is proper division of labour. Ha! ha!'

Tarvin wrote his message, which ran thus:—

'*Getting   there.   Remember   Three   C.'s—* TARVIN.'

It was addressed to Mrs. Mutrie at the address she had given him in Denver.

'Rush it!' he said, as he handed it back over the table to the smiling image.

'All right; no fear. I am here for that,'

returned the native, understanding in general terms from the cabalistic word that his customer was in haste.

'Will the thing ever get there?' drawled Tarvin, as he leaned over the table and met the gaze of the satin-clothed being with an air of good comradeship, which invited him to let him into the fraud, if there was one.

'Oh yes; to-morrow. Denver is in the United States America,' said the native, looking up at Tarvin with childish glee in the sense of knowledge.

'Shake!' exclaimed Tarvin, offering him a hairy fist. 'You've been well brought up.'

He stayed half an hour fraternising with the man on the foundation of this common ground of knowledge, and saw him work the message off on his instrument, his heart going out on that first click all the way home. In the midst of the conversation the native suddenly dived into the cluttered drawer of the dressing-table, and drew forth a telegram covered with dust, which he offered to Tarvin's scrutiny.

'You knowing any new Englishman coming to Rhatore name Turpin?' he asked.

Tarvin stared at the address a moment, and then tore open the envelope to find, as he expected, that it was for him. It was from Mrs. Mutrie, congratulating him on his election to the Colorado legislature by a majority of 1518 over Sheriff.

Tarvin uttered an abandoned howl of joy, executed a war-dance on the white floor of the mosque, snatched the astounded operator from

behind his table, and whirled him away into a mad
waltz. Then, making a low salaam to the now
wholly bewildered native, he rushed from the
building, waving his cable in the air, and went
capering up the road.

When he was back at the rest-house again, he
retired to a bath to grapple seriously with the dust
of the desert, while the commercial travellers without discussed his comings and goings. He plunged
about luxuriously in a gigantic bowl of earthen-
ware ; while a brown-skinned water-carrier sluiced
the contents of a goat-skin over his head.

A voice in the verandah, a little louder than the
others, said, 'He's probably come prospecting for
gold, or boring for oil, and won't tell.'

Tarvin winked a wet left eye.

VII

There is pleasure in the wet, wet clay,
    When the artist's hand is potting it ;
There is pleasure in the wet, wet lay,
    When the poet's pad is blotting it ;
There is pleasure in the shine of your picture on the line
    At the Royal Acade-my ;
But the pleasure felt in these is as chalk to Cheddar cheese,
    When it comes to a well-made Lie :
        To a quite unwreckable Lie,
        To a most impeccable Lie,
To a water-tight, fireproof, angle-iron, sunk-hinge, time-lock,
    steel-faced Lie !
        Not a private hansom Lie,
        But a pair and brougham Lie,
Not a little place at Tooting, but a country-house with
    shooting,
        And a ring-fence, deer-park Lie.

                           —*Op.* 3.

A COMMON rest-house in the desert is not over-
stocked with furniture or carpets. One table, two
chairs, a rack on the door for clothing, and a list
of charges, are sufficient for each room ; and the
traveller brings his own bedding. Tarvin read the
tariff with deep interest before falling asleep that
night, and discovered that this was only in a
distant sense a hotel, and that he was open to the
danger of being turned out at twelve hours' notice,

after he had inhabited his unhomely apartment for a day and a night.

Before he went to bed he called for pen and ink, and wrote a letter to Mrs. Mutrie on the note-paper of his land and improvement company. Under the map of Colorado, at the top, which confidently showed the railroad system of the State converging at Topaz, was the legend, 'N. Tarvin, Real Estate and Insurance Agent.' The tone of his letter was even more assured than the map.

He dreamed that night that the Maharajah was swapping the Naulahka with him for town lots. His Majesty backed out just as they were concluding the deal, and demanded that Tarvin should throw in his own favourite mine, the 'Lingering Lode,' to boot. In his dream Tarvin had kicked at this, and the Maharajah had responded, 'All right, my boy; no Three C.'s then,' and Tarvin had yielded the point, had hung the Naulahka about Mrs. Mutrie's neck, and in the same breath had heard the Speaker of the Colorado legislature declaring that since the coming of the Three C.'s he officially recognised Topaz as the metropolis of the West. Then, perceiving that he himself was the Speaker, Tarvin began to doubt the genuineness of these remarks, and awoke, with aloes in his mouth, to find the dawn spreading over Rhatore, and beckoning him out to the conquests of reality.

He was confronted in the verandah by a grizzled, bearded, booted native soldier on a camel, who handed down to him a greasy little brown book, bearing the legend, *Please write 'seen.'*

Tarvin looked at this new development from the heated landscape with interest, but not with an outward effect of surprise. He had already learned one secret of the East—never to be surprised at anything. He took the book and read, on a thumbed page, the announcement, 'Divine services conducted on Sundays in the drawing-room of the residency at 7.30 A.M. Strangers are cordially invited to attend. (Signed) L. R. Estes, American Presbyterian Mission.'

'They don't get up early for nothing in this country,' mused Tarvin. ' Church " at 7.30 A.M." When do they have dinner? Well, what do I do about this?' he asked the man aloud. The trooper and camel looked at him together, and grunted as they went away. It was no concern of theirs.

Tarvin addressed a remark of confused purport to the retreating figures. This was plainly not a country in which business could be done at red heat. He hungered for the moment when, with the necklace in his pocket and Kate by his side, he should again set his face westward.

The shortest way to that was to go over to call on the missionary. He was an American, and could tell him about the Naulahka if anybody could ; Tarvin had also a shrewd suspicion that he could tell him something about Kate.

The missionary's home, which was just without the city walls, was also of red sandstone, one storey high, and as bare of vines or any living thing as the station at Rawut Junction. But he presently found that there were living beings inside the house, with warm hearts and a welcome for him. Mrs. Estes turned out to be that motherly and kindly woman, with the instinct for housekeeping, who would make a home of a cave. She had a round, smooth face, a soft skin, and quiet, happy eyes. She may have been forty. Her still untinged brown hair was brushed smoothly back; her effect was sedate and restful.

Their visitor had learned that they came from Bangor, Maine, had founded a tie of brotherhood on the fact that his father had been born on a farm down Portland way, and had been invited to breakfast before he had been ten minutes in the house. Tarvin's gift of sympathy was irresistible. He was the kind of man to whom men confide their heart-secrets, and the cankers of their inmost lives, in hotel smoking-rooms. He was the repository of scores of tales of misery and error which he could do nothing to help, and of a few which he could help, and had helped. Before breakfast was ready he had from Estes and his wife the whole picture of their situation at Rhatore. They told him of their troubles with the Maharajah and with the Maharajah's wives, and of the exceeding unfruitfulness of their work; and then of their children, living in the exile of Indian children, at home. They explained that they meant Bangor; they were there with an aunt, receiving their education at the hands of a public school.

'It's five years since we saw them,' said Mrs. Estes, as they sat down to breakfast. 'Fred was only six when he went, and Laura was eight.

They are eleven and thirteen now—only think!
We hope they haven't forgotten us ; but how can
they remember ?   They are only children.'

And then she told him stories of the renewal
of filial ties in India, after such absences, that made
his blood run cold.

The breakfast woke a violent home-sickness in
Tarvin.   After a month at sea, two days of the
chance railroad meals between Calcutta and Rawut
Junction, and a night at the rest-house, he was
prepared to value the homely family meal, and
the abundance of an American breakfast.   They
began with a water-melon, which did not help him
to feel at home, because water-melons were next
to an unknown luxury at Topaz, and when known,
did not ripen in grocers' windows in the month of
April.   But the oatmeal brought him home again,
and the steak and fried potatoes, the coffee and
the hot brown pop-overs, with their beguiling
yellow interiors, were reminders far too deep
for tears.   Mrs. Estes, enjoying his enjoyment,
said they must have out the can of maple syrup,
which had been sent them all the way from
Bangor ; and when the white-robed, silent-moving
servant in the red turban came in with the waffles,
she sent him for it.   They were all very happy
together over this, and said pleasant things about
the American republic, while the punkah sang its
droning song over their heads.

Tarvin had a map of Colorado in his pocket, of
course, and when the talk, swinging to one part
of the United States and another, worked westward, he spread it out on the breakfast-table,

between the waffles and the steak, and showed them the position of Topaz. He explained to Estes how a new railroad, running north and south, would make the town, and then he had to say affectionately what a wonderful town it really was, and to tell them about the buildings they had put up in the last twelve months, and how they had picked themselves up after the fire and gone to building the next morning. The fire had brought $100,000 into the town in insurance, he said. He exaggerated his exaggerations in unconscious defiance of the hugeness of the empty landscape lying outside the window. He did not mean to let the East engulf him or Topaz.

'We've got a young lady coming to us, I think, from your State,' interrupted Mrs. Estes, to whom all Western towns were alike. 'Wasn't it Topaz, Lucien? I'm almost sure it was.'

She rose and went to her work-basket for a letter, from which he confirmed her statement. 'Yes; Topaz. A Miss Sheriff. She comes to us from the Zenana Mission. Perhaps you know her?'

Tarvin's head bent over the map, which he was refolding. He answered shortly, 'Yes; I know her. When is she likely to be here?'

'Most any day now,' said Mrs. Estes.

'It seems a pity,' said Tarvin, 'to bring a young girl out here all alone, away from her friends— though I'm sure you'll be friends to her,' he added quickly, seeking Mrs. Estes' eyes.

'We shall try to keep her from getting home-sick,' said Mrs. Estes, with the motherly note in her voice. 'There's Fred and Laura home in Bangor, you know,' she added after a pause.

'That will be good of you,' said Tarvin, with more feeling than the interests of the Zenana Mission demanded.

'May I ask what your business is here?' inquired the missionary, as he passed his cup to his wife to be refilled. He had a rather formal habit of speech, and his words came muffled from the depths of a dense jungle of beard—iron-grey and unusually long. He had a benevolently grim face, a precise but friendly manner, and a good way of looking one in the eye which Tarvin liked. He was a man of decided opinions, particularly about the native races of India.

'Well, I'm prospecting,' Tarvin said, in a leisurely tone, glancing out of the window as if he expected to see Kate start up out of the desert.

'Ah! For gold?'

'W-e-l-l, yes; as much that as anything.'

Estes invited him out upon the verandah to smoke a cigar with him; his wife brought her sewing and sat with them; and as they smoked Tarvin asked him his questions about the Naulahka. Where was it? What was it? he inquired boldly. But he found that the missionary, though an American, was no wiser about it than the lazy commercial travellers at the rest-house. He knew that it existed, but knew no man who had seen it save the Maharajah. Tarvin got at this through much talk about other things which interested him less; but he began to see an idea in the gold-mining to which the missionary persistently returned. Estes said he meant to engage in placer-mining, of course ?

'Of course,' assented Tarvin.

'But you won't find much gold in the Amet River, I fancy. The natives have washed it spasmodically for hundreds of years. There is nothing to be found but what little silt washes down from the quartz rocks of the Gungra Hills. But you will be undertaking work on a large scale, I judge ?' said the missionary, looking at him curiously.

'Oh, on a large scale, of course.'

Estes added that he supposed he had thought of the political difficulties in his way. He would have to get the consent of Colonel Nolan, and through him the consent of the British Government, if he meant to do anything serious in the State. In fact, he would have to get Colonel Nolan's consent to stay in Rhatore at all.

'Do you mean that I shall have to make it worth the British Government's while to let me alone ?'

'Yes.'

'All right ; I'll do that too.'

Mrs. Estes looked up quickly at her husband from under her eyebrows. Woman-like, she was thinking.

VIII

When a Lover hies abroad,
  Looking for his Love,
Azrael smiling sheathes his sword,
  Heaven smiles above.
    Earth and Sea
    His servants be,
And to lesser compass round,
That his Love be sooner found.
                Chorus from Libretto to Naulahka.

TARVIN learned a number of things within the
next week; and with what the West calls
'adaptability,' put on, with the complete suit of
white linen which he donned the second day, an
initiation into a whole new system of manners,
usages, and traditions. They were not all agree-
able, but they were all in a good cause, and he
took pains to see that his new knowledge should
not go for nothing, by securing an immediate
presentation to the only man in the State of whom
it was definitely assertable that he had seen the
object of his hopes. Estes willingly presented
him to the Maharajah. The missionary and he
rode one morning up the steep slopes of the rock
on which stood the palace, itself rock - hewn.
Passing through a deep archway, they entered a

marble - flagged courtyard, and there found the
Maharajah, attended by one ragged and out-at-
elbow menial, discussing the points of a fox-terrier,
which was lying before him on the flags.

Tarvin, unversed in kings, had expected a
certain amount of state from one who did not pay
his bills, and might be reasonably expected to
cultivate reserve ; but he was not prepared for the
slovenly informality of a ruler in his everyday
garb, released from the duty of behaving with
restraint in the presence of a viceroy, nor for the
picturesque mixture of dirt and decoration about
the court. The Maharajah proved a large and
amiable despot, brown and bush-bearded, arrayed
in a gold-sprigged, green velvet dressing-gown,
who appeared only too delighted to meet a man
who had no connection with the Government of
India, and who never mentioned the subject of
money.

The disproportionate smallness of his hands and
feet showed that the ruler of Gokral Seetarun came
of the oldest blood in Rajputana ; his fathers had
fought hard and ridden far with sword-hilts and
stirrups that would hardly serve an English child.
His face was bloated and sodden, and the dull eyes
stared wearily above deep, rugged pouches. To
Tarvin, accustomed to read the motives of Western
men in their faces, there seemed to be neither fear
nor desire in those eyes—only an everlasting weariness. It was like looking at an extinct volcano—a
volcano that rumbled in good English.

Tarvin had a natural interest in dogs, and the
keenest possible desire to ingratiate himself with the

ruler of the State. As a king he considered him something of an imposture, but as a brother dog-fancier, and the lord of the Naulahka, he was to Tarvin more than a brother ; that is to say, the brother of one's beloved. He spoke eloquently and to the point.

'Come again,' said the Maharajah, with a light of real interest in his eyes, as Estes, a little scandalised, drew off his guest. 'Come again this evening after dinner. You have come from new countries.'

His Majesty, later, carried away by the evening draught of opium, without which no Rajput can talk or think, taught this irreverent stranger, who told him tales of white men beyond the seas, the royal game of pachisi. They played it far into the night, in the marble-flagged courtyard, sur-rounded by green shutters from behind which Tarvin could hear, without turning his head, the whisper of watching women and the rustle of silken robes. The palace, he saw, was all eyes.

Next morning, at dawn, he found the King waiting at the head of the main street of his city for a certain notorious wild boar to come home. The game laws of Gokral Seetarun extended to the streets of walled towns, and the wild pig rooted unconcerned at night in the alley-ways. The pig came, and was dropped, at a hundred yards, by his Majesty's new Express rifle. It was a clean shot, and Tarvin applauded cordially. Had his Majesty the King ever seen a flying coin hit by a pistol bullet? The weary eyes brightened with childish delight. The King had not seen this feat, and had not the coin. Tarvin flung an American quarter skyward, and clipped it with his revolver as it fell. Thereupon the King begged him to do it again, which Tarvin, valuing his reputation, politely declined to do unless one of the court officials would set the example.

The King was himself anxious to try, and Tarvin threw the coin for him. The bullet whizzed unpleasantly close to Tarvin's ear, but the quarter on the grass was dented when he picked it up. The King liked Tarvin's dent as well as if it had been his own, and Tarvin was not the man to undeceive him.

The following morning the royal favour was completely withdrawn, and it was not until he had conferred with the disconsolate drummers in the rest-house that Tarvin learned that Sitabhai had been indulging one of her queenly rages. On this he transferred himself and his abundant capacity for interesting men off-hand to Colonel Nolan, and made that weary white-haired man laugh as he had not laughed since he had been a subaltern over an account of the King's revolver practice. Tarvin shared his luncheon, and discovered from him in the course of the afternoon the true policy of the Government of India in regard to the State of Gokral Seetarun. The Government hoped to elevate it; but as the Maharajah would not pay for the means of civilisation, the progress was slow. Colonel Nolan's account of the internal policy of the palace, given with official caution, was absolutely different from the missionary's, which again differed entirely from the profane account of the men in the rest-house.

G

At twilight the Maharajah pursued Tarvin with a mounted messenger, for the favour of the royal countenance was restored, and he required the presence of the tall man who clipped coins in the air, told tales, and played pachisi. There was more than pachisi upon the board that night, and his Majesty the King grew pathetic, and confided to Tarvin a long and particular account of his own and the State's embarrassments, which presented everything in a fourth new light. He concluded with an incoherent appeal to the President of the United States, on whose illimitable powers and far-reaching authority Tarvin dwelt, with a patriotism extended for the moment to embrace the nation to which Topaz belonged. For many reasons he did not conceive that this was an auspicious time to open negotiations for the transfer of the Naulahka. The Maharajah would have given away half his kingdom, and appealed to the Resident in the morning.

The next day, and many succeeding days, brought to the door of the rest-house, where Tarvin was still staying, a procession of rainbow-clad Orientals, ministers of the court each one, who looked with contempt on the waiting commercial travellers, and deferentially made themselves known to Tarvin, whom they warned in fluent and stilted English against trusting anybody except themselves. Each confidence wound up with, ' And I am your true friend, sir '; and each man accused his fellows to the stranger of every crime against the State, or ill-will toward the Government of India, that it had entered his own brain to conceive.

Tarvin could only faintly conjecture what all this meant. It seemed to him no extraordinary mark of court favour to play pachisi with the King, and the mazes of Oriental diplomacy were dark to him. The ministers were equally at a loss to understand him. He had walked in upon them from out the sky-line, utterly self-possessed, utterly fearless, and, so far as they could see, utterly disinterested; the greater reason, therefore, for suspecting that he was a veiled emissary of the Government, whose plans they could not fathom. That he was barbarously ignorant of everything pertaining to the Government of India only confirmed their belief. It was enough for them to know that he went to the King in secret, was closeted with him for hours, and possessed, for the time being, the royal ear.

These smooth-voiced, stately, mysterious strangers filled Tarvin with weariness and disgust, and he took out his revenge upon the commercial travellers, to whom he sold stock in his land and improvement company between their visits. The yellow-coated man, as his first friend and adviser, he allowed to purchase a very few shares in the 'Lingering Lode,' on the dead quiet. It was before the days of the gold boom in Lower Bengal, and there was still faith in the land.

These transactions took him back in fancy to Topaz, and made him long for some word about the boys at home, from whom he had absolutely cut himself off by this secret expedition, in which he was playing, necessarily alone, for the high stake common to them both. He would have given all the rupees in his pocket at any moment for a sight of the *Topaz Telegram*, or even for a look at a Denver daily. What was happening to his mines —to the 'Mollie K.,' which was being worked on a lease ; to the 'Mascot,' which was the subject of a legal dispute; to the 'Lingering Lode,' where they had been on the point of striking it very rich when he left ; and to his 'Garfield' claim, which Fibby Winks had jumped ? What had become of the mines of all his friends, of their cattle-ranches, of their deals? What, in fine, had become of Colorado and of the United States of America ? They might have legislated silver out of existence at Washington, for all he knew, and turned the republic into a monarchy at the old stand.

His single resource from these pangs was his visits to the house of the missionary, where they talked Bangor, Maine, in the United States. To that house he knew that every day was bringing nearer the little girl he had come half way round the world to keep in sight.

In the splendour of a yellow and violet morning, ten days after his arrival, he was roused from his sleep by a small, shrill voice in the verandah de-manding the immediate attendance of the new Englishman. The Maharaj Kunwar, heir-apparent to the throne of Gokral Seetarun, a wheat-coloured child, aged nine, had ordered his miniature court, which was held quite distinct from his father's, to equip his C-spring barouche, and to take him to the rest-house.

Like his jaded father, the child required amuse-ment. All the women of the palace had told him

that the new Englishman made the King laugh.
The Maharaj Kunwar could speak English much
better than his father—French, too, for the matter
of that—and he was anxious to show off his
accomplishments to a court whose applause he had
not yet commanded.

Tarvin obeyed the voice because it was a
child's, and came out to find an apparently empty
barouche, and an escort of ten gigantic troopers.

'How do you do? *Comment vous portez-vous?*
I am the prince of this State. I am the Maharaj
Kunwar. Some day I shall be king. Come for a
drive with me.'

A tiny mittened hand was extended in greeting.
The mittens were of the crudest magenta wool,
with green stripes at the wrist; but the child was
robed in stiff gold brocade from head to foot, and
in his turban was set an aigrette of diamonds six
inches high, while emeralds in a thick cluster fell
over his eyebrow. Under all this glitter the dark
onyx eyes looked out, and they were full of pride
and of the loneliness of childhood.

Tarvin obediently took his seat in the barouche.
He was beginning to wonder whether he should
ever wonder at anything again.

'We will drive beyond the race-course on the
railway road,' said the child. 'Who are you?'
he asked, softly laying his hand on Tarvin's wrist.

'Just a man, sonny.'

The face looked very old under the turban, for
those born to absolute power, or those who have
never known a thwarted desire, and reared under
the fiercest sun in the world, age even more swiftly

than the other children of the East, who are self-possessed men when they should be bashful babes.

'They say you come here to see things.'

'That's true,' said Tarvin.

'When I'm king I shall allow nobody to come here—not even the viceroy.'

'That leaves me out,' remarked Tarvin, laughing.

'You shall come,' returned the child, measuredly, 'if you make me laugh. Make me laugh now.'

'Shall I, little fellow? Well—there was once —I wonder what *would* make a child laugh in this country. I've never seen one do it yet. W-h-e-w!' Tarvin gave a low, long-drawn whistle. 'What's that over there, my boy?'

A little puff of dust rose very far down the road. It was made by swiftly moving wheels, consequently it had nothing to do with the regular traffic of the State.

'That is what I came out to see,' said the Maharaj Kunwar. 'She will make me well. My father, the Maharajah, said so. I am not well now.' He turned imperiously to a favourite groom at the back of the carriage. 'Soor Singh' —he spoke in the vernacular—'what is it when I become without sense? I have forgotten the English.' The groom leaned forward.

'Heaven-born, I do not remember,' he said.

'Now I remember,' said the child suddenly. 'Mrs. Estes says it is fits. What are fits?'

Tarvin put his hand tenderly on the child's shoulder, but his eyes were following the dust-cloud. 'Let us hope she'll cure them, anyway, young 'un, whatever they are. But who is *she?*'

'I do not know the name, but she will make me well. See! My father has sent a carriage to meet her.'

An empty barouche was drawn up by the side of the road as the rickety, straining mail-cart drew nearer, with frantic blasts upon a battered key-bugle.

'It's better than a bullock-cart anyway,' said Tarvin to himself, standing up in the carriage, for he was beginning to choke.

'Young man, don't you know who she is?" he asked huskily again.

'She was sent,' said the Maharaj Kunwar.

'Her name's Kate,' said Tarvin in his throat, 'and don't you forget it.' Then to himself in a contented whisper, '*Kate!*'

The child waved his hand to his escort, who, dividing, lined either side of the road, with all the ragged bravery of irregular cavalry. The mail-carriage halted, and Kate, crumpled, dusty, dishevelled from her long journey, and red-eyed from lack of sleep, drew back the shutters of the palanquin-like carriage, and stepped dazed into the road. Her numbed limbs would have doubled under her, but Tarvin, leaping from the barouche, caught her to him, regardless of the escort and of the calm-eyed child in the golden drapery, who was shouting, 'Kate! Kate!'

'Run along home, bub,' said Tarvin. 'Well, Kate?'

But Kate had only her tears for him and a gasping 'You! You! *You!*'

IX

We meet in an evil land,
   That is near to the gates of Hell—
I wait for thy command,
To serve, to speed, or withstand ;
   And thou sayest I do not well !

Oh, love, the flowers so red
   Be only blossoms of flame,
The earth is full of the dead,
The new-killed, restless dead,
There is danger beneath and o'erhead ;
   And I guard at thy gates in fear
      Of peril and jeopardy,
   Of words thou canst not hear,
      Of signs thou canst not see—
And thou sayest 't is ill that I came ?

In Shadowland.

TEARS stood again in Kate's eyes as she uncoiled
her hair before the mirror in the room Mrs. Estes
had prepared against her coming—tears of vex-
ation. It was an old story with her that the world
wants nothing done for it, and visits with dis-
pleasure those who must prod up its lazy content.
But in landing at Bombay she had supposed herself
at the end of outside hindrances and obstacles ;
what was now to come would belong to the

wholesome difficulties of real work. And here
was Nick!

She had made the journey from Topaz in a
long mood of exaltation. She was launched; it
made her giddy and happy, like the boy's first
taste of the life of men. She was free at last.
No one could stop her. Nothing could keep her
from the life to which she had promised herself.
A little moment and she might stretch forth her
hand and lay it fast upon her work. A few days
and she should stoop eye to eye above the pain
that had called to her across seas. In her dreams
piteous hands of women were raised in prayer to
her, and dry, sick palms were laid in hers. The
steady urge of the ship was too slow for her; she
counted the throbs of the screw. Standing far in
the prow, with wind-blown hair, straining her eyes
toward India, her spirit went longingly forth
toward those to whom she was going; and her
life seemed to release itself from her, and sped far,
far over the waves, until it reached them and gave
itself to them. For a moment, as she set foot on
land, she trembled with a revulsion of feeling.
She drew near her work; but was it for her?
This old fear, which had gone doubtfully with
her purpose from the beginning, she put behind
her with a stern refusal to question there. She
was for so much of her work as heaven would let
her do; and she went forward with a new, strong,
humble impulse of devotion filling and uplifting
her.

It was in this mood that she stepped out of the
coach at Rhatore into Tarvin's arms.

She did justice to the kindness that had brought him over all these leagues, but she heartily wished that he had not come. The existence of a man who loved her, and for whom she could do nothing, was a sad and troubling fact enough fourteen thousand miles away. Face to face with it, alone in India, it enlarged itself unbearably, and thrust itself between her and all her hopes of bringing serious help to others. Love literally did not seem to her the most important thing in the world at that moment, and something else did ; but that didn't make Nick's trouble unimportant, or prevent it, while she braided her hair, from getting in the way of her thoughts. On the morrow she was to enter upon the life which she meant should be a help to those whom it could reach, and here she was thinking of Nicholas Tarvin.

It was because she foresaw that she would keep on thinking of him that she wished him away. He was the tourist wandering about behind the devotee in the cathedral at prayers ; he was the other thought. In his person he represented and symbolised the life she had left behind ; much worse, he represented a pain she could not heal. It was not with the haunting figure of love attendant that one carried out large purposes. Nor was it with a divided mind that men conquered cities. The intent with which she was aflame needed all of her. She could not divide herself even with Nick. And yet it was good of him to come, and like him. She knew that he had not come merely in pursuit of a selfish hope ; it was as he had said—he couldn't sleep nights, knowing

what might befall her.   That was *really* good of
him.

Mrs. Estes had invited Tarvin to breakfast the
day before, when Kate was not expected, but
Tarvin was not the man to decline an invitation
at the last moment on that account, and he faced
Kate across the breakfast-table next morning with
a smile which evoked an unwilling smile from her.
In spite of a sleepless night she was looking very
fresh and pretty in the white muslin frock which
had replaced her travelling dress, and when he
found himself alone with her after breakfast on the
verandah (Mrs. Estes having gone to look after
the morning affairs of a housekeeper, and Estes
having betaken himself to his mission-school, inside
the city walls), he began to make her his compliments upon the cool white, unknown to the West.
But Kate stopped him.

'Nick,' she said, facing him, 'will you do something for me?'

Seeing her much in earnest, Tarvin attempted
the parry humorous; but she broke in—

'No; it is something I want very much, Nick.
Will you do it for me?'

'Is there anything I wouldn't do for you?' he
asked seriously.

'I don't know; this, perhaps.   But you must
do it.'

'What is it?'

'Go away.'

He shook his head.

'But you must.'

'Listen, Kate,' said Tarvin, thrusting his hands

deep into the big pockets of his white coat; 'I can't. You don't know the place you've come to. Ask me the same question a week hence. I won't agree to go. But I'll agree to talk it over with you then.'

'I know now everything that counts,' she answered. 'I want to do what I've come here for. I shan't be able to do it if you stay. You understand, don't you, Nick? Nothing can change that.'

'Yes, it can. *I* can. I'll behave.'

'You needn't tell me you'll be kind. I know it. But even you can't be kind enough to help hindering me. Believe that, now, Nick, and go. It isn't that I want you to go, you know.'

'Oh!' observed Tarvin, with a smile.

'Well—you know what I mean,' returned Kate, her face unrelaxed.

'Yes; I know. But if I'm good it won't matter. I know that too. You'll see,' he said gently. 'Awful journey, isn't it?'

'You promised me not to take it.'

'I didn't take it,' returned Tarvin, smiling, and spreading a seat for her in the hammock, while he took one of the deep verandah chairs himself. He crossed his legs and fixed the white pith helmet he had lately adopted on his knee. 'I came round the other way on purpose.'

'What do you mean?' asked Kate, dropping tentatively into the hammock.

'San Francisco and Yokohama, of course. You told me not to follow you.'

'*Nick!*' She gathered into the single syllable the reproach and reproof, the liking and despair, with which the least and the greatest of his audacities alike affected her.

Tarvin had nothing to say for once, and in the pause that fell she had time to reassure herself of her abhorrence of his presence here, and time to still the impulse of pride, which told her that it was good to be followed over half the earth's girdle for love, and the impulse of admiration for that fine devotion—time, above all—for this was worst and most shameful—to scorn the sense of loneliness and far-awayness that came rolling in on her out of the desert like a cloud, and made the protecting and home-like presence of the man she had known in the other life seem for a moment sweet and desirable.

'Come, Kate, you didn't expect me to stay at home, and let you find your way out here to take the chances of this old sand-heap, did you? It would be a cold day when I let you come to Gokral Seetarun all by your lone, little girl—freezing cold, I've thought since I've been here, and seen what sort of camp it is.'

'Why didn't you tell me you were coming?'

'You didn't seem particularly interested in what I did, when I last saw you.'

'Nick! I didn't want you to come here, and I had to come myself.'

'Well, you've come.   I hope you'll like it,' said he, grimly.

'Is it so bad?' she asked.   'Not that I shall mind.'

'Bad!   Do you remember Mastodon?'

Mastodon was one of those Western towns

which have their future behind them—a city without an inhabitant, abandoned and desolate.

'Take Mastodon for deadness, and fill it with ten Leadvilles for wickedness—Leadville the first year—and you've got a tenth of it.'

He went on to offer her an exposition of the history, politics, and society of Gokral Seetarun, from his own point of view, dealing with the dead East from the standpoint of the living West, and dealing with it vividly. It was a burning theme, and it was a happiness to him to have a listener who could understand his attitude, even if she could not entirely sympathise with it. His tone besought her to laugh at it with him a little, if only a little, and Kate consented to laugh; but she said it all seemed to her more mournful than amusing.

Tarvin could agree to this readily enough, but he told her that he laughed to avoid weeping. It made him tired to see the fixedness, the apathy, and lifelessness of this rich and populous world, which should be up and stirring by rights—trading, organising, inventing, building new towns, making the old ones keep up with the procession, laying new railroads, going in for fresh enterprises, and keeping things humming.

'They've got resources enough,' he said. 'It isn't as if they had the excuse that the country's poor. It's a good country. Move the population of a lively Colorado town to Rhatore, set up a good local paper, organise a board of trade, and let the world know what there is here, and we'd have a boom in six months that would shake the empire.

But what's the use? They're dead. They're mummies. They're wooden images. There isn't enough real, old-fashioned downright rustle and razzle-dazzle and "git up and git" in Gokral Seetarun to run a milk-cart.'

'Yes, yes,' she murmured, half to herself, with illumined eyes. 'It's for that I've come.'

'How's that?'

'Because they are *not* like us,' she answered, turning her lustrous face on him. 'If they were clever, if they were wise, what could we do for them? It is because they are lost, stumbling, foolish creatures that they need us.' She heaved a deep sigh. 'It is good to be here.'

'It's good to have you,' said Tarvin.

She started. 'Don't say such things any more, please, Nick,' she said.

'Oh, well!' he groaned.

'But it's this way, Nick,' she said earnestly, but kindly. 'I don't belong to such things any more—not even to the possibility of them. Think of me as a nun. Think of me as having renounced all such happiness, and all other kinds of happiness but my work.'

'H'm. May I smoke?' At her nod he lighted a cigar. 'I'm glad I'm here for the ceremony.'

'What ceremony?' she asked.

'Seeing you take the veil. But you won't take it.'

'Why not?'

He grumbled inarticulately over his cigar a moment. Then he looked up. 'Because I've got

big wealth that says you won't. I know you, I
know Rhatore, and I know——'

'What? Who?'

'Myself,' he said, looking up.

She clasped her hands in her lap. 'Nick,' she
said, leaning toward him, 'you know I like you.
I like you too well to let you go on thinking—
you talk of not being able to sleep. How do you
suppose I can sleep with the thought always by me
that you are laying up a pain and disappointment
for yourself—one that I can't help, unless I can
help it by begging you to go away now. I do
beg it. *Please* go!'

Tarvin pulled at his cigar musingly for some
seconds. 'Dear girl, I'm not afraid.'

She sighed, and turned her face away toward
the desert. 'I wish you were,' she said hopelessly.

'Fear is not for legislators,' he retorted oracu-
larly.

She turned back to him with a sudden motion.
'Legislators! O Nick, are you——?'

'I'm afraid I am—by a majority of 1518.'
He handed her the cable-despatch.

'Poor father !'

'Well, I don't know.'

'Oh ! Well, I congratulate you, of course.'

'Thanks.'

'But I'm not sure it will be a good thing for
you.'

'Yes ; that's the way it had struck me. If I
spend my whole term out here, like as not my
constituents won't be in a mood to advance my
political career when I get back.'

' All the more reason——'

' No ; the more reason for fixing the real thing first. I can make myself solid in politics any time. But there isn't but one time to make myself solid with you, Kate. It's here. It's now.' He rose and bent over her. ' Do you think I can postpone that, dear ? I can adjourn it from day to day, and I do cheerfully, and you shan't hear any more of it until you're ready to. But you like me, Kate. I know that. And I—well, I like you. There isn't but one end to that sort of thing.' He took her hand. ' Good-bye. I'll come and take you for a look at the city to-morrow.'

Kate gazed long after his retreating figure, and then took herself into the house, where a warm, healthful chat with Mrs. Estes, chiefly about the children at Bangor, helped her to a sane view of the situation she must face with the reappearance of Tarvin. She saw that he meant to stay, and if she didn't mean to go, it was for her to find the brave way of adjusting the fact to her hopes. His perversity complicated an undertaking which she had never expected to find simple in itself ; and it was finally only because she trusted all that he said implicitly that she was able to stay herself upon his promise to ' behave.' Liberally interpreted, this really meant much from Tarvin ; perhaps it meant all that she need ask.

When all was said, there remained the impulse to flight ; but she was ashamed to find, when he came in the morning, that a formidable pang of home-sickness drew her toward him, and made his definite and cheerful presence a welcome sight.

Mrs. Estes had been kind. The two women had made friends, and found each other's heart with instant sympathy. But a home face was different, and perhaps Nick's was even more different. At all events, she willingly let him carry out his plan of showing her the city.

In their walk about it Tarvin did not spare her the advantage of his ten days' residence in Rhatore preceding her coming ; he made himself her guide, and stood on rocks overlooking things and spouted his second-hand history with an assurance that the oldest Political Resident might have envied. He was interested in the problems of the State, if not responsible for their solution. Was he not a member of a governing body ? His ceaseless and fruitful curiosity about all new things had furnished him, in ten days, with much learning about Rhatore and Gokral Seetarun, enabling him to show to Kate, with eyes scarcely less fresh than her own, the wonders of the narrow, sand-choked streets, where the footfalls of camels and men alike fell dead. They lingered by the royal menagerie of starved tigers, and the cages of the two tame hunting leopards, hooded like hawks, that slept, and yawned, and scratched on their two bedsteads by the main gate of the city ; and he showed her the ponderous door of the great gate itself, studded with foot-long spikes against the attacks of that living battering-ram, the elephant. He led her through the long lines of dark shops planted in and among the ruins of palaces, whose builders had been long since forgotten, and about the straggling barracks, past knots of fantastically

attired soldiers, who hung their day's marketing
from the muzzle of the Brown Bess or flint-lock;
and then he showed her the mausoleum of the
kings of Gokral Seetarun, under the shadow of the
great temple where the children of the Sun and
Moon went to worship, and where the smooth,
black stone bull glared across the main square at
the cheap bronze statue of Colonel Nolan's pre-
decessor—an offensively energetic and very plain
Yorkshireman. Lastly, they found beyond the
walls the clamouring caravansary of traders by the
gateway of the Three Gods, whence the caravans
of camels filed out with their burdens of glistening
rock-salt for the railroad, and where by day and
by night cloaked and jaw-bound riders of the
desert, speaking a tongue that none could understand, rode in from God knows what fastness
beyond the white hillocks of Jeysulmir.

As they went along, Tarvin asked her about
Topaz. How had she left it? How was the dear
old town looking? Kate said she had only left it
three days after his departure.

'Three days! Three days is a long time in
the life of a growing town.'

Kate smiled. 'I didn't see any changes,' she
said.

'No? Peters was talking about breaking
ground for his new brick saloon on G Street the
day after I left; Parsons was getting in a new
dynamo for the city's electric light plant; they
were just getting to work on the grading of
Massachusetts Avenue, and they had planted the
first tree in my twenty-acre plot. Kearney, the

druggist, was putting in a plate-glass window, and I shouldn't wonder if Maxim had got his new post-office boxes from Meriden before you left. Didn't you notice?'

Kate shook her head. 'I was thinking of something else just then.'

'Pshaw! I'd like to know. But no matter. I suppose it *is* asking too much to expect a woman to play her own hand, and keep the run of improvements in the town,' he mused. 'Women aren't built that way. And yet I used to run a political canvass and a business or two, and something else in that town.' He glanced humorously at Kate, who lifted a warning hand. 'Forbidden subject? All right. I *will* be good. But they had to get up early in the morning to do anything to it without letting me into it. What did your father and mother say at the last?'

'Don't speak of that,' begged Kate.

'Well, I won't.'

'I wake up at night, and think of mother. It's dreadful. At the last I suppose I should have stayed behind and shirked if some one had said the right word—or the wrong one—as I got on board the train, and waved my handkerchief to them.'

'Good heaven! Why didn't I stay!' he groaned.

'You couldn't have said it, Nick,' she told him quietly.

'You mean your father could. Of course he could, and if he had happened to be some one else he would. When I think of that I want to——!'

'Don't say anything against father, please,' she said, with a tightening of the lips.

'Oh, dear child!' he murmured contritely, 'I didn't mean that. But I have to say something against somebody. Give me somebody to curse, and I'll be quiet.'

'Nick!'

'Well, I'm not a block of wood,' he growled.

'No; you are only a very foolish man.'

Tarvin smiled. 'Now you're shouting.'

She asked him about the Maharaj Kunwar, to change the subject, and Tarvin told her that he was a little brick. But he added that the society of Rhatore wasn't all as good.

'You ought to see Sitabhai!'

He went on to tell her about the Maharajah and the people of the palace with whom she would come in contact. They talked of the strange mingling of impassiveness and childishness in the people, which had already impressed Kate, and spoke of their primitive passions and simple ideas —simple as the massive strength of the Orient is simple.

'They aren't what we should call cultured. They don't know Ibsen a little bit, and they don't go in for Tolstoi for sour apples,' said Tarvin, who did not read three newspapers a day at Topaz for nothing. 'If they really knew the modern young woman, I suppose her life wouldn't be worth an hour's purchase. But they've got some rattling good old-fashioned ideas, all the same—the sort I used to hear once upon a time at my dear old mother's knee, away back in the State of Maine. Mother believed in marriage, you know; and that's where she agreed with me and with the fine old-style natives of India. The venerable, ramshackle, tumble-down institution of matrimony is still in use here, you know.'

'But I never said I sympathised with Nora, Nick,' exclaimed Kate, leaping all the chasms of connection.

'Well, then, that's where you are solid with the Indian Empire. The *Doll's House* glanced right off this blessed old-timey country. You wouldn't know where it had been hit.'

'But I don't agree with all your ideas either,' she felt bound to add.

'I can think of one,' retorted Tarvin, with a shrewd smile. 'But I'll convert you to my views there.'

Kate stopped short in the street along which they were walking. 'I trusted you, Nick!' she said reproachfully.

He stopped, and gazed ruefully at her for a moment. 'O Lord!' he groaned. 'I trusted myself! But I'm always thinking of it. What can you expect? But I tell you what, Kate, this shall be the end—last, final, ultimate. I'm done. From this out I'm a reformed man. I don't promise not to think, and I'll have to go on feeling, just the same. But I'll be quiet. Shake on it.' He offered his hand, and Kate took it.

They walked on for some moments in silence until Tarvin said mournfully, 'You didn't see Heckler just before you came away, did you?'

She shook her head.

'No; Jim and you never did get along much together. But I wish I knew what he's thinking about me. Didn't hear any rumour, any report, going around about what had become of me, I suppose?'

'They thought in town that you had gone to San Francisco to see some of the Western directors of the Colorado and California Central, I think. They thought that because the conductor of your train brought back word that you said you were going to Alaska, and they didn't believe that. I wish you had a better reputation for truth-telling at Topaz, Nick.'

'So do I, Kate; so do I,' exclaimed Tarvin heartily. 'But if I had, how would I ever get the right thing believed? That's just what I wanted them to think—that I was looking after their interests. But where would I be if I had sent that story back? They would have had me working a land-grab in Chile before night. That reminds me—don't mention that I'm here in writing home, please. Perhaps they'll figure that out, too, by the rule of contraries, if I give them the chance. But I don't want to give them the chance.'

'I'm not likely to mention it,' said Kate, flushing.

A moment later she recurred to the subject of her mother. In the yearning for home that came upon her anew in the midst of all the strangeness through which Tarvin was taking her, the thought of her mother, patient, alone, looking for some word from her, hurt her as if for the first time. The memory was for the moment intolerable to her; but when Tarvin asked her why she had come at all if she felt that way, she answered with the courage of better moments—'Why do men go to war?'

Kate saw little of Tarvin during the next few days. Mrs. Estes made her known at the palace, and she had plenty to occupy her mind and heart. There she stepped bewilderedly into a land where it was always twilight—a labyrinth of passages, courtyards, stairs, and hidden ways, all overflowing with veiled women, who peered at her and laughed behind her back, or childishly examined her dress, her helmet, and her gloves. It seemed impossible that she should ever know the smallest part of the vast warren, or distinguish one pale face from another in the gloom, as the women led her through long lines of lonely chambers where the wind sighed alone under the glittering ceilings, to hanging gardens two hundred feet above the level of the ground, but still jealously guarded by high walls, and down again by interminable stairways, from the glare and the blue of the flat roofs to silent subterranean chambers hewn against the heat of the summer sixty feet into the heart of the living rock. At every step she found women and children, and yet more women and children. The palace was reported to hold within its walls four thousand living, and no man knew how many buried, dead.

There were many women—how many she did not know—worked upon by intrigues she could not comprehend, who refused her ministrations absolutely. They were not ill, they said, and

the touch of the white woman meant pollution.
Others there were who thrust their children before
her and bade her bring colour and strength back
to these pale buds born in the darkness ; and
terrible, fierce-eyed girls who leaped upon her out
of the dark, overwhelming her with passionate
complaints that she did not and dared not understand. Monstrous and obscene pictures glared at
her from the walls of the little rooms, and the
images of shameless gods mocked her from their
greasy niches above the doorways. The heat and
the smell of cooking, faint fumes of incense, and
the indescribable taint of overcrowded humanity,
caught her by the throat. But what she heard
and what she guessed sickened her more than any
visible horror. Plainly it was one thing to be
stirred to generous action by a vivid recital of the
state of the women of India, another to face the
unutterable fact in the isolation of the women's
apartments of the palace of Rhatore.

Tarvin meanwhile was going about spying out
the land on a system which he had contrived for
himself. It was conducted on the principle of
exhaustion of the possibilities in the order of their
importance — every movement which he made
having the directest, though not always the most
obvious, relation to the Naulahka.

He was free to come and go through the royal
gardens, where innumerable and very seldom paid
gardeners fought with water-skin and well-wheel
against the destroying heat of the desert. He was
welcomed in the Maharajah's stables, where eight
hundred horses were littered down nightly, and

was allowed to watch them go out for their morning exercise, four hundred at a time, in a whirlwind of dust. In the outer courts of the palace it was open to him to come and go as he chose—to watch the toilets of the elephants when the Maharajah went out in state, to laugh with the quarter-guard, and to unearth dragon-headed, snake-throated pieces of artillery, invented by native artificers, who, here in the East, had dreamed of the *mitrailleuse*. But Kate could go where he was forbidden to venture. He knew the life of a white woman to be as safe in Rhatore as in Topaz; but on the first day she disappeared, untroubled and unquestioning, behind the darkness of the veiled door leading to the apartments of the women of the palace, he found his hand going instinctively to the butt of his revolver.

The Maharajah was an excellent friend, and no bad hand at pachisi; but as Tarvin sat opposite him, half an hour later, he reflected that he should not recommend the Maharajah's life for insurance if anything happened to his love while she remained in those mysterious chambers from which the only sign that came to the outer world was a ceaseless whispering and rustling. When Kate came out, the little Maharaj Kunwar clinging to her hand, her face was white and drawn, and her eyes full of indignant tears. She had seen.

Tarvin hastened to her side, but she put him from her with the imperious gesture that women know in deep moments, and fled to Mrs. Estes.

Tarvin felt himself for the moment rudely thrust out of her life. The Maharaj Kunwar

found him that evening pacing up and down the
verandah of the rest-house, almost sorry that he
had not shot the Maharajah for bringing that look
into Kate's eyes.   With deep-drawn breath he
thanked his God that he was there to watch
and defend, and, if need were, to carry off, at
the last, by force.   With a shudder he fancied
her here alone, save for the distant care of Mrs.
Estes.

'I have brought this for Kate,' said the child,
descending from his carriage cautiously, with a
parcel that filled both his arms.   'Come with me
there.'

Nothing loth, Tarvin came, and they drove
over to the house of the missionary.

'All the people in my palace,' said the child as
they went, 'say that she's your Kate.'

'I'm glad they know that much,' muttered
Tarvin to himself savagely.   'What's this you
have got for her?' he asked the Maharaj aloud,
laying his hand on the parcel.

'It is from my mother, the Queen—the real
Queen, you know, because I am the Prince.   There
is a message, too, that I must not tell.'   He began
to whisper, childlike, to himself, to keep the
message in mind.   Kate was in the verandah when
they arrived, and her face brightened a little at
sight of the child.

'Tell my guard to stand back out of the garden.
Go, and wait in the road.'

The carriage and troopers withdrew.   The child,
still holding Tarvin's hand, held out the parcel to
Kate.

'It is from my mother,' he said. 'You have seen her. This man need not go. He is'—he hesitated a little—'of your heart, is he not? Your speech is his speech.'

Kate flushed, but did not attempt to set the child right. What could she say?

'And I am to tell this,' he continued, 'first before everything, till you quite understand.' He spoke hesitatingly, translating out of his own vernacular as he went on, and drawing himself to his full height, as he cleared the cluster of emeralds from his brow. 'My mother, the Queen—the real Queen—says, "I was three months at this work. It is for you, because I have seen your face. That which has been made may be unravelled against our will, and a gipsy's hands are always picking. For the love of the gods look to it that a gipsy unravels nothing that I have made, for it is my life and soul to me. Protect this work of mine that comes from me—a cloth nine years upon the loom." I know more English than my mother,' said the child, dropping into his ordinary speech.

Kate opened the parcel, and unrolled a crude yellow and black comforter, with a violent crimson fringe, clumsily knitted. With such labours the queens of Gokral Seetarun were wont to beguile their leisure.

'That is all,' said the child. But he seemed unwilling to go. There was a lump in Kate's throat, as she handled the pitiful gift. Without warning the child, never loosening for a moment his grip on Tarvin's hand, began to repeat the message word by word, his little fingers tightening on Tarvin's fist as he went on.

'Say I am very grateful indeed,' said Kate, a little puzzled, and not too sure of her voice.

'That was not the answer,' said the child ; and he looked appealingly at his tall friend, the new Englishman.

The idle talk of the commercial travellers in the verandah of the rest-house flashed through Tarvin's mind. He took a quick pace forward, and laid his hand on Kate's shoulder, whispering huskily—

'Can't you see what it means ? It's the boy— the cloth nine years on the loom.'

'But what can I do ?' cried Kate, bewildered.

'Look after him. Keep on looking after him. You are quick enough in most things. Sitabhai wants his life. See that she doesn't get it.'

Kate began to understand a little. Everything was possible in that awful palace, even child-murder. She had already guessed the hate that lives between childless and mother queens. The Maharaj Kunwar stood motionless in the twilight, twinkling in his jewelled robes.

'Shall I say it again ?' he asked.

'No, no, no, child ! No !' she cried, flinging herself on her knees before him, and snatching his little figure to her breast, with a sudden access of tenderness and pity. 'O Nick ! what shall we do in this horrible country ?' She began to cry.

'Ah !' said the Maharaj, utterly unmoved, 'I was to go when I saw that you cried.' He lifted up his voice for the carriage and troopers, and departed, leaving the shabby comforter on the floor.

Kate was sobbing in the half darkness.   Neither Mrs. Estes nor her husband was within just then. That little 'we' of hers went through Tarvin with a sweet and tingling ecstasy.   He stooped and took her in his arms, and for that which followed Kate did not rebuke him.

'We'll pull through together, little girl,' he whispered to the shaken head on his shoulder.

X

Ye know the Hundred Danger Time when, gay with paint
    and flowers,
Your household gods are bribed to help the bitter, helpless
    hours ;
Ye know the worn and rotten mat whereon your daughter
    lies,
Ye know the *Sootak*-room unclean, the cell wherein she dies;

Dies with the babble in her ear of midwife's muttered charm,
Dies, spite young life that strains to stay, the suckling on
    her arm—
Dies in the four-fold heated room, parched by the Birth-
    Fire's breath—
Foredoomed, ye say, lest anguish lack, to haunt her home
    in death.

                    A Song of the Women.

'DEAR FRIEND—That was very unkind of you,
and you have made my life harder. I know I was
weak. The child upset me. But I must do what
I came for, and I want you to strengthen me,
Nick, not hinder me. Don't come for a few days,
please. I need all I am or hope to be for the work
I see opening here. I think I can really do some
good. Let me, please. KATE.'

Tarvin read fifty different meanings into this

letter, received the following morning, and read
them out again.   At the end of his conjectures he
could be sure only of one thing—that in spite of
that moment's weakness, Kate was fixed upon her
path.   He could not yet prevail against her stead-
fast gentleness, and perhaps it would be better not
to try.   Talks in the verandah, and sentinel-like
prowlings about her path when she went to the
palace, were pleasant enough, but he had not come
to Rhatore to tell her that he loved her.   Topaz,
in whose future the other half of his heart was
bound up, knew that secret long ago, and—Topaz
was waiting for the coming of the Three C.'s, even
as Nick was waiting on Kate's comings and goings.
The girl was unhappy, overstrained, and despairing, but since—he thanked God always—he was
at hand to guard her from the absolute shock of
evil fate, she might well be left for the moment to
Mrs. Estes' comfort and sympathy.

   She had already accomplished something in the
guarded courts of the women's quarters, for the
Maharaj Kunwar's mother had entrusted her only
son's life to her care (who could help loving and
trusting Kate?); but for his own part, what had
he done for Topaz beyond—he looked toward the
city—playing pachisi with the Maharajah?   The
low morning sun flung the shadow of the rest-
house before him.   The commercial travellers
came out one by one, gazed at the walled bulk of
Rhatore, and cursed it.   Tarvin mounted his
horse, of which much more hereafter, and ambled
toward the city to pay his respects to the Maharajah.
It was through him, if through any one, that he

must possess himself of the Naulahka; he had
been anxiously studying him, and shrewdly measuring the situation, and he now believed that he had
formed a plan through which he might hope to
make himself solid with the Maharajah—a plan
which, whether it brought him the Naulahka or
not, would at least allow him the privilege of
staying at Rhatore. This privilege certain broad
hints of Colonel Nolan's had seemed to Tarvin of
late plainly to threaten, and it had become clear to
him that he must at once acquire a practical and
publishable object for his visit, if he had to rip up
the entire State to find it. To stay, he must do
something in particular. What he had found to
do was particular enough; it should be done forthwith, and it should bring him first the Naulahka,
and then—if he was at all the man he took himself
for—Kate!

As he approached the gates he saw Kate, in a
brown habit, riding with Mrs. Estes out of the
missionary's garden.

'You needn't be afraid, dear. I shan't bother
you,' he said to himself, smiling at the dust-cloud
rising behind her, as he slackened his pace. 'But
I wonder what's taking you out so early.'

The misery within the palace walls which had
sent her half weeping to Mrs. Estes represented
only a phase of the work for which Kate had come.
If the wretchedness was so great under the shadow
of the throne, what must the common folk endure?
Kate was on her way to the hospital.

'There is only one native doctor at the hospital,'
Mrs. Estes was saying, as they went along, 'and,

of course, he's only a native ; that is to say, he is idle.'

' How can any one be idle here ? ' her companion cried, as the stored heat from under the city gates beat across their temples.

'Every one grows idle so soon in Rhatore,' returned Mrs. Estes, with a little sigh, thinking of Lucien's high hopes and strenuous endeavours, long since subdued to a mild apathy.

Kate sat her horse with the assured seat of a Western girl who has learned to ride and to walk at the same time. Her well-borne little figure had advantages on horseback. The glow of resolve lighting her simply framed face at the moment lent it a spiritual beauty ; and she was warmed by the consciousness that she drew near her purpose and the goal of two years' working and dreaming. As they rounded a curve in the main street of the city, a crowd was seen waiting at the foot of a flight of red sandstone steps rising to the platform of a whitewashed house three storeys in height, on which appeared the sign, 'State Dispensary.' The letters leaned against one another, and drooped down over each side of the door.

A sense of the unreality of it all came over Kate as she surveyed the crowd of women, clad in vermilion, dull-red, indigo, saffron, blue, pink, and turquoise garments of raw silk. Almost every woman held a child on her hip, and a low wailing cry rose up as Kate drew rein. The women clustered about her stirrup, caught at her foot, and thrust their babies into her arms. She took

one little one to her breast, and hushed it tenderly ;
it was burnt and dry with fever.

'Be careful,' said Mrs. Estes ; 'there is small-
pox in the hills behind us, and these people have
no notion of precautions.'

Kate, listening to the cry of the women, did
not answer. A portly, white-bearded native, in
a brown camel's hair dressing-gown and patent
leather boots, came out of the dispensary, thrusting the women right and left, and bowing profoundly.

'You are new lady doctor ?' he said. 'Hospital
is quite ready for inspection. Stand back from
the miss sahib !' he shouted in the vernacular, as
Kate slipped to the ground, and the crowd closed
about her. Mrs. Estes remained in the saddle,
watching the scene.

A woman of the desert, very tall, gold-coloured,
and scarlet-lipped, threw back her face-cloth,
caught Kate by the wrist, and made as if she
would drag her away, crying aloud fiercely in the
vernacular. The trouble in her eyes was not to
be denied. Kate followed unresisting, and, as the
crowd parted, saw a camel kneeling in the road-
way. On its back a gaunt skeleton of a man was
muttering, and picking aimlessly at the nail-studded
saddle. The woman drew herself up to full height,
and, without a word, flung herself down upon the
ground, clasping Kate's feet. Kate stooped to
raise her, her underlip quivering, and the doctor
from the steps shouted cheerfully—

'Oh, that is all right. He is confirmed lunatic,
her husband. She is always bringing him here.'

'Have you done nothing, then?' cried Kate, turning on him angrily.

'What *can* do? She will not leave him here for treatment so I may blister him.'

'Blister him!' murmured Kate to herself, appalled, as she caught the woman's hands and held them firmly. 'Tell her that I say he must be left here,' she said aloud. The doctor conveyed the command. The woman took a deep breath, and stared at Kate under level brows for a full half-minute. Then she carried Kate's hand to the man's forehead, and sat down in the dust, veiling her head.

Kate, dumb under these strange expressions of the workings of the Eastern mind, stared at her for a moment, with an impulse of the compassion which knows no race, before she bent and kissed her quietly on the forehead.

'Carry this man up,' she said, pointing; and he was carried up the steps and into the hospital, his wife following like a dog. Once she turned and spoke to her sisters below, and there went up a little chorus of weeping and laughter.

'She says,' said the doctor, beaming, 'that she will kill any one who is impolite to you. Also, she will be the nurse of your son.'

Kate paused to say a word to Mrs. Estes, who was bound on an errand further into the city; then she mounted the steps with the doctor.

'Now, will you see the hospital?' he asked. 'But first let me introduce. I am Lalla Dhunpat Rai, Licentiate Medicine, from the Duff College.

I was first native my province that took that degree. That was twenty years ago.'

Kate looked at him wonderingly. ' Where have you been since ? ' she asked.

'Some time I stayed in my father's house. Then I was clerk in medical stores in British India. But his Highness have graciously given me this appointment, which I hold now.'

Kate lifted her eyebrows. This, then, was to be her colleague. They passed into the hospital together in silence, Kate holding the skirt of her riding-habit clear of the accumulated grime of the floor.

Six roughly made pallets, laced with hide and string, stood in the filthy central courtyard of the house, and on each cot a man, swathed in a white sheet, tossed and moaned and jabbered. A woman entered with a pot full of rancid native sweetmeats, and tried vainly to make one of the men eat of her delicacies. In the full glare of the sunlight stood a young man almost absolutely unclothed, his hands clasped behind his head, trying to outstare the sun. He began a chant, broke off, and hurried from bed to bed, shouting to each words that Kate could not understand. Then he returned to his place in the centre, and took up his interrupted song.

' He is confirmed lunatic, also,' said the doctor. ' I have blistered and cupped him very severely, but he will not go away. He is quite harmless, except when he does not get his opium.'

' Surely you don't allow the patients opium ! ' exclaimed Kate.

'*Of course* I allow opium.   Otherwise they would die.   All Rajputs eat opium.'

'And you?' asked Kate, with horror.

'Once I did not—when I first came.   But now——' He drew a smooth-worn tin tobacco-box from his waist, and took from it what appeared to Kate a handful of opium pills.

Despair was going over her in successive waves. 'Show me the women's ward,' she said wearily.

'Oh, they are all upstairs and downstairs and roundabout,' returned the doctor casually.

'And the maternity cases?' she asked.

'They are in casual ward.'

'Who attends to them?'

'They do not like me; but there is very clever woman from the outside—she comes in.'

'Has she any training—any education?'

'She is much esteemed in her own village,' said the doctor.   'She is here now, if you wish to see.'

'Where?' demanded Kate.

Dhunpat Rai, somewhat uneasy in his mind, made haste to lead the way up a narrow staircase to a closed door, from behind which came the wail of a new life.

Kate flung the door open wrathfully.   In that particular ward of the State Hospital were the clay and cow-dung images of two gods, which the woman in charge was besprinkling with marigold buds.   Every window, every orifice that might admit a breath of air, was closed, and the birth-fire blazed fiercely in one corner, its fumes nearly asphyxiating Kate as she entered.

What happened between Kate and the much-esteemed woman will never be known. The girl did not emerge for half an hour. But the woman came out much sooner, dishevelled, and cackling feebly.

After this Kate was prepared for anything, even for the neglected condition of the drugs in the dispensary — the mortar was never cleaned, and every prescription carried to the patient many more drugs than were written for him — and for the foul, undrained, uncleaned, unlighted, and unventilated rooms which she entered one after another hopelessly. The patients were allowed to receive their friends as they would, and to take from their hands whatever misguided kindness offered. When death came, the mourners howled in chorus about the cot, and bore the naked body through the courtyard, amid the jeers of the lunatic, to carry to the city what infection Heaven willed.

There was no isolation of infectious cases during the progress of the disease, and children scourged with ophthalmia played light-heartedly with the children of the visitors or among diphtheria beds. At one point, and one point only, the doctor was strong; he was highly successful in dealing with the very common trouble entered on the day-book as 'loin bite.' The woodcutters and small traders who had occasion to travel through the lonely roads of the State were not infrequently struck down by tigers, and in these cases the doctor, discarding the entire English pharmacopœia, fell back on simples of proved repute in the neighbouring villages, and wrought wonders. None the less, it was necessary to convey to him that in future there would be only one head of the State Hospital, that her orders must be obeyed without question, and that her name was Miss Kate Sheriff.

The doctor, reflecting that she attended on the women of the court, offered no protest. He had been through many such periods of reform and reorganisation, and knew that his own inertia and a smooth tongue would carry him through many more. He bowed and assented, allowing Kate's reproaches to pass over his head, and parrying all questions with the statement—

'This hospital only allowed one hundred and fifty rupees per mensem from State revenues. How can get drugs all the way from Calcutta for that?'

'*I* am paying for this order,' said Kate, writing out a list of needed drugs and appliances on the desk in the bath-room, which was supposed to serve as an office; 'and I shall pay for whatever else I think necessary.'

'Order going through me offeecially?' suggested Dhunpat Rai, with his head on one side.

Unwilling to raise unnecessary obstacles, Kate assented. With those poor creatures lying in the rooms about her unwatched, untended, at the mercy of this creature, it was not a time to argue about commissions.

'Yes,' she said decidedly; 'of course.' And the doctor, when he saw the size and scope of the order, felt that he could endure much at her hands.

At the end of the three hours Kate came away, fainting with weariness, want of food, and bitter heartache.

XI

Who speaks to the King carries his life in his hand.
Native Proverb.

TARVIN found the Maharajah, who had not yet taken his morning allowance of opium, sunk in the deepest depression. The man from Topaz gazed at him shrewdly, filled with his purpose.

The Maharajah's first words helped him to declare it. 'What have you come here for?' he asked.

'To Rhatore?' inquired Tarvin, with a smile that embraced the whole horizon.

'Yes; to Rhatore,' grunted the Maharajah. 'The agent sahib says you do not belong to any government, and that you have come here only to see things and write lies about them. Why have you come?'

'I have come to turn your river. There is gold in it,' he said steadily.

The Maharajah answered him with brevity. 'Go and speak to the Government,' he said sulkily.

'It's your river, I guess,' returned Tarvin cheerfully.

'Mine! Nothing in the State is mine. The shopkeeper people are at my gates day and night.

The agent sahib won't let me collect taxes as my
fathers used to do. I have no army.'

'That's perfectly true,' assented Tarvin, under
his breath. 'I'll run off with it some morning.'

'And if I had,' continued the Maharajah,
'I have no one to fight against. I am only
an old wolf, with all my teeth drawn. Go
away!'

They were talking in the flagged courtyard immediately outside that wing of the palace occupied
by Sitabhai. The Maharajah was sitting in a
broken Windsor chair, while his grooms brought
up successive files of horses, saddled and bridled,
in the hope that one of the animals might be
chosen for his Majesty's ride. The stale, sick
air of the palace drifted across the marble flags
before the morning wind, and it was not a wholesome smell.

Tarvin, who had drawn rein in the courtyard
without dismounting, flung his right leg over the
pony's withers, and held his peace. He had seen
something of the effect of opium upon the Maharajah. A servant was approaching with a small
brass bowl full of opium and water. The Maharajah swallowed the draught with many wry faces,
dashed the last brown drops from his moustache
and beard, and dropped back into the chair, staring
with vacant eyes. In a few minutes he sprang to
his feet, erect and smiling.

'Are you here, Sahib?' said he. 'You are
here, or I should not feel ready to laugh. Do
you go riding this morning?'

'I'm your man.'

'Then we will bring out the Foxhall colt. He will throw you.'

'Very good,' said Tarvin leisurely.

'And I will ride my own Cutch mare. Let us get away before the agent sahib comes,' said the Maharajah.

The blast of a bugle was heard without the courtyard, and a clatter of wheels, as the grooms departed to saddle the horses.

The Maharaj Kunwar ran up the steps and pattered toward the Maharajah, his father, who picked him up in his lap, and fondled him.

'What brings thee here, Lalji?' asked the Maharajah. Lalji, the Beloved, was the familiar name by which the Prince was known within the palace.

'I came to exercise my guard. Father, they are giving me bad saddlery for my troopers from the State arsenal. Jeysingh's saddle-peak is mended with string, and Jeysingh is the best of my soldiers. Moreover, he tells me nice tales,' said the Maharaj Kunwar, speaking in the vernacular, with a friendly little nod toward Tarvin.

'Hai! Hai! Thou art like all the rest,' said the King. 'Always some fresh demand upon the State. And what is it now?'

The child joined his little hands together, and caught his father fearlessly by his monstrous beard, which, in the manner of a Rajput, was brushed up over his ears. 'Only ten little new saddles,' said the child. 'They are in the big saddle-rooms. I have seen them. But the keeper of the horses said that I was first to ask the King.'

The Maharajah's face darkened, and he swore a
great oath by his gods.

'The King is a slave and a servant,' he growled
—'the servant of the agent sahib and this woman-
talking English Raj ; but, by Indur ! the King's
son is at least a King's son. What right had
Saroop Singh to stay thee from anything that thou
desiredst, Prince ?'

'I told him,' said the Maharaj Kunwar, 'that
my father would not be pleased. But I said no
more, because I was not very well, and thou
knowest'—the boy's head drooped under the
turban—'I am only a little child. I may have the
saddles ?'

Tarvin, to whom no word of this conversation
was intelligible, sat at ease on his pony, smiling at
his friend the Maharaj. The interview had begun
in the dead dawn-silence of the courtyard—a
silence so intense that he could hear the doves
cooing on a tower a hundred and fifty feet above
his head. But now all four sides of the green-
shuttered courtyard were alive, awake, and intent
about him. He could hear muffled breathings, the
rustle of draperies, and the faintest possible jarring
of shutters, cautiously opened from within. A
heavy smell of musk and jasmine came to his
nostrils and filled him with uneasiness, for he knew,
without turning his head or his eyes, that Sitabhai
and her women were watching all that went on.
But neither the King nor the Prince heeded. The
Maharaj Kunwar was very full of his English
lessons, learned at Mrs. Estes' knee, and the King
was as interested as he. Lest Tarvin should fail to

understand, the Prince began to speak in English
again, but very slowly and distinctly, that his
father also might comprehend.

'And this is a new verse,' he said, 'which I
learned only yesterday.'

'Is there any talk of their gods in it?' asked
the Maharajah suspiciously. 'Remember thou art
a Rajput.'

'No; oh no!' said the Prince. 'It is only
English, and I learned it very quickly.'

'Let me hear, little Pundit. Some day thou
wilt become a scribe, and go to the English
colleges, and wear a long black gown.'

The child slipped quickly back into the
vernacular. 'The flag of our State has five
colours,' he said. 'When I have fought for that,
perhaps I will become an Englishman.'

'There is no leading of armies afield any more,
little one; but say thy verses.'

The subdued rustle of unseen hundreds grew
more intense. Tarvin leaned forward with his chin
in his hand, as the Prince slid down from his
father's lap, put his hands behind him, and began,
without pauses or expression—

> 'Tiger, tiger, burning bright
> In the forests of the night,
> What immortal hand or eye
> Framed thy fearful symmetry?
> When thy heart began to beat
> What dread hand made thy dread feet?

'There is more that I have forgotten,' he went
on, 'but the last line is—

> 'Did He who made the lamb make thee?

I learned it all very quickly.' And he began to applaud himself with both hands, while Tarvin followed suit.

'I do not understand; but it is good to know English. Thy friend here speaks such English as I never knew,' said the Maharajah in the vernacular.

'Ay,' rejoined the Prince. 'But he speaks with his face and his hands alive—so; and I laugh before I know why. Now Colonel Nolan Sahib speaks like a buffalo, with his mouth shut. I cannot tell whether he is angry or pleased. But, father, what does Tarvin Sahib do here?'

'We go for a ride together,' returned the King. 'When we return, perhaps I will tell thee. What do the men about thee say of him?'

'They say he is a man of clean heart; and he is always kind to me.'

'Has he said aught to thee of me?'

'Never in language that I could understand. But I do not doubt that he is a good man. See, he is laughing now.'

Tarvin, who had pricked up his ears at hearing his own name, now resettled himself in the saddle, and gathered up his reins, as a hint to the King that it was time to be moving.

The grooms brought up a long, switch-tailed English thoroughbred and a lean, mouse-coloured mare. The Maharajah rose to his feet.

'Go back to Saroop Singh and get the saddles, Prince,' said he.

'What are you going to do to-day, little man?' asked Tarvin.

'I shall go and get new equipment,' answered the child, 'and then I shall come to play with the prime minister's son here.'

Again, like the hiss of a hidden snake, the rustle behind the shutters increased. Evidently some one there understood the child's words.

'Shall you see Miss Kate to-day?'

'Not to-day. 'Tis holiday for me. I do not go to Mrs. Estes to-day.'

The King turned on Tarvin swiftly, and spoke under his breath.

'Must he see that doctor lady every day? All my people lie to me, in the hope of winning my favour; even Colonel Nolan says that the child is very strong. Speak the truth. He is my first son.'

'He is not strong,' answered Tarvin calmly. 'Perhaps it would be better to let him see Miss Sheriff this morning. You don't lose anything by keeping your weather eye open, you know.'

'I do not understand,' said the King; 'but go to the missionary's house to-day, my son.'

'I am to come here and play,' answered the Prince petulantly.

'You don't know what Miss Sheriff's got for you to play with,' said Tarvin.

'What is it?' asked the Maharaj sharply.

'You've got a carriage and ten troopers,' replied Tarvin. 'You've only got to go there and find out.'

He drew a letter from his breast-pocket, glancing with liking at the two-cent American stamp, and scribbled a note to Kate on the envelope, which ran thus :—

'Keep the little fellow with you to-day.
There's a wicked look about things this morning.
Find something for him to do ; get up games for
him ; do anything, but keep him away from the
palace. I got your note. All right. I understand.'

He called the Maharaj to him, and handed
him the note. 'Take this to Miss Kate, like a
little man, and say I sent you,' he said.

'My son is not an orderly,' said the King
surlily.

'Your son is not very well, and I'm the first to
speak the truth to you about him, it seems to me,'
said Tarvin. 'Gently on that colt's mouth—you.'
The Foxhall colt was dancing between his grooms.

'You'll be thrown,' said the Maharaj Kunwar,
in an ecstasy of delight. 'He throws all his
grooms.'

At that moment a shutter in the courtyard
clicked distinctly three times in the silence.

One of the grooms passed to the off-side of the
plunging colt deftly. Tarvin put his foot into
the stirrup to spring up, when the saddle turned
completely round. Some one let go of the horse's
head, and Tarvin had just time to kick his foot
free as the animal sprang forward.

'I've seen slicker ways of killing a man than
that,' he said quietly. 'Bring my friend back,' he
added to one of the grooms ; and when the
Foxhall colt was under his hands again he cinched
him up as the beast had not been girt since he had
first felt the bit. 'Now,' he said, and leaped into

the saddle, as the King clattered out of the court-yard.

The colt reared on end, landed stiffly on his forefeet, and lashed out. Tarvin, sitting him with the cow-boy seat, said quietly to the child, who was still watching his movements, 'Run along, Maharaj. Don't hang around here. Let me see you started for Miss Kate.'

The boy obeyed, with a regretful glance at the prancing horse. Then the Foxhall colt devoted himself to unseating his rider. He refused to quit the courtyard, though Tarvin argued with him, first behind the saddle, and then between the indignant ears. Accustomed to grooms who slipped off at the first sign of rebellion, the Foxhall colt was wrathful. Without warning, he dashed through the archway, wheeled on his haunches, and bolted in pursuit of the Maharajah's mare. Once in the open, sandy country, he felt that he had a field worthy of his powers. Tarvin also saw his opportunity. The Maharajah, known in his youth as a hard rider among a nation of perhaps the hardest riders on earth, turned in his saddle and watched the battle with interest.

'You ride like a Rajput,' he shouted, as Tarvin flew past him. 'Breathe him on a straight course in the open.'

'Not till he's learned who's boss,' replied Tarvin, and he wrenched the colt around.

'*Shabash! Shabash!* Oh, well done! Well done!' cried the Maharajah, as the colt answered the bit. 'Tarvin Sahib, I'll make you colonel of my regular cavalry.'

K

'Ten million irregular devils!' said Tarvin impolitely. 'Come back, you brute! Back!'

The horse's head was bowed on his lathering chest under the pressure of the curb; but before obeying he planted his forefeet, and bucked as viciously as one of Tarvin's own broncos. 'Both feet down and chest extended,' he murmured gaily to himself, as the creature see-sawed up and down. He was in his element, and dreamed himself back in Topaz.

'*Maro! Maro!*' exclaimed the King. 'Hit him hard! Hit him well!'

'Oh, let him have his little picnic,' said Tarvin easily. 'I like it.'

When the colt was tired he was forced to back for ten yards. 'Now we'll go on,' said Tarvin, and fell into a trot by the side of the Maharajah. 'That river of yours is full of gold,' he said, after a moment's silence, as if continuing an uninterrupted conversation.

'When I was a young man,' said the King, 'I rode pig here. We chased them with the sword in the springtime. That was before the English came. Over there, by that pile of rock, I broke my collar-bone.'

'Full of gold, Maharajah Sahib. How do you propose to get it out?'

Tarvin knew something already of the King's discursiveness; he did not mean to give way to it.

'What do I know?' answered the King solemnly. 'Ask the agent sahib.'

'But, look here, who *does* run this State, you or Colonel Nolan?'

'You know,' returned the Maharajah. 'You have seen.' He pointed north and south. 'There,' he said, 'is one railway line ; yonder is another. I am a goat between two wolves.'

'Well, anyway, the country between is your own. Surely you can do what you like with that.'

They had ridden some two or three miles beyond the city, parallel with the course of the Amet River, their horses sinking fetlock-deep in the soft sand. The King looked along the chain of shining pools, the white, scrub-tipped hillocks of the desert, and the far distant line of low granite-topped hills, whence the Amet sprang. It was not a prospect to delight the heart of a King.

'Yes ; I am lord of all this country,' he said. 'But look you, one-fourth of my revenue is swallowed up by those who collect it ; one-fourth those black-faced camel-breeders in the sand there will not pay, and I must not march troops against them ; one-fourth I myself, perhaps, receive ; but the people who should pay the other fourth do not know to whom it should be sent. Yes ; I am a very rich king.'

'Well, any way you look at it, the river ought to treble your income.'

The Maharajah looked at Tarvin intently.

'What would the Government say ?' he asked.

'I don't quite see where the Government comes in. You can lay out orange-gardens and take canals around them.' (There was a deep-set twinkle of comprehension in his Majesty's eye.) 'Working the river would be much easier. You've tried placer-mining here, haven't you ?'

'There was some washing in the bed of the river one summer. My jails were too full of convicts, and I feared rebellion. But there was nothing to see, except those black dogs digging in the sand. That year I won the Poona cup with a bay pony.'

Tarvin brought his hand down on his thigh with an unguarded smack. What was the use of talking business to this wearied man, who would pawn what the opium had left to him of soul for something to see? He shifted his ground instantly.

'Yes; that sort of mining is nothing to look at. What you want is a little dam up Gungra way.'

'Near the hills?'

'Yes.'

'No man has ever dammed the Amet,' said the King. 'It comes out of the ground, and sinks back into the ground, and when the rain falls it is as big as the Indus.'

'We'll have the whole bed of it laid bare before the rains begin—bare for twelve miles,' said Tarvin, watching the effect on his companion.

'No man has dammed the Amet,' was the stony reply.

'No *man* has ever tried. Give me all the labour I want, and *I* will dam the Amet.'

'Where will the water go?' inquired the King.

'I'll take it around another way, as you took the canal around the orange-garden, of course.'

'Ah! *Then* Colonel Nolan talked to me as if I were a child.'

'You know why, Maharajah Sahib,' said Tarvin placidly.

The King was frozen for a moment by this audacity. He knew that all the secrets of his domestic life were common talk in the mouths of the city, for no man can bridle three hundred women; but he was not prepared to find them so frankly hinted at by this irreverent stranger, who was and was not an Englishman.

'Colonel Nolan will say nothing this time,' continued Tarvin. 'Besides, it will help your people.'

'Who are also his,' said the King.

The opium was dying out of his brain, and his head fell forward upon his chest.

'Then I shall begin to-morrow,' said Tarvin. 'It will be something to see. I must find the best place to dam the river, and I daresay you can lend me a few hundred convicts.'

'But why have you come here at all,' asked the King, 'to dam my rivers, and turn my State upside down?'

'Because it's good for you to laugh, Maharajah Sahib. You know that as well as I do. I will play pachisi with you every night until you are tired, and I can speak the truth—a rare commodity in these parts.'

'Did you speak truth about the Maharaj Kunwar? Is he indeed not well?'

'I have told you he isn't quite strong. But there's nothing the matter with him that Miss Sheriff can't put right.'

'Is that the truth?' demanded the King. 'Remember, he has my throne after me.'

'If I know Miss Sheriff, he'll have that throne. Don't you fret, Maharajah Sahib.'

'You are great friend of hers?' pursued his companion. 'You both come from one country?'

'Yes,' assented Tarvin; 'and one town.'

'Tell me about that town,' said the King curiously.

Tarvin, nothing loth, told him—told him at length, in detail, and with his own touches of verisimilitude, forgetting in the heat of admiration and affection that the King could understand, at best, not more than one word in ten of his vigorous Western colloquialisms. Half way through his rhapsody the King interrupted.

'If it was so good, why did you not stay there?'

'I came to see you,' said Tarvin quickly. 'I heard about you there.'

'Then it is true, what my poets sing to me, that my fame is known in the four corners of the earth? I will fill Bussant Rao's mouth with gold if it is so.'

'You can bet your life. Would you like me to go away, though? Say the word!' Tarvin made as if to check his horse.

The Maharajah remained sunk in deep thought, and when he spoke it was slowly and distinctly, that Tarvin might catch every word. 'I hate all the English,' he said. 'Their ways are not my ways, and they make such trouble over the killing of a man here and there. *Your* ways are not my ways; but you do not give so much trouble, and you are a friend of the doctor lady.'

' Well, I hope I'm a friend of the Maharaj
Kunwar's too,' said Tarvin.

' Are you a true friend to him?' asked the
King, eyeing him closely.

' That's all right. I'd like to see the man who
tried to lay a hand on the little one. He'd vanish,
King ; he'd disappear ; he wouldn't be. I'd mop
up Gokral Seetarun with him.'

' I have seen you hit that rupee. Do it again.'

Without thinking for a moment of the Foxhall
colt, Tarvin drew his revolver, tossed a coin into
the air, and fired. The coin fell beside them—a
fresh one this time—marked squarely in the centre.
The colt plunged furiously, and the Cutch mare
curveted. There was a thunder of hoofs behind
him. The escort, which, till now, had waited
respectfully a quarter of a mile behind, were racing
up at full speed, with levelled lances. The King
laughed a little contemptuously.

' They are thinking you have shot me," he said.
' So they will kill you, unless I stop them. Shall
I stop them ?'

Tarvin thrust out his under jaw with a motion
peculiar to himself, wheeled the colt, and waited
without answering, his empty hands folded on the
pommel of his saddle. The troop swept down in
an irregular mob, each man crouching, lance in
rest, over his saddle-bow, and the captain of the
troop flourishing a long, straight Rajput sword.
Tarvin felt rather than saw the lean, venomous
lance-heads converging on the breast of the colt.
The King drew off a few yards, and watched him
where he stood alone in the centre of the plain,

waiting. For that single moment, in which he faced death, Tarvin thought to himself that he preferred any customer to a Maharajah.

Suddenly his Highness shouted once, the lance-butts fell as though they had been smitten down, and the troop, opening out, whirled by on each side of Tarvin, each man striving as nearly as might be to brush the white man's boot.

The white man stared in front of him without turning his head, and the King gave a little grunt of approval.

'Would you have done that for the Maharaj Kunwar?' he asked, wheeling his mare in again beside him, after a pause.

'No,' said Tarvin placidly. 'I should have begun shooting long before.'

'What! Fifty men?'

'No; the captain.'

The King shook in his saddle with laughter, and held up his hand. The commandant of the troop trotted up.

'*Ohé*, Pertab Singh-Ji, he says he would have shot thee.' Then, turning to Tarvin, smiling, 'That is my cousin.'

The burly Rajput captain grinned from ear to ear, and, to Tarvin's surprise, answered in perfect English—'That would do for irregular cavalry—to kill the subalterns, you understand—but we are drilled exclusively on English model, and I have my commission from the Queen. Now, in the German army——'

Tarvin looked at him in blank amazement.

'But you are not connected with the military,'

said Pertab Singh-Ji politely. ' I have heard how
you shoot, and I saw what you were doing. But
you must please excuse. When a shot is fired near
his Highness it is our order always to come up.'

He saluted, and withdrew to his troop.

The sun was growing unpleasantly hot, and the
King and Tarvin trotted back toward the city.

'How many convicts can you lend me?' asked
Tarvin, as they went.

'All my jails full, if you want them,' was the
enthusiastic answer. 'By God, sahib, I never saw
anything like that. I would give you anything.'

Tarvin took off his hat, and mopped his forehead, laughing.

'Very good, then. I'll ask for something that
will cost you nothing.'

The Maharajah grunted doubtfully. People
generally demanded of him things he was not
willing to part with.

'That talk is new to me, Tarvin Sahib,' said he.

'You'll see I'm in earnest when I say I only
want to look at the Naulahka. I've seen all your
State diamonds and gold carriages, but I haven't
seen that.'

The Maharajah trotted fifty yards without replying. Then—

'Do they speak of it where you come from?'

'Of course. All Americans know that it's the
biggest thing in India. It's in all the guide-books,'
said Tarvin brazenly.

'Do the books say where it is? The English
people are so wise.' The Maharajah stared straight
in front of him, and almost smiled.

'No; but they say you know, and I'd like to
see it.'

'You must understand, Tarvin Sahib'—the
Maharajah spoke meditatively—'that this is not *a*
State jewel, but *the* State jewel—the jewel of the
State. It is a holy thing. Even I do not keep
it, and I cannot give you any order to see it.'

Tarvin's heart sank.

'But,' the Maharajah continued, 'if I say where
it is, you can go at your own risk, without Government interfering. I have seen you are not afraid
of risk, and I am a very grateful man. Perhaps
the priests will show you; perhaps they will not.
Or perhaps you will not find the priests at all.
Oh, I forgot; it is not in *that* temple that I was
thinking of. No; it must be in the Gye-Mukh
—the Cow's Mouth. But there are no priests
there, and nobody goes. Of course it is in the
Cow's Mouth. I thought it was in this city,'
resumed the Maharajah. He spoke as if he were
talking of a dropped horse-shoe or a mislaid
turban.

'Oh, of course. The Cow's Mouth,' repeated
Tarvin, as if this also were in the guide-books.

Chuckling with renewed animation, the King
went on—'By God, only a very brave man would
go to the Gye-Mukh; such a brave man as yourself, Tarvin Sahib,' he added, giving his companion
a shrewd look. 'Ho, ho! Pertab Singh-Ji would
not go. No; not with all his troops that you
conquered to-day.'

'Keep your praise until I've earned it, Maharajah
Sahib,' said Tarvin. 'Wait until I've dammed that

river.' He was silent for a while, as if digesting this newest piece of information.

'Now, you have a city like this city, I suppose?' said the Maharajah interrogatively, pointing to Rhatore.

Tarvin had overcome, in a measure, his first feeling of contempt for the State of Gokral Seetarun and the city of Rhatore. He had begun to look upon them both, as was his nature in the case of people and things with which he dwelt, with a certain kindness.

'Topaz is going to be bigger,' he explained.

'And when you are there what is your offeecial position?' asked the Maharajah.

Tarvin, without answering, drew from his breast-pocket the cable from Mrs. Mutrie, and handed it in silence to the King. Where an election was concerned even the sympathy of an opium-soaked Rajput was not indifferent to him.

'What does it mean?' asked the King, and Tarvin threw up his hands in despair.

He explained his connection with the government of his State, making the Colorado legislature appear as one of the parliaments of America. He owned up to being the Hon. Nicholas Tarvin, if the Maharajah really wanted to give him his full title.

'Such as the members of provincial councils that come here?' suggested the Maharajah, remembering the grey-headed men who visited him from time to time, charged with authority only little less than that of a viceroy. 'But still you will not write letters to that legislature about my government,' queried he suspiciously, recalling again over-curious emissaries from the British Parliament over seas, who sat their horses like sacks, and talked interminably of good government when he wished to go to bed. 'And above all,' he added slowly, as they drew near to the palace, 'you are most true friend of the Maharaj Kunwar? And your friend, the lady doctor, will make him well?'

'That,' said Tarvin, with a sudden inspiration, 'is what we are both here for!'

XII

This I saw when the rites were done,
And the lamps were dead and the Gods alone,
And the grey snake coiled on the altar stone—
Ere I fled from a Fear that I could not see,
And the Gods of the East made mouths at me.
                                   In Seeonee.

WHEN he left the King's side, Tarvin's first impulse was to set the Foxhall colt into a gallop, and forthwith depart in search of the Naulahka. He mechanically drove his heels home, and shortened his rein under the impulse of the thought ; but the colt's leap beneath him recalled him to his senses, and he restrained himself and his mount with the same motion.

His familiarity with the people's grotesque nomenclature left him unimpressed by the Cow's Mouth as a name for a spot, but he gave some wonder to the question why the thing should be *in* the Cow's Mouth. This was a matter to be laid before Estes.

'These heathen,' he said to himself, 'are just the sort to hide it away in a salt-lick, or bury it in a hole in the ground. Yes ; a hole is about their size. They put the State diamonds in cracker-

boxes tied up with boot-laces.   The Naulahka is
probably hanging on a tree.'

As he trotted toward the missionary's house, he
looked at the hopeless landscape with new interest,
for any spur of the low hills, or any roof in the
jumbled city, might contain his treasure.

Estes, who had outlived many curiosities, and
knew Rajputana as a prisoner knows the bricks of
his cell, turned on Tarvin, in reply to the latter's
direct question, a flood of information.   There
were mouths of all kinds in India, from the Burning Mouth in the north, where a jet of natural gas
was worshipped by millions as the incarnation of a
divinity, to the Devil's Mouth among some forgotten Buddhist ruins in the furthest southern
corner of Madras.

There was also a Cow's Mouth some hundreds
of miles away, in the courtyard of a temple at
Benares, much frequented by devotees ; but as far
as Rajputana was concerned, there was only one
Cow's Mouth, and that was to be found in a
dead city.

The missionary launched into a history of wars
and rapine, extending over hundreds of years, all
centring round one rock-walled city in the wilderness, which had been the pride and the glory of the
kings of Mewar.   Tarvin listened with patience as
infinite as his weariness—ancient history had no
charm for the man who was making his own town
—while Estes enlarged upon the past, and told
stories of voluntary immolation on the pyre in
subterranean palaces by thousands of Rajput women
who, when the city fell before a Mohammedan, and

their kin had died in the last charge of defence, cheated the conquerors of all but the empty glory of conquest. Estes had a taste for archæology, and it was a pleasure to him to speak of it to a fellow-countryman.

By retracing the ninety-six miles to Rawut Junction, Tarvin might make connection with a train that would carry him sixty-seven miles westward to yet another junction, where he would change and go south by rail for a hundred and seven miles ; and this would bring him within four miles of this city, its marvellous nine-storeyed tower of glory, which he was to note carefully, its stupendous walls and desolate palaces. The journey would occupy at least two days. At this point Tarvin suggested a map, and a glance at it showed him that Estes proposed an elaborate circus round three sides of a square, whereas a spider-like line ran more or less directly from Rhatore to Gunnaur.

'This seems shorter,' he said.

'It's only a country road, and you have had some experience of roads in this State. Fifty-seven miles on a *kutcha* road in this sun would be fatal.'

Tarvin smiled to himself. He had no particular dread of the sun, which, year by year, had stolen from his companion something of his vitality.

'I think I'll ride, anyhow. It seems a waste to travel half round India to get at a thing across the road, though it *is* the custom of the country.'

He asked the missionary what the Cow's Mouth was like, and Estes explained archæologically, architecturally, and philologically to such good purpose that Tarvin understood that it was some sort of a hole in the ground—an ancient, a remarkably ancient, hole of peculiar sanctity, but nothing more than a hole.

Tarvin decided to start without an hour's delay. The dam might wait until he returned. It was hardly likely that the King's outburst of generosity would lead him to throw open his jails on the morrow. Tarvin debated for a while whether he should tell him of the excursion he was proposing to himself, and then decided that he would look at the necklace first, and open negotiations later. This seemed to suit the customs of the country. He returned to the rest-house with Estes' map in his pocket to take stock of his stable. Like other men of the West, he reckoned a horse a necessity before all necessities, and had purchased one mechanically immediately after his arrival. It had been a comfort to him to note all the tricks of all the men he had ever traded horses with faithfully reproduced in the lean, swarthy Cabuli trader, who had led his kicking, plunging horse up to the verandah one idle evening ; and it had been a greater comfort to battle with them as he had battled in the old days. The result of the skirmish, fought out in broken English and expressive American, was an unhandsome, doubtful-tempered, mouse-coloured Kathiawar stallion, who had been dismissed for vice from the service of his Majesty, and who weakly believed that, having eaten pieces of the troopers of the Deolee Irregular Horse, ease and idleness awaited him. Tarvin had undeceived him leisurely, in such moments as he most felt the need of doing something, and the Kathiawar, though

never grateful, was at least civil. He had been
christened Fibby Winks in recognition of un-
gentlemanly conduct and a resemblance which
Tarvin fancied he detected between the beast's
lean face and that of the man who had jumped his
claim.

Tarvin threw back the loin cloth as he came
upon Fibby drowsing in the afternoon sun behind
the rest-house.

'We're going for a little walk down town,
Fibby,' he said.

The Kathiawar squealed and snapped.

'Yes; you always were a loafer, Fibby.'

Fibby was saddled by his nervous native attendant, while Tarvin took a blanket from his room
and rolled up into it an imaginative assortment of
provisions. Fibby was to find his rations where
Heaven pleased. Then he set out as light-
heartedly as though he were going for a canter
round the city. It was now about three in the
afternoon. All Fibby's boundless reserves of ill-
temper and stubborn obstinacy Tarvin resolved
should be devoted, by the aid of his spurs, to
covering the fifty-seven miles to Gunnaur in the
next ten hours, if the road were fair. If not, he
should be allowed another two hours. The return
journey would not require spurs. There was a
moon that night, and Tarvin knew enough of
native roads in Gokral Seetarun, and rough trails
elsewhere, to be certain that he would not be confused by cross-tracks.

It being borne into Fibby's mind that he was
required to advance, not in three directions at

once, but in one, he clicked his bit comfortably in his mouth, dropped his head, and began to trot steadily. Then Tarvin pulled him up, and addressed him tenderly.

'Fib, my boy, we're not out for exercise—you'll learn that before sundown. Some galoot has been training you to waste your time over the English trot. I'll be discussing other points with you in the course of the campaign; but we'll settle this now. We don't begin with crime. Drop it, Fibby, and behave like a man-horse.'

Tarvin was obliged to make further remarks on the same subject before Fibby returned to the easy native lope, which is also a common Western pace, tiring neither man nor beast. By this he began to understand that a long journey was demanded of him, and, lowering his tail, buckled down to it.

At first he moved in a cloud of sandy dust with the cotton wains and the country carts that were creaking out to the far distant railway at Gunnaur. As the sun began to sink, his gaunt shadow danced like a goblin across low-lying volcanic rock tufted with shrubs, and here and there an aloe.

The carters unyoked their cattle on the roadside, and prepared to eat their evening meal by the light of dull red fires. Fibby cocked one ear wistfully toward the flames, but held on through the gathering shadows, and Tarvin smelt the acrid juice of bruised camel-thorn beneath his horse's hoofs. The moon rose in splendour behind him, and, following his lurching shadow, he overtook a

naked man who bore over his shoulder a stick
loaded with jingling bells, and fled panting and
perspiring from one who followed him armed with
a naked sword. This was the mail-carrier and his
escort running to Gunnaur. The jingling died
away on the dead air, and Fibby was ambling
between interminable lines of thorn bushes that
threw mad arms to the stars, and cast shadows as
solid as themselves across the road. Some beast
of the night plunged through the thicket alongside,
and Fibby snorted in panic. Then a porcupine
crossed under his nose with a rustle of quills, and
left an evil stench to poison the stillness for a
moment. A point of light gleamed ahead, where
a bullock-cart had broken down, and the drivers
were sleeping peacefully till daylight should show
the injury. Here Fibby stopped, and Tarvin,
through the magic of a rupee, representing fortune
to the rudely awakened sleepers, procured food
and a little water for him, eased the girths, and
made as much of him as he was disposed to permit.
On starting again, Fibby found his second wind,
and with it there woke the spirit of daring and
adventure inherited from his ancestors, who were
accustomed to take their masters thirty leagues in
a day for the sacking of a town, to sleep by a lance
driven into the earth as a picket, and to return
whence they had come before the ashes of the
houses had lost heat. So Fibby lifted his tail
valiantly, neighed, and began to move.

The road descended for miles, crossing the dry
beds of many water-courses and once a broad river,
where Fibby stopped for another drink, and would

have lain down to roll in a melon-bed but that his
rider spurred him on up the slope. The country
grew more fertile at every mile, and rolled in
broader waves. Under the light of the setting
moon, the fields showed silver - white with the
opium-poppy, or dark with sugar-cane.

Poppy and sugar ceased together, as Fibby
topped a long, slow ascent, and with distended
nostrils, snuffed for the wind of the morning. He
knew that the day would bring him rest. Tarvin
peered forward where the white line of the road
disappeared in the gloom of velvety scrub. He
commanded a vast level plain flanked by hills of
soft outline—a plain that in the dim light seemed
as level as the sea. Like the sea, too, it bore on
its breast a ship, like a gigantic monitor with a
sharp bow, cutting her way from north to south ;
such a ship as man never yet has seen—two miles
long, with three or four hundred feet freeboard,
lonely, silent, mastless, without lights, a derelict of
the earth.

'We are nearly there, Fib, my boy,' said Tarvin,
drawing rein, and scanning the monstrous thing
by the starlight. ' We'll get as close as we can,
and then wait for the daylight before going aboard.'

They descended the slope, which was covered
with sharp stones and sleeping goats. Then the
road turned sharply to the left, and began to run
parallel to the ship. Tarvin urged Fibby into a
more direct path, and the good horse blundered
piteously across the scrub-covered ground, cut up
and channelled by the rains into a network of six-
foot ravines and gulches.

Here he gave out with a despairing grunt. Tarvin took pity on him, and, fastening him to a tree, bade him think of his sins till breakfast-time, and dropped from his back into a dry and dusty water-hole. Ten steps further, and the scrub was all about him, whipping him across the brows, hooking thorns into his jacket, and looping roots in front of his knees as he pushed on up an ever-steepening incline.

At last Tarvin was crawling on his hands and knees, grimed from head to foot, and hardly to be distinguished from the wild pigs that passed like slate-coloured shadows through the tangle of the thickets on their way to their rest. Too absorbed to hear them grunt, he pulled and screwed himself up the slope, tugging at the roots as though he would rend the Naulahka from the bowels of the earth, and swearing piously at every step. When he stopped to wipe the sweat from his face, he found, more by touch than by eye, that he knelt at the foot of a wall that ran up into the stars. Fibby, from the tangle below, was neighing dolefully.

'You're not hurt, Fibby,' he gasped, spitting out some fragments of dry grass ; ' you aren't on in this scene. Nobody's asking *you* to fly to-night,' he said, looking hopelessly up at the wall again, and whistling softly in response to an owl's hooting overhead.

He began to pick his way between the foot of the wall and the scrub that grew up to it, pressing one hand against the huge cut stones, and holding the other before his face. A fig-seed had found foothold between two of the gigantic slabs, and, undisturbed through the centuries, had grown into an arrogant, gnarled tree, that writhed between the fissures and heaved the stonework apart. Tarvin considered for a while whether he could climb into the crook of the lowest branch, then moved on a few steps, and found the wall rent from top to bottom through the twenty feet of its thickness, allowing passage for the head of an army.

'Like them, exactly like them!' he mused. 'I might have expected it. To build a wall sixty feet high, and put an eighty-foot hole in it! The Naulahka must be lying out on a bush, or a child's playing with it, and—I can't get it!'

He plunged through the gap, and found himself amid scattered pillars, slabs of stone, broken lintels, and tumbled tombs, and heard a low, thick hiss almost under his riding-boots. No man born of woman needs to be instructed in the voice of the serpent.

Tarvin jumped, and stayed still. Fibby's neigh came faintly now. The dawn-wind blew through the gap in the wall, and Tarvin wiped his forehead with a deep sigh of relief. He would do no more till the light came. This was the hour to eat and drink; also to stand very still, because of that voice from the ground.

He pulled food and a flask from his pocket, and, staring before him in every direction, ate hungrily. The loom of the night lifted a little, and he could see the outline of some great building a few yards away. Beyond this were other shadows, faint as the visions in a dream—the shadows of yet more temples and lines of houses; the wind, blowing among them, brought back a rustle of tossing hedges.

The shadows grew more distinct : he could see that he was standing with his face to some decayed tomb. Then his jaw fell, for, without warning or presage, the red dawn shot up behind him, and there leaped out of the night the city of the dead. Tall-built, sharp-domed palaces, flushing to the colour of blood, revealed the horror of their emptiness, and glared at the day that pierced them through and through.

The wind passed singing down the empty streets, and, finding none to answer, returned, chasing before it a muttering cloud of dust, which presently whirled itself into a little cyclone-funnel, and lay down with a sigh.

A screen of fretted marble lay on the dry grass, where it had fallen from some window above, and a gecko crawled over it to sun himself. Already the dawn flush had passed. The hot light was everywhere, and a kite had poised himself in the parched blue sky. The day, new-born, might have been as old as the city. It seemed to Tarvin that he and it were standing still to hear the centuries race by on the wings of the purposeless dust.

As he took his first step into the streets, a peacock stepped from the threshold of a lofty red house, and spread his tail in the splendour of the sun. Tarvin halted, and with perfect gravity took off his hat to the royal bird, where it blazed against the sculptures on the wall, the sole living thing in sight.

The silence of the place and the insolent naked-ness of the empty ways lay on him like a dead weight. For a long time he did not care to whistle, but rambled aimlessly from one wall to another, looking at the gigantic reservoirs, dry and neglected, the hollow guard-houses that studded the battlements, the time-riven arches that spanned the streets, and, above all, the carven tower with a shattered roof that sprang a hundred and fifty feet into the air, for a sign to the country-side that the royal city of Gun-naur was not dead, but would one day hum with men.

It was from this tower, encrusted with figures in high relief of beast and man, that Tarvin, after a heavy climb, looked out on the vast sleeping land in the midst of which the dead city lay. He saw the road by which he had come in the night, dipping and reappearing again over thirty miles of country, saw the white poppy-fields, the dull-brown scrub, and the unending plain to the northward, cut by the shining line of the rail. From his eyrie he peered forth as a man peers from a crow's-nest at sea ; for, once down there below in the city, all view was cut off by the battlements that rose like bulwarks. On the side nearest to the railroad, sloping causeways, paved with stone, ran down to the plain under many gates, as the gangway of a ship when it is let down, and through the gaps in the walls — time and the trees had torn their way to and fro — there was nothing to be seen except the horizon, which might have been the deep sea.

He thought of Fibby waiting in the scrub for his breakfast, and made haste to descend to the streets again. Remembering the essentials of his talk with Estes as to the position of the Cow's Mouth, he passed up a side lane, disturbing the squirrels and monkeys that had taken up their quarters in the cool dark of the rows of empty houses. The last house ended in a heap of ruins among a tangle of mimosa and tall grass, through which ran a narrow foot-track.

Tarvin marked the house as the first actual ruin he had seen. His complaint against all the others, the temples and the palaces, was that they were not ruined, but dead—empty, swept, and garnished, with the seven devils of loneliness in riotous possession. In time—in a few thousand years perhaps—the city would crumble away. He was distinctly glad that one house at least had set the example.

The path dropped beneath his feet on a shelf of solid rock that curved over like the edge of a waterfall. Tarvin took only one step, and fell, for the rock was worn into deep gutters, smoother than ice, by the naked feet of millions who had trodden that way for no man knew how many years. When he rose he heard a malignant chuckle, half suppressed, which ended in a choking cough, ceased, and broke out anew. Tarvin registered an oath to find that scoffer when he had found the necklace, and looked to his foothold more carefully. At this point it seemed that the Cow's

Mouth must be some sort of disused quarry fringed to the lips with rank vegetation.

All sight of what lay below him was blocked by the thick foliage of trees that leaned forward, bowing their heads together as night-watchers huddle over a corpse. Once upon a time there had been rude steps leading down the almost sheer descent, but the naked feet had worn them to glassy knobs and lumps, and blown dust had made a thin soil in their chinks. Tarvin looked long and angrily, because the laugh came from the bottom of this track, and then, digging his heel into the mould, began to let himself down step by step, steadying himself by the tufts of grass. Before he had realised it, he was out of reach of the sun, and neck deep in tall grass. Still there was a sort of pathway under his feet, down the almost perpendicular side. He gripped the grass, and went on. The earth beneath his elbows grew moist, and the rock where it cropped out showed rotten with moisture and coated with moss. The air grew cold and damp. Another plunge downward revealed to him what the trees were guarding, as he drew breath on a narrow stone ledge. They sprang from the masonry round the sides of a square tank of water so stagnant that it had corrupted past corruption, and lay dull blue under the blackness of the trees. The drought of summer had shrunk it, and a bank of dried mud ran round its sides. The head of a sunken stone pillar, carved with monstrous and obscene gods, reared itself from the water like the head of a tortoise swimming to land. The birds moved in

the sunlit branches of the trees far overhead.
Little twigs and berries dropped into the water,
and the noise of their fall echoed from side to side
of the tank that received no sunlight.

The chuckle that had so annoyed Tarvin broke
out again as he listened. This time it was behind
him, and wheeling sharply, he saw that it came
from a thin stream of water that spurted fitfully
from the rudely carved head of a cow, and dripped
along a stone spout into the heavy blue pool.
Behind that spout the moss-grown rock rose sheer.
This, then, was the Cow's Mouth.

The tank lay at the bottom of a shaft, and the
one way down to it was that by which Tarvin had
come—a path that led from the sunlight to the
chill and mould of a vault.

'Well, this is kind of the King, anyhow,' he
said, pacing the ledge cautiously, for it was almost
as slippery as the pathway on the rocks. 'Now,
what's the use of this?' he continued, returning.
The ledge ran only round one side of the tank,
and, unless he trusted to the mudbanks on the
other three, there was no hope of continuing his
exploration further. The Cow's Mouth chuckled
again, as a fresh jet of water forced its way
through the formless jaws.

'Oh, dry up!' he muttered impatiently, staring
through the half light that veiled all.

He dropped a piece of rock on the mud under
the lip of the ledge, then tested it with a cautious
foot, found that it bore, and decided to walk
round the tank. As there were more trees to the
right of the ledge than to the left, he stepped off

on the mud from the right, holding cautiously to the branches and the tufts of grass in case of any false step.

When the tank was first made its rock walls had been perfectly perpendicular, but time and weather and the war of the tree roots had broken and scarred the stone in a thousand places, giving a scant foothold here and there.

Tarvin crept along the right side of the tank, resolved, whatever might come, to go round it. The gloom deepened as he came directly under the largest fig-tree, throwing a thousand arms across the water, and buttressing the rock with snake-like roots as thick as a man's body. Here, sitting on a root, he rested and looked at the ledge. The sun, shooting down the path that he had trampled through the tall grass, threw one patch of light on the discoloured marble of the ledge and on the blunt muzzle of the cow's head ; but where Tarvin rested under the fig-tree there was darkness, and an intolerable scent of musk. The blue water was not inviting to watch ; he turned his face inward to the rock and the trees, and looking up, caught the emerald-green of a parrot's wing moving among the upper branches. Never in his life had Tarvin so acutely desired the blessed sunshine. He was cold and damp, and conscious that a gentle breeze was blowing in his face from between the snaky tree roots.

It was the sense of space more than actual sight that told him that there was a passage before him shrouded by the roots on which he sat, and it was his racial instinct of curiosity rather than any love

of adventure that led him to throw himself at the
darkness, which parted before and closed behind
him. He could feel that his feet were treading
on cut stone overlaid with a thin layer of dried
mud, and, extending his arms, found masonry on
either side. Then he lighted a match, and con-
gratulated himself that his ignorance of cows'
mouths had not led him to bring a lantern with
him. The first match flickered in the draught
and went out, and before the flame had died he
heard a sound in front of him like the shivering
backward draw of a wave on a pebbly beach.
The noise was not inspiriting, but Tarvin pressed
on for a few steps, looking back to see that the
dull glimmer of the outer day was still behind
him, and lighted another match, guarding it with
his hands. At his next step he shuddered from
head to foot. His heel had crashed through a
skull on the ground.

The match showed him that he had quitted
the passage, and was standing in a black space of
unknown dimensions. He fancied that he saw
the outline of a pillar, or rows of pillars, flickering
drunkenly in the gloom, and was all too sure that
the ground beneath him was strewn with bones.
Then he became aware of pale emerald eyes
watching him fixedly, and perceived that there
was deep breathing in the place other than his
own. He flung the match down, the eyes retreated, there was a wild rattle and crash in the
darkness, a howl that might have been bestial or
human, and Tarvin, panting between the tree
roots, swung himself to the left, and fled back

over the mud-banks to the ledge, where he stood, his back to the Cow's Mouth and his revolver in his hand.

In that moment of waiting for what might emerge from the hole in the side of the tank, Tarvin tasted all the agonies of pure physical terror. Then he noted with the tail of his eye that a length of mud-bank to his left—half the mud-bank, in fact—was moving slowly into the water. It floated slowly across the tank, a long welt of filth and slime. Nothing came out of the hole between the fig-tree roots, but the mud-bank grounded under the ledge almost at Tarvin's feet, and opened horny eyelids, heavy with green slime.

The Western man is familiar with many strange things, but the alligator does not come within the common range of his experiences. A second time Tarvin moved from point to point without being able to explain the steps he took to that end. He found himself sitting in the sunshine at the head of the slippery path that led downwards. His hands were full of the wholesome jungle grass and the clean dry dust. He could see the dead city about him, and he felt that it was home.

The Cow's Mouth chuckled and choked out of sight as it had chuckled since the making of the tank, and that was at the making of time. A man, old, crippled, and all but naked, came through the high grass leading a little kid, and calling mechanically from time to time, ' *Ao, Bhai! Ao!* ' 'Come, brother! Come!' Tarvin marvelled first at his appearance on earth at all, and next that he could so unconcernedly descend the path to the darkness and the horror below. He did not know that the sacred crocodile of the Cow's Mouth was waiting for his morning meal, as he had waited in the days when Gunnaur was peopled, and its queens never dreamed of death.

XIII

Beat off in our last fight were we ?
The greater need to seek the sea ;
For Fortune changeth as the moon
To caravel and picaroon.
Then, Eastward Ho ! or Westward Ho !
Whichever wind may meetest blow.
Our quarry sails on either sea,
Fat prey for such bold lads as we.
And every sun-dried buccaneer
Must hand and reef and watch and steer,
And bear great wrath of sea and sky
Before the plate-ships wallow by.
Now, as our tall bow takes the foam,
Let no man turn his heart to home,
Save to desire land the more,
And larger warehouse for his store,
When treasure won from Santos Bay
Shall make our sea-washed village gay.

Blackbeard.

FIBBY and Tarvin ate their breakfast together,
half an hour later, in the blotched shadows of the
scrub below the wall. The horse buried his nose
into his provender, and said nothing. The man
was equally silent. Once or twice he rose to his
feet, scanned the irregular line of wall and bastion,
and shook his head. He had no desire to return
there. As the sun grew fiercer he found a resting-

place in the heart of a circle of thorn, tucked the saddle under his head, and lay down to sleep. Fibby, rolling luxuriously, followed his master's example. The two took their rest while the air quivered with heat and the hum of insects, and the browsing goats clicked and pattered through the water-channels.

The shadow of the Tower of Glory lengthened, fell across the walls, and ran far across the plain ; the kites began to drop from the sky by twos and threes ; and naked children, calling one to another, collected the goats and drove them to the smoky villages before Tarvin roused himself for the homeward journey.

He halted Fibby once for a last look at Gunnaur as they reached the rising ground. The sunlight had left the walls, and they ran black against the misty levels and the turquoise-blue of the twilight. Fires twinkled from a score of huts about the base of the city, but along the ridge of the desolation itself there was no light.

' Mum's the word, Fibby,' said Tarvin, picking up his reins. ' We don't think well of this picnic, and we won't mention it at Rhatore.'

He chirruped, and Fibby went home as swiftly as he could lay hoof to stone, only once suggesting refreshment. Tarvin said nothing till the end of the long ride, when he heaved a deep sigh of relief as he dismounted in the fresh sunlight of the morning.

Sitting in his room, it seemed to him a waste of a most precious opportunity that he had not manufactured a torch in Gunnaur and thoroughly explored the passage. But the memory of the green eyes and the smell of musk came back to him, and he shivered. The thing was not to be done. Never again, for any consideration, under the wholesome light of the sun, would he, who feared nothing, set foot in the Cow's Mouth.

It was his pride that he knew when he had had enough. He had had enough of the Cow's Mouth ; and the only thing for which he still wished in connection with it was to express his mind about it to the Maharajah. Unhappily, this was impossible. That idle monarch, who, he now saw plainly, had sent him there either in a mood of luxurious sportiveness or to throw him off the scent of the necklace, remained the only man from whom he could look for final victory. It was not to the Maharajah that he could afford to say all that he thought.

Fortunately the Maharajah was too much entertained by the work which Tarvin immediately instituted on the Amet River to inquire particularly whether his young friend had sought the Naulahka at the Gye Mukh. Tarvin had sought an audience with the King the morning after his return from that black spot, and, with the face of a man who had never known fear and who lacks the measure of disappointments, gaily demanded the fulfilment of the King's promise. Having failed in one direction on a large scale, he laid the first brick on the walls of a new structure without delay, as the people of Topaz had begun to build their town anew the morning after the fire. His experience at the Gye Mukh only sharpened his determination, adding to it a grim willingness to get even with the man who had sent him there.

The Maharajah, who felt in especial need of amusement that morning, was very ready to make good his promise, and ordered that the long man who played pachisi should be granted all the men he could use. With the energy of disgust, and with a hot memory of the least assured and comfortable moments of his life burning in his breast, Tarvin flung himself on the turning of the river and the building of his dam. It was necessary, it seemed, in the land upon which he had fallen, to raise a dust to hide one's ends. He would raise a dust, and it should be on the same scale as the catastrophe which he had just encountered—thorough, business-like, uncompromising.

He raised it, in fact, in a stupendous cloud. Since the State was founded no one had seen anything like it. The Maharajah lent him all the convict labour of his jails, and Tarvin marched the little host of leg-ironed *kaidies* into camp at a point five miles beyond the city walls, and solemnly drew up his plans for the futile damming of the barren Amet. His early training as a civil engineer helped him to lay out a reasonable plan of operations, and to give a semblance of reality to his work. His notion was to back up the river by means of a dam at a point where it swept around a long curve, and to send it straight across the plain by excavating a deep bed for it. When this was completed the present bed of the river would lie bare for several miles, and if there were any gold there, as Tarvin said to himself, then would be the time to pick it up. Meanwhile his operations vastly entertained the King, who rode out every morning and watched him directing his small army for an hour or more. The marchings and counter-marchings of the mob of convicts with baskets, hoes, shovels, and pannier-laden donkeys, the prodigal blasting of rocks, and the general bustle and confusion, drew the applause of the King, for whom Tarvin always reserved his best blasts. This struck him as only fair, as the King was paying for the powder, and, indeed, for the entire entertainment.

Among the unpleasant necessities of his position was the need of giving daily to Colonel Nolan, to the King, and to all the drummers at the rest-house, whenever they might choose to ask him, his reasons for damming the Amet. The great Indian Government itself also presently demanded his reasons, in writing, for damming the Amet; Colonel Nolan's reasons, in writing, for allowing the Amet to be dammed; and the King's reasons for allowing anybody but a duly authorised agent of the Government to dam the Amet. This was accompanied by a request for further information. To these inquiries Tarvin, for his part, returned an evasive answer, and felt that he was qualifying himself for his political career at home. Colonel Nolan explained officially to his superiors that the convicts were employed in remunerative labour, and, unofficially, that the Maharajah had been so phenomenally good for some time past (being kept amused by this American stranger), that it would be a thousand pities to interrupt the operations. Colonel Nolan was impressed by the fact that Tarvin was the Hon. Nicholas Tarvin, and a member of the legislature of one of the United States.

The Government, knowing something of the irrepressible race who stride booted into the council-halls of kings, and demand concessions for oil-boring from Arracan to the Peshin, said no more, but asked to be supplied with information from time to time as to the progress of the stranger's work. When Tarvin heard this he sympathised with the Indian Government. He understood this thirst for information ; he wanted some himself as to the present whereabouts of the Naulahka ; also touching the time it would take Kate to find out that she wanted him more than the cure of any misery whatever.

At least twice a week, in fancy, he gave up the Naulahka definitely, returned to Topaz, and resumed the business of a real estate and insurance agent. He drew a long breath after each of these decisions, with the satisfying recollection that there was still one spot on the earth's surface where a man might come directly at his desires if he possessed the sand and the hustle ; where he could walk a straight path to his ambition ; and where he did not by preference turn five corners to reach an object a block away.

Sometimes, as he grilled patiently in the river bed under the blighting rays of the Indian sun, he would heretically blaspheme the Naulahka, refusing to believe in its existence, and persuading himself

that it was as grotesque a lie as the King's parody
of a civilised government, or as Dhunpat Rai's
helpful surgery. Yet from a hundred sources he
heard of the existence of that splendour, only
never in reply to a direct question.

Dhunpat Rai, in particular (once weak enough
to complain of the new lady doctor's 'excessive
zeal and surplusage administration'), had given
him an account that made his mouth water. But
Dhunpat Rai had not seen the necklace since the
crowning of the present King, fifteen years before.
The very convicts on the works, squabbling over
the distribution of food, spoke of millet as being
as costly as the Naulahka. Twice the Maharaj
Kunwar, babbling vaingloriously to his big friend
of what he would do when he came to the throne,
concluded his confidences with, 'And then I shall
wear the Naulahka in my turban all day long.'

But when Tarvin asked him where that precious
necklace lived, the Maharaj Kunwar shook his
head, answering sweetly, 'I do not know.'

The infernal thing seemed to be a myth, a
word, a proverb—anything rather than the finest
necklace in the world. In the intervals of blasting
and excavation he would make futile attempts to
come upon its track. He took the city ward by
ward, and explored every temple in each ; he
rode, under pretence of archæological study, to
the outlying forts and ruined palaces that lay
beyond the city in the desert, and roved restlessly
through the mausoleums that held the ashes of the
dead kings of Rhatore. He told himself a
hundred times that he knew each quest to be

hopeless ; but he needed the consolation of persistent search. And the search was always vain.

Tarvin fought his impatience when he rode abroad with the Maharajah. At the palace, which he visited at least once a day under pretence of talking about the dam, he devoted himself more sedulously than ever to pachisi. It pleased the Maharajah in those days to remove himself from the white marble pavilion in the orange garden, where he usually spent the spring months, to Sitabhai's wing of the red-stone palace, and to sit in the courtyard watching trained parrots firing little cannons, and witnessing combats between fighting quail or great grey apes dressed in imitation of English officers. When Colonel Nolan appeared the apes were hastily dismissed ; but Tarvin was allowed to watch the play throughout, when he was not engaged on the dam. He was forced to writhe in inaction and in wonder about his necklace, while these childish games went forward ; but he constantly kept the corner of an eye upon the movements of the Maharaj Kunwar. There, at least, his wit could serve some one.

The Maharajah had given strict orders that the child should obey all Kate's instructions. Even his heavy eyes noted an improvement in the health of the little one, and Tarvin was careful that he should know that the credit belonged to Kate alone. With impish perversity the young Prince, who had never received an order in his life before, learned to find joy in disobedience, and devoted his wits, his escort, and his barouche to gambolling in the wing of the palace belonging to Sitabhai. There he found grey-headed flatterers by the score, who abased themselves before him, and told him what manner of king he should be in the years to come. There also were pretty dancing-girls, who sang him songs, and would have corrupted his mind but that it was too young to receive corruption. There were, besides, apes and peacocks and jugglers—new ones every day—together with dancers on the slack-rope, and wonderful packing-cases from Calcutta, out of which he was allowed to choose ivory-handled pistols and little gold-hilted swords with seed pearls set in a groove along the middle, and running musically up and down as he waved the blade round his head. Finally, the sacrifice of a goat in an opal and ivory temple in the heart of the women's quarters, which he might watch, allured him that way. Against these entice-ments Kate, moody, grave, distracted, her eyes full of the miseries on which it was her daily lot to look, and her heart torn with the curelessness of it all, could offer only little childish games in the missionary's drawing-room. The heir-apparent to the throne did not care for leap-frog, which he deemed in the highest degree undignified; nor yet for puss-in-the-corner, which seemed to him over-active; nor for tennis, which he understood was played by his brother princes, but which to him appeared no part of a Rajput's education. Some-times, when he was tired (and on rare occasions when he escaped to Sitabhai's wing it was observ-able that he returned very tired indeed), he would listen long and intently to the stories of battle and

siege which Kate read to him, and would scandalise
her at the end of the tale by announcing, with
flashing eye—

'When I am king I will make my army do *all*
those things.'

It was not in Kate's nature—she would have
thought it in the highest degree wrong—to refrain
from some little attempt at religious instruction.
But here the child retreated into the stolidity of
the East, and only said—

'All these things are very good for you, Kate,
but all my gods are very good for me; and if
my father knew, he would be angry.'

'And what *do* you worship?' asked Kate, pity-
ing the young pagan from the bottom of her
heart.

'My sword and my horse,' answered the Maharaj Kunwar; and he half drew the jewelled sabre
that was his inseparable companion, returning it
with a resolute clank that closed the discussion.

But it was impossible, he discovered, to evade
the long man Tarvin as he evaded Kate. He
resented being called 'bub,' nor did he approve of
'little man.' But Tarvin could drawl the word
'Prince' with a quiet deference that made the
young Rajput almost suspect himself the subject of
a jest. And yet Tarvin Sahib treated him as a
man, and allowed him, under due precautions, to
handle his mighty 'gun,' which was not a gun,
but a pistol. And once, when the Prince had
coaxed the keeper of the horse into allowing him
to bestride an unmanageable mount, Tarvin, riding
up, had picked him out of the depths of the velvet

saddle, set him on his own saddle-bow, and, in the same cloud of dust, shown him how, in his own country, they laid the reins on one side or the other of the neck of their cattle-ponies to guide them in pursuit of a steer broken from the herd.

The trick of being lifted from his saddle, appealing to the 'circus' latent in the boy breast even of an Eastern prince, struck the Maharaj as so amusing that he insisted on exhibiting it before Kate; and as Tarvin was a necessary figure in the performance, he allured him into helping him with it one day before the house of the missionary. Mr. and Mrs. Estes came out upon the verandah with Kate and watched the exhibition, and the missionary pursued it with applause and requests for a repetition, which, having been duly given, Mrs. Estes asked Tarvin if he would not stay to dinner with them since he was there. Tarvin glanced doubtfully at Kate for permission, and, by a process of reasoning best known to lovers, construed the veiling of her eyes and the turning of her head into assent.

After dinner, as they sat on the verandah in the starlight, 'Do you really mind?' he asked.

'What?' asked she, lifting her sober eyes and letting them fall upon him.

'My seeing you sometimes. I know you don't like it; but it will help me to look after you. You must see by this time that you need looking after.'

'Oh no.'

'Thank you,' said Tarvin, almost humbly.

'I mean I don't need looking after.'

'But you don't dislike it?'

'It's good of you,' she said impartially.

'Well, then, it will be bad of you not to like it.'

Kate had to smile. 'I guess I like it,' she replied.

'And you will let me come once in a while? You can't think what the rest-house is. Those drummers will kill me yet. And the coolies at the dam are not in my set.'

'Well, since you're here. But you ought *not* to be here. Do me a real kindness, and go away, Nick.'

'Give me an easier one.'

'But *why* are you here? You can't show any rational reason.'

'Yes; that's what the British Government says. But I brought my reason along.'

He confessed his longing for something homely and natural and American after a day's work under a heathen and raging sun; and when he put it in this light, Kate responded on another side. She had been brought up with a sense of responsibility for making young men feel at home; and he certainly felt at home when she was able to produce, two or three evenings later, a Topaz paper sent her by her father. Tarvin pounced on it, and turned the flimsy four pages inside out, and then back again.

He smacked his lips. 'Oh, good, good, *good!*' he murmured relishingly. 'Don't the advertisements look nice? What's the matter with Topaz?' cried he, holding the sheet from him at arm's length, and gazing ravenously up and down its columns. 'Oh, *she's* all right.' The cooing,

musical sing-song in which he uttered this consecrated phrase was worth going a long way to
hear. 'Say, we're coming on, aren't we? We're
not lagging nor loafing, nor fooling our time away,
if we *haven't* got the Three C.'s *yet*. We're keeping up with the procession. Hi-yi! look at the
"Rustler Rootlets"—just about a stickful! Why,
the poor old worm-eaten town is going sound,
sound asleep in her old age, isn't she? Think of
taking a railroad there! Listen to this :—

' " Milo C. Lambert, the owner of 'Lambert's
Last Ditch,' has a car-load of good ore on the
dump, but, like all the rest of us, don't find it pays
to ship without a railroad line nearer than fifteen
miles. Milo says Colorado won't be good enough
for him after he gets his ore away."

'I should think not. Come to Topaz, Milo!
And this :—

' " When the Three C.'s comes into the city in
the fall we shan't be hearing this talk about hard
times. Meantime it's an injustice to the town,
which all honest citizens should resent and do their
best to put down, to speak of Rustler as taking a
back seat to any town of its age in the State. As
a matter of fact, Rustler was never more prosperous.
With mines which produced last year ore valued
at a total of $1,200,000, with six churches of dif-
ferent denominations, with a young but prosperous and growing academy which is destined to
take a front rank among American schools, with a

record of new buildings erected during the past year equal if not superior to any town in the mountains, and with a population of lively and determined business men, Rustler bids fair in the coming year to be worthy of her name."

' Who said " afraid " ? We're not hurt. Hear us whistle. But I'm sorry Heckler let that into his correspondence,' he added, with a momentary frown. 'Some of our Topaz citizens might miss the fun of it, and go over to Rustler to wait for the Three C.'s. Coming in the fall, is it? Oh, dear! Oh, dear, dear, dear! This is the way they amuse themselves while they dangle their legs over Big Chief Mountain and wait for it :—

' " Our merchants have responded to the recent good feeling which has pervaded the town since word came that President Mutrie, on his return to Denver, was favourably considering the claims of Rustler. Robbins has his front windows prettily decorated and filled with fancy articles. His store seems to be the most popular for the youngsters who have a nickel or two to spend."

' I should murmur ! Won't you like to see the Three C.'s come sailing into Topaz one of these fine mornings, little girl? ' asked Tarvin suddenly, as he seated himself on the sofa beside her, and opened out the paper so that she could look over his shoulder.

' Would you like it, Nick ? '

' *Would* I ! '

'Then, of course, I should. But I think you
will be better off if it doesn't. It will make you
too rich. See father.'

'Well, I'd put on the brakes if I found myself
getting real rich. I'll stop just after I've passed
the Genteel Poverty Station. Isn't it good to see
the old heading again—Heckler's name as large as
life just under "oldest paper in Divide County,"
and Heckler's fist sticking out all over a rousing
editorial on the prospects of the town? Home-
like, isn't it? He's got two columns of new
advertising ; that shows what the town's doing.
And look at the good old "ads." from the Eastern
agencies. How they take you back! I never
expected to thank Heaven for a Castoria advertise-
ment ; did you, Kate? But I swear it makes me
feel good all over. I'll read the patent inside if
you say much.'

Kate smiled. The paper gave her a little pang
of home-sickness too. She had her own feeling
for Topaz ; but what reached her through the
Telegram's lively pages was the picture of her
mother sitting in her kitchen in the long after-
noons (she had sat in the kitchen so long in the
poor and wandering days of the family that she did
it now by preference), gazing sadly out at white-
topped Big Chief, and wondering what her daughter
was doing at that hour. Kate remembered well
that afternoon hour in the kitchen when the work
was done. She recalled from the section-house
days the superannuated rocker, once a parlour
chair, which her mother had hung with skins and
told off for kitchen service. Kate remembered

with starting tears that her mother had always
wanted her to sit in it, and how good it had been
to see from her own hassock next the oven the
little mother swallowed up in its deeps. She heard
the cat purring under the stove, and the kettle
singing ; the clock ticked in her ear, and the
cracks between the boards in the floor of the hastily
built section-house blew the cold prairie air against
her heels.

She gazed over Tarvin's shoulder at the two
cuts of Topaz which appeared in every issue of the
Telegram—the one representing the town in its
first year, the other the town of to-day—and a
lump rose in her throat.

'Quite a difference, isn't there ?' said Tarvin,
following her eye. 'Do you remember where
your father's tent used to stand, and the old section-
house, just here by the river ?' He pointed, and
Kate nodded without speaking. 'Those were
good days, weren't they ? Your father wasn't as
rich as he is now, and neither was I ; but we were
all mighty happy together.'

Kate's thought drifted back to that time, and
called up other visions of her mother expending
her slight frame in many forms of hard work.
The memory of the little characteristic motion with
which she would shield with raised hand the worn
young-old face when she would be broiling above
an open fire, or frying doughnuts, or lifting the
stove lid, forced her to gulp down the tears. The
simple picture was too clear, even to the light of
the fire on the face, and the pink light shining
through the frail hand.

'Hello!' said Tarvin, casting his eye up and down the columns, 'they've had to put another team on to keep the streets clean. We had one. Heckler don't forget the climate either. And they are doing well at the Mesa House. That's a good sign. The tourists will all have to stop over at Topaz when the new line comes through, and we have the right hotel. Some towns might think we had a little tourist traffic now. Here's Loomis dining fifty at the Mesa the other day—through express. They've formed a new syndicate to work the Hot Springs. Do you know, I shouldn't wonder if they made a town down there. Heckler's right. It *will* help Topaz. We don't mind a town that near. It makes a suburb of it.'

He marked his sense of the concession implied in letting him stay that evening by going early; but he did not go so early on the following evening, and as he showed no inclination to broach forbidden subjects, Kate found herself glad to have him there, and it became a habit of his to drop in, in the evenings, and to join the group that gathered, with open doors and windows, about the family lamp. In the happiness of seeing visible effects from her labours blossoming under her eyes, Kate regarded his presence less and less. Sometimes she would let him draw her out upon the verandah under the sumptuous Indian night—nights when the heat-lightning played like a drawn sword on the horizon, and the heavens hovered near the earth, and the earth was very still. But commonly they sat within, with the missionary and his wife, talking of Topaz, of the hospital, of the Maharaj

Kunwar, of the dam, and sometimes of the Estes children at Bangor. For the most part, however, when the talk was among the group, it fell upon the infinitesimal gossip of a sequestered life, to the irritation and misery of Tarvin.

When the conversation lagged in these deeps he would fetch up violently with a challenge to Estes on the subject of the tariff or silver legislation, and after that the talk was at least lively. Tarvin was, by his training, largely a newspaper-educated man. But he had also been taught at first hand by life itself, and by the habit of making his own history; and he used the hairy fist of horse-sense in dealing with the theories of newspaper politics and the systems of the schools.

Argument had no allurements for him, however; it was with Kate that he talked when he could, and oftenest, of late, of the hospital, since her progress there had begun to encourage her. She yielded at last to his entreaties to be allowed to see this paragon, and to look for himself upon the reforms she had wrought.

Matters had greatly improved since the days of the lunatic and the 'much-esteemed woman,' but only Kate knew how much remained to be done. The hospital was at least clean and sweet if she inspected it every day, and the people in their fashion were grateful for kinder tending and more skilful treatment than they had hitherto dreamed of. Upon each cure a rumour went abroad through the country-side of a new power in the land, and other patients came; or the convalescent herself would bring back a sister, a child, or a

mother with absolute faith in the power of the
White Fairy to make all whole. They could not
know all the help that Kate brought in the train
of her quiet movements, but for what they knew
they blessed her as they lay. Her new energy
swept even Dhunpat Rai along the path of reform.
He became curious in the limewashing of stonework, the disinfecting of wards, the proper airing
of bed-linen, and even the destruction by fire
of the bedsteads, once his perquisite, on which
smallpox patients had died. Native-like, he
worked best for a woman with the knowledge
that there was an energetic white man in the background. Tarvin's visits, and a few cheery words
addressed to him by that capable outsider, supplied
him with this knowledge.

Tarvin could not understand the uncouth talk
of the out-patients, and did not visit the women's
wards; but he saw enough to congratulate Kate
unreservedly. She smiled contentedly. Mrs.
Estes was sympathetic, but in no way enthusiastic;
and it was good to be praised by Nick, who had
found so much to blame in her project.

'It's clean and it's wholesome, little girl,' he
said, peering and sniffing; 'and you've done
miracles with these jellyfish. If you'd been on the
opposition ticket instead of your father I shouldn't
be a member of the legislature.'

Kate never talked to him about that large part
of her work which lay among the women of the
Maharajah's palace. Little by little she learned
her way about such portions of the pile as she was
permitted to traverse. From the first she had

understood that the palace was ruled by one
Queen, of whom the women spoke under their
breath, and whose lightest word, conveyed by the
mouth of a grinning child, set the packed mazes
humming. Once only had she seen this Queen,
glimmering like a tiger-beetle among a pile of
kincob cushions—a lithe, black-haired young girl,
it seemed, with a voice as soft as running water at
night, and with eyes that had no shadow of fear
in them. She turned lazily, the jewels clinking
on ankle, arm, and bosom, and looked at Kate for
a long time without speaking.

'I have sent that I may see you,' she said at
last. 'You have come here across the water to
help these cattle?'

Kate nodded, every instinct in her revolting at
the silver-tongued splendour at her feet.

'You are not married?' The Queen put her
hands behind her head and looked at the painted
peacocks on the ceiling.

Kate did not reply, but her heart was hot.

'Is there any sickness here?' she asked at last
sharply. 'I have much to do.'

'There is none, unless it may be that you yourself are sick. There are those who sicken without
knowing it.'

The eyes turned to meet Kate's, which were
blazing with indignation. This woman, lapped in
idleness, had struck at the life of the Maharaj
Kunwar; and the horror of it was that she was
younger than herself.

'*Achcha*,' said the Queen, still more slowly,
watching her face. 'If you hate me so, why

do you not say so? You white people love truth.'

Kate turned on her heel to leave the room. Sitabhai called her back for an instant, and, moved by some royal caprice, would have caressed her, but she fled indignant, and was careful never again to venture into that wing of the palace. None of the women there called for her services, and not once but several times, when she passed the mouth of the covered way that led to Sitabhai's apartments, she saw a little naked child flourishing a jewelled knife, and shouting round the headless carcass of a goat whose blood was flooding the white marble. 'That,' said the women, 'is the gipsy's son. He learns to kill daily. A snake is a snake, and a gipsy is a gipsy, till they are dead.'

There was no slaughter of goats, singing of songs, or twangling of musical instruments in the wing of the palace that made itself specially Kate's own. Here lived, forgotten by the Maharajah and mocked by Sitabhai's maidens, the mother of the Maharaj Kunwar. Sitabhai had taken from her—by the dark arts of the gipsies, so the Queen's adherents said; by her own beauty and knowledge in love, they sang in the other wing of the palace —all honour and consideration due to her as the Queen Mother. There were scores of empty rooms where once there had been scores of waiting-women, and those who remained with the fallen Queen were forlorn and ill-favoured. She herself was a middle-aged woman, by Eastern standards; that is to say, she had passed twenty-five, and had never been more than ordinarily comely.

Her eyes were dull with much weeping, and her mind was full of superstitions—fears for every hour of the night and the day, and vague terrors, bred of loneliness, that made her tremble at the sound of a footfall.   In the years of her prosperity she had been accustomed to perfume herself, put on her jewels, and with braided hair await the Maharajah's coming.   She would still call for her jewels, attire herself as of old, and wait amid the respectful silence of her attendants till the long night gave way to the dawn, and the dawn showed the furrows on her cheeks.   Kate had seen one such vigil, and perhaps showed in her eyes the wonder that she could not repress, for the Queen Mother fawned on her timidly after the jewels had been put away, and begged her not to laugh.

'You do not understand, Miss Kate,' she pleaded.   'There is one custom in your country and another in ours ; but still you are a woman, and you will know.'

'But you know that no one will come,' Kate said tenderly.

'Yes, I know ; but—no, you are not a woman, only a fairy that has come across the water to help me and mine.'

Here again Kate was baffled.   Except in the message sent by the Maharaj Kunwar, the Queen Mother never referred to the danger that threatened her son's life.   Again and again Kate had tried to lead up to the subject—to gain some hint, at least, of the nature of the plot.

'I know nothing,' the Queen would reply. 'Here behind the curtain no one knows anything.

Miss Kate, if my own women lay dead out there
in the sun at noon'—she pointed downwards
through the tracery of her window to the flagged
path below—'I should know nothing. Of what
I said I know nothing ; but surely it is allowed '—
she lowered her voice to a whisper—'oh, surely it
is allowed to a mother to bid another woman look
to her son. He is so old now that he thinks himself a man, and wanders far, and so young that he
thinks the world will do him no harm. *Ahi!*
And he is so wise that he knows a thousand times
more than I : he speaks English like an Englishman. How can I control him with my little
learning and my very great love ? I say to you,
Be good to my son. That I can say aloud, and
write it upon a wall, if need were. There is no
harm in that. But if I said more, look you, the
plaster between the stones beneath me would gape
to suck it in, and the wind would blow all my
words across to the villages. I am a stranger here
—a Rajputni from Kulu, a thousand thousand koss
away. They bore me here in a litter to be married
—in the dark they bore me for a month ; and
except that some of my women have told me, I
should not know which way the home wind blows
when it goes to Kulu. What can a strange cow
do in the byre ? May the gods witness.'

'Ah, but tell me what you think ? '

'I think nothing,' the Queen would answer
sullenly. 'What have women to do with thinking ? They love and they suffer. I have said all
that I may say. Miss Kate, some day you will
bear a little son. As you have been good to my son,

so may the gods be good to yours when that time comes, and you know how the heart is full of love.'

'If I am to protect him, I must know. You leave me in the dark.'

'And I also am in the dark—and the darkness is full of danger.'

Tarvin himself was much about the palace, not only because he perceived that it was there he might most hopefully keep his ear to the ground for news of the Naulahka, but because it enabled him to observe Kate's comings and goings, and with his hand ready for a rapid movement to his pistol-pocket.

His gaze followed her at these times, as at others, with the longing look of the lover; but he said nothing, and Kate was grateful to him. It was a time, as it seemed to him, to play the part of the Tarvin who had carried water for her long ago at the end of the section; it was a time to stand back, to watch, to guard, but not to trouble her.

The Maharaj Kunwar came often under his eye, and he was constantly inventing amusing things for him to do remote from Sitabhai's courtyard; but the boy would occasionally break away, and then it was Tarvin's task to go after him and make sure that he came to no harm. One afternoon when he had spent some time in coaxing the child away, and had finally resorted to force, much to the child's disgust, a twelve-foot baulk of teakwood, as he was passing out under an arch in process of repair, crashed down from the scaffolding just in front of Fibby's nose. The horse retired into the courtyard on his hind legs, and Tarvin heard the rustle of the women behind the shutters.

He reflected on the incurable slackness of these people, stopped to swear at the workmen crouched on the scaffolding in the hollow of the arch, and went on. They were no less careless about the dam—it was in the blood, he supposed—for the headman of a coolie gang who must have crossed the Amet twenty times, showed him a new ford across a particularly inviting channel, which ended in a quicksand ; and when Tarvin had flung himself clear, the gang spent half the day in hauling Fibby out with ropes. They could not even build a temporary bridge without leaving the boards loose, so that a horse's hoof found its way between ; and the gangs seemed to make a point of letting bullock-carts run down the steep embankments into the small of Tarvin's back, when, at infrequent intervals, that happened to be turned.

Tarvin was filled with great respect for the British Government, which worked on these materials, and began to understand the mild-faced melancholy and decisive views of Lucien Estes about the native population, as well as to sympathise more keenly than ever with Kate.

This curious people were now, he learned with horror, to fill the cup of their follies by marrying the young Maharaj Kunwar to a three-year-old babe, brought from the Kulu hills, at vast expense, to be his bride. He sought out Kate at the missionary's, and found her quivering with indignation. She had just heard.

'It's like them to waste a wedding where it isn't

wanted,' said Tarvin soothingly. Since he saw
Kate excited, it became his part to be calm.
'Don't worry your overworked head about it,
Kate. You are trying to do too much, and you
are feeling too much. You will break down before
you know it, from sheer exhaustion of the
chord of sympathy.'

'Oh no!' said Kate. 'I feel quite strong
enough for anything that may come. I mustn't
break down. Think of this marriage coming on.
The Maharaj will need me more than ever. He
has just told me that he won't get any sleep for
three days and three nights while their priests are
praying over him.'

'Crazy! Why, it's a quicker way of killing
him than Sitabhai's. Heavens! I daren't think of
it. Let's talk of something else. Any papers
from your father lately? This kind of thing
makes Topaz taste sort of good.'

She gave him a package received by the last
post, and he fell silent as he ran his eye hastily over
a copy of the *Telegram* six weeks old; but he
seemed to find little comfort in it. His brows
knitted.

'Pshaw!' he exclaimed with irritation, 'this
won't do!'

'What is it?'

'Heckler bluffing about the Three C.'s, and
not doing it well. That isn't like Jim. He talks
about it as a sure thing as hard as if he didn't
believe in it, and had a private tip from somewhere
that it wasn't coming after all. I've no doubt he
has. But he needn't give it away to Rustler like

that. Let's look at the real estate transfers. Ah! that tells the story,' he exclaimed excitedly, as his eye rested on the record of the sale of a parcel of lots on G Street. 'Prices are going down— away, 'way down. The boys are caving. They're giving up the fight.' He leaped up and marched about the room nervously. 'Heavens! if I could only get word to them!'

'Why—what, Nick? What word do you want to send them?'

He pulled himself up instantly.

'To let them know that *I* believe in it,' he said. 'To get them to hold on.'

'But suppose the road doesn't come to Topaz after all. How can you know, away off here in India?'

'Come to Topaz, little girl!' he shouted. 'Come to Topaz! It's coming if I have to lay the rails!'

But the news about the temper of the town vexed and disconcerted him notwithstanding, and after he left Kate that night he sent a cable to Heckler, through Mrs. Mutrie, desiring her to forward the despatch from Denver, as if that were the originating office of the message.

'HECKLER, TOPAZ.—*Take a brace, for God's sake. Got dead cinch on Three C.'s. Trust me, and boom like* —— TARVIN.'

XIV

Because I sought it far from men,
   In deserts and alone,
I found it burning overhead,
   The jewel of a throne.

Because I sought—I sought it so
   And spent my days to find—
It blazed one moment ere it left
   The blacker night behind.
                              The Crystals of Iswara.

A CITY of tents had grown up in three days
without the walls of Rhatore—a city greened with
far-brought lawns of turf, and stuck about with
hastily transplanted orange-trees, wooden lamp-
posts painted in gaudy colours, and a cast-iron
fountain of hideous design. Many guests were
expected at Rhatore to grace the marriage of the
Maharaj Kunwar—barons, princes, thakurs, lords
of waste fortresses and of hopeless crags of the
north and the south, fiefs from the fat, poppy-
blazoned plains of Mewar, and brother rajahs of
the King. They came accompanied by their escorts,
horse and foot.

In a land where genealogies, to be respectable,
must run back without a break for eight hundred

years, it is a delicate matter not to offend ; and all
were desperately jealous of the place and precedence
of their neighbours in the camp. Lest the task
should be too easy, the household bards of the
princes came with them, and squabbled with the
court officials of Gokral Seetarun. Behind the
tents stretched long lines of horse-pickets, where
the fat pink-and-blue-spotted stallions neighed and
squealed at one another, under their heavy velvet
trappings, all day long ; and the ragged militia of
twenty tiny native states smoked and gambled
among their saddles, or quarrelled at the daily
distribution of food furnished by the generosity of
the Maharajah. From hundreds of miles about,
vagrant and mendicant priests of every denomina-
tion had flocked into the city, and their salmon-
coloured raiment, black blankets, or ash-smeared
nudity gave Tarvin many minutes of untrammelled
entertainment as he watched them roaming fearlessly
from tent to tent, their red eyes rolling in their
heads, alternately threatening or fawning for gifts.
The rest-house, as Tarvin discovered, was crammed
with fresh contingents of commercial travellers.
His Highness was not likely to pay at such a
season, but fresh orders would be plentiful. The
city itself was brilliant with coats of pink-and-white
lime-wash, and the main streets were obstructed
with the bamboo scaffoldings of fireworks. Every
house-front was swept and newly luted with clean
mud, and the doorways were hung with marigolds
and strings of jasmine-buds. Through the crowds
tramped the sweating sweetmeat-dealers, vendors
of hawks, dealers in cheap jewellery and glass

bracelets and little English mirrors, while camels, loaded with wedding gifts of far-off kings, ploughed through the crowd, or the mace-bearers of the State cleared a path with their silver staves for the passage of the Maharajah's carriages. Forty barouches were in use, and, as long as horse-flesh held out, or harness could be patched with string, it did not beseem the dignity of the State to provide less than four horses to each. As these horses were untrained, and as the little native boys, out of sheer lightness of heart, touched off squibs and crackers at high noon, the streets were animated.

The hill on which the palace stood seemed to smoke like a volcano, for the little dignitaries came without cessation, each expecting the salute of cannon due to his rank. Between the roars of the ordnance, strains of uncouth music would break from the red walls, and presently some officer of the court would ride out of one of the gates, followed by all his retinue, each man gorgeous as a cock-pheasant in spring, his moustache fresh oiled and curled fiercely over his ears ; or one of the royal elephants, swathed in red velvet and bullion from shoulder to ankle, would roll out under the weight of his silver howdah, and trumpet till the streets were cleared for his passage. Seventy elephants were fed daily by the King—no mean charge, since each beast consumed as much green fodder daily as he could carry on his back, as well as thirty or forty pounds of flour. Now and again one of the monsters, maddened by the noise and confusion, and by the presence of strange rivals, would be overtaken with paroxysms of blind fury.

Then he would be hastily stripped of his trappings, bound with ropes and iron chains, hustled out of the city between two of his fellows, and tied down half a mile away by the banks of the Amet, to scream and rage till the horses in the neighbouring camps broke their pickets and stampeded wildly among the tents. Pertab Singh, commandant of his Highness's body-guard, was in his glory. Every hour of the day gave him excuse for charging with his troop on mysterious but important errands between the palace and the tents of the princes. The formal interchange of visits alone occupied two days. Each prince with his escort would solemnly drive to the palace, and half an hour later the silver state barouche and the Maharajah himself, jewelled from head to heel, would return the visit, while the guns gave word of the event to the city of houses and to the city of tents.

When night fell on the camp there was no silence till near the dawn, for strolling players, singers of songs, and tellers of stories, dancing girls, brawny Oudh wrestlers, and camp followers beyond counting, wandered from tent to tent making merry. When these had departed, the temples in the city sent forth the hoarse cries of conchs, and Kate, listening, seemed to hear in every blast the wail of the little Maharaj Kunwar, who was being prepared for his marriage by interminable prayers and purifications. She saw as little of the boy as Tarvin did of the King. In those days every request for an audience was met with, 'He is with his priests.' Tarvin cursed all the priests of Rhatore, and condemned to every variety of

perdition the hang-dog fakirs that prowled about
his path.

'I wish to goodness they'd come to a point
with this fool business,' he said to himself. 'I
haven't got a century to spend in Rhatore.'

After nearly a week of uninterrupted clamour,
blazing sunshine, and moving crowds clad in
garments, the colours of which made Tarvin's eyes
ache, there arrived, by the same road that had
borne Kate to the city, two carriages containing
five Englishmen and three Englishwomen, who,
later, walked about the city with lack-lustre eyes,
bored by the official duty which compelled them
to witness in the hot weather a crime which it was
not only beyond them to hinder, but to which they
were obliged to lend their official patronage.

The agent to the Governor-General—that is to
say, the official representative of the Viceroy in
Rajputana—had some time before represented to
the Maharajah that he might range himself in the
way of progress and enlightenment by ordering
that his son should not be given in marriage for
another ten years. The Maharajah, pleading the
immemorial custom of his land and the influence
of the priests, gilded his refusal by a generous
donation to a women's hospital in Calcutta which
was not in want of funds.

For his own part, Tarvin could not comprehend
how any government could lend its countenance
to this wicked farce, calling itself a marriage, which
was presently to be played out with the assistance
of two children. He was presently introduced
to the agent of the Governor - General, who was

anxious to learn more about the damming of the
Amet. To be asked about the damming of the
Amet, when he was making no more progress than
at present with the Naulahka, seemed to Tarvin,
however, the last touch of insult, and he was not
communicative, asking the agent, instead, a number
of urgent questions about the approaching infamy
at the palace. The agent declaring the marriage
to be a political necessity, the destination suggested
by Tarvin for political necessities of this sort
caused the official to stiffen, and to look this wild
American up and down with startled curiosity.
They parted on poor terms.

With the rest of the party Tarvin was more at
ease. The agent's wife, a tall brunette, belonging
to one of those families which from the earliest
days of the East India Company have administered
the fortunes of India, solemnly inspected Kate's
work at the hospital ; and being only a woman,
and not an official, was attracted, and showed that
she was attracted, by the sad-eyed little woman
who did not talk about her work. Therefore
Tarvin devoted himself to the amusement and entertainment of the agent's wife, and she pronounced
him an extraordinary person. 'But, then, all
Americans are extraordinary, you know, though
they're so clever.'

Not forgetting in the midst of this tumultuous
pageant that he was a citizen of Topaz, Tarvin
told her about that blessed city of the plain, away
off there under the Sauguache Range, where half
his heart lay. He called it 'the magic city,' im-
plying that the dwellers of the Western continent

had agreed to call it so by general consent. She
was not bored ; she enjoyed it. Talk of land and
improvement companies, boards of trade, town
lots, and the Three C.'s was fresh to her, and it
became easy to lead up to what Tarvin actually
had in mind. What about the Naulahka ? Had
she ever seen it ? He asked these questions
boldly.

No ; she knew nothing of the Naulahka. Her
thoughts were bounded by the thought of going
home in the spring. Home for her meant a little
house near Sydenham, close to the Crystal Palace,
where her three-year-old boy was waiting for her ;
and the interests of the other English men and
women seemed equally remote from Rajputana—
not to mention the Naulahka. It was only infer-
entially that Tarvin could gather that they had
spent the greater part of their working lives within
the limits of the country. They talked as gipsies
might talk by the roadside a little before the horses
are put into the caravan. The ways were hot,
they implied, and very dusty ; and they hoped one
day to be able to rest. The wedding was only
one more weary incident on the line of march, and
they devoutly wished it over. One of them even
envied Tarvin for coming to the State with his
fresh eye and his lively belief in the possibility of
getting something out of the land besides a harvest
of regrets.

The last day of the marriage ceremonies began
and ended with more cannon, more fireworks,more
clattering of hoofs, more trumpeting of elephants,
and with the clamour of bands trying to play ' God

Save the Queen.' The Maharaj Kunwar was to appear in the evening (in an Indian state wedding the bride is neither mentioned nor seen) at a banquet, where the agent of the Governor-General would propose his health and that of his father. The Maharaj was to make a speech in his best English. A court scribe had already composed a long oration to be used by his father. Tarvin was beginning seriously to doubt whether he should ever see the child alive again ; and, before the banquet, rode out into the seething city to reconnoitre. It was twilight, and the torches were flaring between the houses. Wild outlanders from the desert, who had never seen a white man before, caught his horse by the bridle, examined him curiously, and with a grunt let him pass. The many-coloured turbans showed under the flickering light like the jewels of a broken necklace, and all the white housetops were crowded with the veiled figures of women. In half an hour the Maharaj Kunwar would make his way from the royal temple to the banqueting-tent at the head of a procession of caparisoned elephants.

Tarvin forced his way inch by inch through the dense crowd that waited at the foot of the temple steps. He merely wished to satisfy himself that the child was well ; he wanted to see him come from the temple. As he looked about him he saw that he was the only white man in the crowd, and pitied his jaded acquaintances, who could find no pleasure in the wild scene under his eyes.

The temple doors were closed, and the torchlight flashed back from the ivory and silver with

which they were inlaid. Somewhere out of sight
stood the elephants, for Tarvin could hear their
deep breathing and an occasional squeal above the
hum of the crowd. Half a troop of cavalry, very
worn and dusty with the day's labours, were trying
to clear an open space before the temple, but they
might as well have tried to divide a rainbow.
From the roofs of the houses the women were
throwing flowers, sweetmeats, and coloured rice
into the crowd, while small bards, not yet attached
to the house of any prince, chanted aloud in praise
of the Maharajah, the Maharaj Kunwar, the
Viceroy, the agent of the Governor‑General,
Colonel Nolan, and any one else who might
possibly reward praise with pence. One of these
men, recognising Tarvin, struck up a chant in his
honour. He had come, said the song, from a far
country to dam an ungovernable river, and fill the
country‑side with gold ; his step was like the step
of a dromedary in the spring ; his eye terrible as
that of an elephant ; and the graces of his person
such that the hearts of all the women of Rhatore
turned to water when he rode upon the public
way. Lastly, he would reward the singer of
this poor song with untold generosity, and his
name and fame should endure in the land so long
as the flag of Gokral Seetarun had five colours,
or as long as the Naulahka adorned the throat of
kings.

Then, with an ear‑splitting shriek of conchs, the
temple doors opened inward, and the voices of the
crowd were hushed into a whisper of awe. Tarvin's
hands tightened on the reins of his horse, and he

leaned forward to stare. The opened doors of the temples framed a square of utter darkness, and to the screeching of the conchs was added a throbbing of innumerable drums. A breath of incense, strong enough to make him cough, drifted across the crowd, which was absolutely silent now.

The next moment the Maharaj Kunwar, alone and unattended, came out of the darkness, and stood in the torchlight with his hands on the hilt of his sword. The face beneath the turban, draped with loops of diamonds under an emerald aigrette, was absolutely colourless. There were purple circles about his eyes, and his mouth was half open ; but the pity Tarvin felt for the child's weariness was silenced by a sudden thrill and leap of his heart, for on the gold cloth of the Maharaj Kunwar's breast lay the Naulahka.

There was no need, this time, to ask any questions. It was not he who saw it ; its great deep eyes seemed to fall on him. It blazed with the dull red of the ruby, the angry green of the emerald, the cold blue of the sapphire, and the white-hot glory of the diamond. But dulling all these glories was the superb radiance of one gem that lay above the great carved emerald on the central clasp. It was the black diamond—black as the pitch of the infernal lake, and lighted from below with the fires of hell.

The thing lay on the boy's shoulders, a yoke of flame. It outshone the silent Indian stars above, turned the tossing torches to smears of dull yellow, and sucked the glitter from the cloth of gold on which it lay.

There was no time to think, to estimate, to appraise, scarcely a moment even to realise, for the conchs suddenly wailed again, the Maharaj stepped back into the darkness, and the doors of the temple were shut.

XV

From small-pox and the Evil Eye, a wasteful marriage-
feast, and the kindness of my co-wife, may the Gods protect
my son.—*Hindu Proverb*.

TARVIN made his way to the banquet with his face
aflame and his tongue dry between his teeth. He
had seen it. It existed. It was not a myth. And
he would have it ; he would take it back with him.
Mrs. Mutrie should hang it about the sculptured
neck that looked so well when she laughed ; and
the Three C.'s should come to Topaz. He would
be the saviour of his town ; the boys at home
would take the horses out of his carriage and drag
him up Pennsylvania Avenue with their own hands ;
and town lots would sell next year in Topaz by the
running inch.

It was worth all the waiting, worth the damming
of a hundred rivers, worth a century of pachisi
playing, and a thousand miles of bullock-cart.
As he drained a glass to the health of the young
Maharaj Kunwar at the banquet that evening, he
renewed his pledge to himself to fight it out on this
line if it took all summer. His pride of success
had lain low of late, and taken many hurts ; but
now that he had seen his prize he esteemed it

already within his grasp, as he had argued at Topaz
that Kate must be his because he loved her.

Next morning he woke with a confused notion
that he stood on the threshold of great deeds ; and
then, in his bath, he wondered whence he had
plucked the certainty and exultation of the night
before. He had, indeed, seen the Naulahka. But
the temple doors had closed on the vision. He
found himself asking whether either temple or
necklace had been real, and in the midst of his
wonder and excitement was half way to the city
before he knew that he had left the rest-house.
When he came to himself, however, he knew well
whither he was going and what he was going for.
If he had seen the Naulahka, he meant to keep it
in sight. It had disappeared into the temple. To
the temple, therefore, he would go.

Fragments of burnt-out torches lay on the
temple steps among trampled flowers and spilt oil,
and the marigold garlands hung limp and wilted on
the fat shoulders of the black stone bulls that
guarded the inner court. Tarvin took off his
white pith helmet (it was very hot, though it was
only two hours after dawn), pushed back the
scanty hair from his high forehead, and surveyed
the remnants of yesterday's feast. The city was
still asleep after its holiday. The doors of the
building were wide open, and he ascended the steps
and walked in, with none to hinder.

The formless, four-faced god Iswara, standing
in the centre of the temple, was smeared and discoloured with stains of melted butter, and the black
smoke of exhausted incense. Tarvin looked at the

figure curiously, half expecting to find the Naulahka hung about one of its four necks. Behind him, in the deeper gloom of the temple, stood other divinities, many-handed and many-headed, tossing their arms aloft, protruding their tongues, and grinning at one another. The remains of many sacrifices lay about them, and in the half light Tarvin could see that the knees of one were dark with dried blood. Overhead the dark roof ran up into a Hindu dome, and there was a soft rustle and scratching of nesting bats.

Tarvin, with his hat on the back of his head and his hands in his pockets, gazed at the image, looking about him and whistling softly. He had been a month in India, but he had not yet penetrated to the interior of a temple. Standing there, he recognised with fresh force how entirely the life, habits, and traditions of this strange people alienated them from all that seemed good and right to him ; and he was vaguely angered to know that it was the servants of these horrors who possessed a necklace which had power to change the destiny of a Christian and civilised town like Topaz.

He knew that he would be expelled without ceremony for profanation, if discovered, and made haste to finish his investigations, with a half-formed belief that the slovenliness of the race might have caused them to leave the Naulahka about somewhere, as a woman might leave her jewels on her dressing-table after a late return from a ball the night before. He peered about and under the gods, one by one, while the bats squeaked above him. Then he returned to the central image of Iswara, and in his former attitude regarded the idol.

It occurred to him that, though he was on level ground, most of his weight was resting on his toes, and he stepped back to recover his balance. The slab of sandstone he had just quitted rolled over slowly, as a porpoise rolls in the still sea, revealing for an instant a black chasm below. Then it shouldered up into its place again without a sound, and Tarvin wiped the cold sweat from his forehead. If he had found the Naulahka at that instant he would have smashed it in pure rage. He went out into the sunlight once more, devoting the country where such things were possible to its own gods ; he could think of nothing worse.

A priest, sprung from an unguessable retreat, came out of the temple immediately afterward, and smiled upon him.

Tarvin, willing to renew his hold on the wholesome world in which there were homes and women, betook himself to the missionary's cottage, where he invited himself to breakfast. Mr. and Mrs. Estes had kept themselves strictly aloof from the marriage ceremony, but they could enjoy Tarvin's account of it, delivered from the Topaz point of view. Kate was unfeignedly glad to see him. She was full of the discreditable desertion of Dhunpat Rai and the hospital staff from their posts. They had all gone to watch the wedding festivities, and for three days had not appeared at the hospital. The entire work of the place had devolved on herself and the wild woman of the

desert who was watching her husband's cure.
Kate was very tired, and her heart was troubled
with misgivings for the welfare of the little Prince,
which she communicated to Tarvin when he drew
her out upon the verandah after breakfast.

'I'm sure he wants absolute rest now,' she said,
almost tearfully. 'He came to me at the end of
the dinner last night—I was in the women's wing
of the palace—and cried for half an hour. Poor
little baby! It's cruel.'

'Oh, well, he'll be resting to-day. Don't
worry.'

'No; to-day they take his bride back to her
own people again, and he has to drive out with
the procession or something—in this sun, too.
It's very wicked. Doesn't it ever make your
head ache, Nick? I sometimes think of you
sitting out on that dam of yours, and wonder
how you can bear it.'

'I can bear a good deal for you, little girl,'
returned Tarvin, looking down into her eyes.

'Why, how is that for me, Nick?'

'You'll see if you live long enough,' he assured
her; but he was not anxious to discuss his dam,
and returned to the safer subject of the Maharaj
Kunwar.

Next day and the day after he rode aimlessly
about in the neighbourhood of the temple, not
caring to trust himself within its walls again, but
determined to keep his eye upon the first and last
spot where he had seen the Naulahka. There
was no chance at present of getting speech with
the only living person, save the King, whom he

definitely knew to have touched the treasure. It was maddening to await the reappearance of the Maharaj Kunwar in his barouche, but he summoned what patience he could. He hoped much from him ; but meanwhile he often looked in at the hospital to see how Kate fared. The traitor Dhunpat Rai and his helpers had returned ; but the hospital was crowded with cases from the furthest portions of the State—fractures caused by the King's reckless barouches, and one or two cases, new in Kate's experience, of men drugged, under the guise of friendship, for the sake of the money they carried with them, and left helpless in the public ways.

Tarvin, as he cast his shrewd eye about the perfectly kept men's ward, humbly owned to himself that, after all, she was doing better work in Rhatore than he. She at least did not run a hospital to cover up deeper and darker designs, and she had the inestimable advantage over him of having her goal in sight. It was not snatched from her after one maddening glimpse ; it was not the charge of a mysterious priesthood, or of an impalpable State ; it was not hidden in treacherous temples, nor hung round the necks of vanishing infants.

One morning, before the hour at which he usually set out for the dam, Kate sent a note over to him at the rest-house asking him to call at the hospital as soon as possible. For one rapturous moment he dreamed of impossible things. But smiling bitterly at his readiness to hope, he lighted a cigar, and obeyed the order.

Kate met him on the steps, and led him into the dispensary.

She laid an eager hand on his arm. 'Do you know anything about the symptoms of hemp-poisoning?' she asked him.

He caught her by both hands quickly, and stared wildly into her face. 'Why? Why? Has any one been daring—— ?'

She laughed nervously. 'No, no. It isn't me. It's him.'

'Who?'

'The Maharaj—the child. I'm certain of it now.' She went on to tell him how, that morning, the barouche, the escort, and a pompous native had hurried up to the missionary's door bearing the almost lifeless form of the Maharaj Kunwar; how she had at first attributed the attack, whatever it might be, to exhaustion consequent upon the wedding festivities; how the little one had roused from his stupor, blue-lipped and hollow-eyed, and had fallen from one convulsion into another, until she had begun to despair; and how, at the last, he had dropped into a deep sleep of exhaustion, when she had left him in the care of Mrs. Estes. She added that Mrs. Estes had believed that the young prince was suffering from a return of his usual malady; she had seen him in paroxysms of this kind twice before Kate came.

'Now look at this,' said Kate, taking down the chart of her hospital cases, on which were recorded the symptoms and progress of two cases of hemp-poisoning that had come to her within the past week.

'These men,' she said, 'had been given sweetmeats by a gang of travelling gipsies, and all their
money was taken from them before they woke up.
Read for yourself.'

Tarvin read, biting his lips. At the end he
looked up at her sharply.

'Yes,' he said, with an emphatic nod of his
head—'yes. Sitabhai?'

'Who else would dare?' answered Kate
passionately.

'I know. I know. But how to stop her going
on! how to bring it home to her!'

'Tell the Maharajah,' responded Kate decidedly.

Tarvin took her hand. 'Good! I'll try it.
But there's no shadow of proof, you know.'

'No matter. Remember the boy. Try. I
must go back to him now.'

The two returned to the house of the missionary
together, saying very little on the way. Tarvin's
indignation that Kate should be mixed up in this
miserable business almost turned to anger at Kate
herself, as he rode beside her; but his wrath was
extinguished at sight of the Maharaj Kunwar.
The child lay on a bed in an inner room at the
missionary's, almost too weak to turn his head.
As Kate and Tarvin entered, Mrs. Estes rose from
giving him his medicine, said a word to Kate by
way of report, and returned to her own work.
The child was clothed only in a soft muslin
coat; but his sword and jewelled belt lay across
his feet.

'Salaam, Tarvin Sahib,' he murmured. 'I am
very sorry that I was ill.'

Tarvin bent over him tenderly. 'Don't try to talk, little one.'

'Nay; I am well now,' was the answer. 'Soon we will go riding together.'

'Were you very sick, little man?'

'I cannot tell. It is all dark to me. I was in the palace laughing with some of the dance-girls. Then I fell. And after that I remember no more till I came here.'

He gulped down the cooling draught that Kate gave him, and resettled himself on the pillows, while one wax-yellow hand played with the hilt of his sword. Kate was kneeling by his side, one arm under the pillow supporting his head; and it seemed to Tarvin that he had never before done justice to the beauty latent in her good, plain, strong features. The trim little figure took softer outlines, the firm mouth quivered, the eyes were filled with a light that Tarvin had never seen before.

'Come to the other side—so,' said the child, beckoning Tarvin in the native fashion, by folding all his tiny fingers into his palms rapidly and repeatedly. Tarvin knelt obediently on the other side of the couch. 'Now I am a king, and this is my court.'

Kate laughed musically in her delight at seeing the boy recovering strength. Tarvin slid his arm under the pillow, found Kate's hand there, and held it.

The portière at the door of the room dropped softly. Mrs. Estes had stolen in for a moment, and imagined that she saw enough to cause her to steal out again. She had been thinking a great deal since the days when Tarvin first introduced himself.

The child's eyes began to grow dull and heavy, and Kate would have withdrawn her arm to give him another draught.

'Nay; stay so,' he said imperiously; and relapsing into the vernacular, muttered thickly—'Those who serve the King shall not lack their reward. They shall have villages free of tax—three, five villages; Sujjain, Amet, and Gungra. Let it be entered as a free gift when they marry. They shall marry, and be about me always—Miss Kate and Tarvin Sahib.'

Tarvin did not understand why Kate's hand was withdrawn swiftly. He did not know the vernacular as she did.

'He is getting delirious again,' said Kate, under her breath. 'Poor, poor little one!'

Tarvin ground his teeth, and cursed Sitabhai between them. Kate was wiping the damp forehead, and trying to still the head as it was thrown restlessly from side to side. Tarvin held the child's hands, which closed fiercely on his own, as the boy was racked and convulsed by the last effects of the hemp.

For some minutes he fought and writhed, calling upon the names of many gods, striving to reach his sword, and ordering imaginary regiments to hang those white dogs to the beams of the palace gate, and to smoke them to death.

Then the crisis passed, and he began to talk to himself and to call for his mother.

The vision of a little grave dug in the open plain sloping to the river, where they had laid out the Topaz cemetery, rose before Tarvin's memory. They were lowering Heckler's first baby into it, in its pine coffin; and Kate, standing by the grave-side, was writing the child's name on the finger's length of smoothed pine which was to be its only headstone.

'Nay, nay, nay!' wailed the Maharaj Kunwar. 'I am speaking the truth; and oh, I was so tired at that pagal dance in the temple, and I only crossed the courtyard. . . . It was a new girl from Lucknow; she sang the song of "The Green Pulse of Mundore." . . . Yes; but only some almond curd. I was hungry, too. A little white almond curd, mother. Why should I not eat when I feel inclined? Am I a sweeper's son, or a prince? Pick me up! pick me up! It is very hot inside my head. . . . Louder. I do not understand. Will they take me over to Kate? She will make all well. What was the message?' The child began to wring his hands despairingly. 'The message! The message! I have forgotten the message. No one in the State speaks English as I speak English. But I have forgotten the message.

> 'Tiger, tiger, burning bright
> In the forests of the night,
> What immortal hand or eye
> Framed thy fearful symmetry?

Yes, mother; till she cries. I am to say the whole of it till she cries. I will not forget. I did not forget the first message. By the great god Har!

I have forgotten this message.' And he began to cry.

Kate, who had watched so long by bedsides of pain, was calm and strong; she soothed the child, speaking to him in a low, quieting voice, administering a sedative draught, doing the right thing, as Tarvin saw, surely and steadily, undisturbed. It was he who was shaken by the agony that he could not alleviate.

The Maharaj Kunwar drew a long, sobbing breath, and contracted his eyebrows.

'*Mahadeo ki jai!*' he shouted. 'It has come back. A gipsy has done this. A gipsy has done this. And I was to say it until she cried.'

Kate half rose, with an awful look at Tarvin. He returned it, and, nodding, strode from the room, dashing the tears from his eyes.

XVI

Heart of my heart, is it meet or wise
To warn a King of his enemies ?
We know what Heaven or Hell may bring,
But no man knoweth the mind of the King.
The Ballad of the King's Jest.

'WANT to see the Maharajah.'
  'He cannot be seen.'
  'I shall wait until he comes.'
  'He will not be seen all day.'
  'Then I shall wait all day.'
Tarvin settled himself comfortably in his saddle,
and drew up in the centre of the courtyard, where
he was wont to confer with the Maharajah.

The pigeons were asleep in the sunlight, and
the little fountain was talking to itself, as a pigeon
coos before settling to its nest. The white marble
flagging glared like hot iron, and waves of heat
flooded him from the green-shaded walls. The
guardian of the gate tucked himself up in his sheet
again and slept. And with him slept, as it seemed,
the whole world in a welter of silence as intense as
the heat. Tarvin's horse champed his bit, and the
echoes of the ringing iron tinkled from side to
side of the courtyard. The man himself whipped

a silk handkerchief round his neck as some slight
protection against the peeling sunbeams, and, scorn-
ing the shade of the archway, waited in the open
that the Maharajah might see there was an urgency
in his visit.

In a few minutes there crept out of the stillness
a sound like the far-off rustle of wind across a
wheat-field on a still autumn day. It came from
behind the green shutters, and with its coming
Tarvin mechanically straightened himself in the
saddle. It grew, died down again, and at last
remained fixed in a continuous murmur, for which
the ear strained uneasily — such a murmur as
heralds the advance of a loud racing tide in a
nightmare, when the dreamer cannot flee nor declare his terror in any voice but a whisper. After
the rustle came the smell of jasmine and musk that
Tarvin knew well.

The palace wing had wakened from its afternoon siesta, and was looking at him with a hundred
eyes. He felt the glances that he could not see,
and they filled him with wrath as he sat immovable,
while the horse swished at the flies. Somebody
behind the shutters yawned a polite little yawn.
Tarvin chose to regard it as an insult, and resolved
to stay where he was till he or the horse dropped.
The shadow of the afternoon sun crept across the
courtyard inch by inch, and wrapped him at last
in stifling shade.

There was a muffled hum—quite distinct from
the rustle—of voices within the palace. A little
ivory inlaid door opened, and the Maharajah rolled
into the courtyard. He was in the ugliest muslin

undress, and his little saffron-coloured Rajput turban was set awry on his head, so that the emerald plume tilted drunkenly. His eyes were red with opium, and he walked as a bear walks when he is overtaken by the dawn in the poppy-field, where he has gorged his fill through the night watches.

Tarvin's face darkened at the sight, and the Maharajah, catching the look, bade his attendants stand back out of earshot.

'Have you been waiting long, Tarvin Sahib?' he asked huskily, with an air of great good-will. 'You know I see no man at this afternoon hour, and—and they did not bring me the news.'

'I can wait,' said Tarvin composedly.

The King seated himself in the broken Windsor chair, which was splitting in the heat, and eyed Tarvin suspiciously.

'Have they given you enough convicts from the jails? Why are you not on the dam, then, instead of breaking my rest? By God! is a King to have no peace because of you and such as you?'

Tarvin let this outburst go by without comment.

'I have come to you about the Maharaj Kunwar,' he said quietly.

'What of him?' said the Maharajah quickly. 'I—I—have not seen him for some days.'

'Why?' asked Tarvin bluntly.

'Affairs of state and urgent political necessity,' murmured the King, evading Tarvin's wrathful eyes. 'Why should I be troubled by these things, when I know that no harm has come to the boy?'

'No harm!'

'How could harm arrive?' The voice dropped into an almost conciliatory whine. 'You yourself, Tarvin Sahib, promised to be his true friend. That was on the day you rode so well, and stood so well against my bodyguard. Never have I seen such riding, and *therefore* why should I be troubled? Let us drink.'

He beckoned to his attendants. One of them came forward with a long silver tumbler concealed beneath his flowing garments, and poured into it an allowance of liqueur brandy that made Tarvin, used to potent drinks, open his eyes. The second man produced a bottle of champagne, opened it with a skill born of long practice, and filled up the tumbler with the creaming wine.

The Maharajah drank deep, and wiped the foam from his beard, saying apologetically—'Such things are not for political agents to see ; but you, Sahib, are true friend of the State. Therefore I let you see. Shall they mix you one like this? '

'Thanks. I didn't come here to drink. I came to tell you that the Maharaj has been very ill.'

'I was told there was a little fever,' said the King, leaning back in his chair. 'But he is with Miss Sheriff, and she will make all well. Just a little fever, Tarvin Sahib. Drink with me.'

'A little hell ! Can you understand what I am saying ? The little chap has been half poisoned.'

'Then it was the English medicines,' said the Maharajah, with a bland smile. 'Once they made me very sick, and I went back to the native hakims. You are always making funny talks, Tarvin Sahib.'

With a mighty effort Tarvin choked down his rage, and tapped his foot with his riding-whip, speaking very clearly and distinctly—'I haven't come here to make funny talk to-day. The little chap is with Miss Sheriff now. He was driven over there ; and somebody in the palace has been trying to poison him with hemp.'

'Bhang !' said the Maharajah stupidly.

'I don't know what you call the mess, but he has been poisoned. But for Miss Sheriff he would have died—your first son would have died. He has been poisoned—do you hear, Maharajah Sahib? —and by some one in the palace.'

'He has eaten something bad, and it has made him sick,' said the King surlily. 'Little boys eat anything. By God ! no man would dare to lay a finger on my son.'

'What would you do to prevent it ?'

The Maharajah half rose to his feet, and his red eyes filled with fury. 'I would tie him to the forefoot of my biggest elephant, and kill him through an afternoon !' Then he relapsed, foaming, into the vernacular, and poured out a list of the hideous tortures that were within his will but not in his power to inflict. 'I would do all these things to any man who touched him,' he concluded.

Tarvin smiled incredulously.

'I know what you think,' stormed the King, maddened by the liquor and the opium. 'You think that because there is an English government I can make trials only by law, and all that nonsense. Stuff ! What do I care for the law that is in books ? Will the walls of my palace tell anything that I do ? '

' They won't. If they did, they might let you know that it is a woman inside the palace who is at the bottom of this.'

The Maharajah's face turned grey under its brown. Then he burst forth anew, almost huskily —' Am I a king or a potter that I must have the affairs of my zenana dragged into the sunlight by any white dog that chooses to howl at me ? Go out, or the guard will drive you out like a jackal.'

' That's all right,' said Tarvin calmly. ' But what has it to do with the Prince, Maharajah Sahib? Come over to Mr. Estes's and I'll show you. You've had some experience of drugs, I suppose. You can decide for yourself. The boy has been poisoned.'

' It was an accursed day for my State when I first allowed the missionaries to come, and a worse day when I did not drive you out.'

' Not in the least. I'm here to look after the Maharaj Kunwar, and I'm going to do it. You prefer leaving him to be killed by your women.'

' Tarvin Sahib, do you know what you say ? '

' Shouldn't be saying it if I didn't. I have all the proof in my hands.'

' But when there is a poisoning there are no proofs of any kind, least of all when a woman poisons ! One does justice on suspicion, and by the English law it is a most illiberal policy to kill on suspicion. Tarvin Sahib, the English have taken away from me everything that a Rajput desires, and I and the others are rolling in idleness like horses that never go to exercise. But at least I am master *there !* '

He waved a hand toward the green shutters, and spoke in a lower key, dropping back into his chair, and closing his eyes.

Tarvin looked at him despairingly.

' No one man would dare—no man would dare,' murmured the Maharajah more faintly. ' And as for the other thing that you spoke of, it is not in your power. By God ! I am a Rajput and a king. I do not talk of the life behind the curtain.'

Then Tarvin took his courage in both hands and spoke.

' I don't want you to talk,' he said ; ' I merely want to warn you against Sitabhai. She's poisoning the Prince.'

The Maharajah shuddered. That a European should mention the name of his queen was in itself sufficient insult, and one beyond all his experience. But that a European should cry aloud in the open courtyard a charge such as Tarvin had just made surpassed imagination. The Maharajah had just come from Sitabhai, who had lulled him to rest with songs and endearments sacred to him alone ; and here was this lean outlander assailing her with vile charges. But for the drugs he would, in the extremity of his rage, have fallen upon Tarvin, who was saying, ' I can prove it quite enough to satisfy Colonel Nolan.'

The Maharajah stared at Tarvin with shiny eyes, and Tarvin thought for a moment that he was going to fall in a fit ; but it was the drink and the opium reasserting their power upon him.

He mumbled angrily. The head fell forward, the words ceased, and he sat in his chair breathing heavily, as senseless as a log.

Tarvin gathered up his reins, and watched the sodden monarch for a long time in silence, as the rustle behind the shutters rose and fell. Then he turned to go, and rode out through the arch, thinking.

Something sprang out of the darkness where the guard slept, and where the King's fighting apes were tethered ; and the horse reared as a grey ape, its chain broken at the waist-band, flung itself on the pommel of the saddle, chattering. Tarvin felt and smelt the beast. It thrust one paw into the horse's mane, and with the other encircled his own throat. Instinctively he reached back, and before the teeth under the grimy blue gums had time to close he had fired twice, pressing the muzzle of the pistol into the hide. The creature rolled off to the ground, moaning like a human being, and the smoke of the two shots drifted back through the hollow of the arch and dissolved in the open courtyard.

XVII

Strangers drawn from the ends of the earth, jewelled and
    plumed were we ;
I was the Lord of the Inca Race, and she was the Queen of
    the Sea.
Under the stars beyond our stars where the reinless meteors
    glow,
Hotly we stormed Valhalla, a million years ago.

Dust of the stars was under our feet, glitter of stars above—
Wrecks of our wrath dropped reeling down as we fought and
    we spurned and we strove ;
Worlds upon worlds we tossed aside, and scattered them to
    and fro,
The night that we stormed Valhalla, a million years ago.

She with the star I had marked for my own—I with my set
    desire—
Lost in the loom of the Night of Nights, 'wildered by worlds
    afire—
Met in a war 'twixt love and hate where the reinless meteors
    glow,
Hewing our way to Valhalla, a million years ago.
                         The Sack of the Gods.

IN summer the nights of the desert are hotter than
the days, for when the sun goes down, earth,
masonry, and marble give forth their stored heat,

and the low clouds, promising rain and never
bringing it, allow nothing to escape.

Tarvin was lying at rest in the verandah of the
rest-house, smoking a cheroot and wondering how
far he had bettered the case of the Maharaj Kunwar
by appealing to the Maharajah. His reflections
were not disturbed ; the last of the commercial
travellers had gone back to Calcutta and Bombay,
grumbling up to the final moment of their stay,
and the rest-house was all his own. Surveying his
kingdom, he meditated, between the puffs of his
cheroot, on the desperate and apparently hopeless
condition of things. They had got to the precise
point where he liked them. When a situation
looked as this one did, only Nicholas Tarvin could
put it through and come out on top. Kate was
obdurate ; the Naulahka was damnably coy ; the
Maharajah was ready to turn him out of the State.
Sitabhai had heard him denounce her. His life
was likely to come to a sudden and mysterious
end, without so much as the satisfaction of knowing that Heckler and the boys would avenge him ;
and if it went on, it looked as though it would
have to go on without Kate, and without the gift
of new life to Topaz — in other words, without
being worth the trouble of living.

The moonlight, shining on the city beyond the
sands, threw fantastic shadows on temple spires and
the watch-towers along the walls. A dog in search
of food snuffed dolefully about Tarvin's chair, and
withdrew to howl at him at a distance. It was a
singularly melancholy howl. Tarvin smoked till
the moon went down in the thick darkness of an

Indian night. She had scarcely set when he was aware of something blacker than the night between him and the horizon.

'Is it you, Tarvin Sahib?' the voice inquired in broken English.

Tarvin sprang to his feet before replying. He was beginning to be a little suspicious of fresh apparitions. His hand went to his hip pocket. Any horror, he argued, might jump out at him from the darkness in a country managed on the plan of a Kiralfy trick spectacle.

'Nay; do not be afraid,' said the voice. 'It is I—Juggut Singh.'

Tarvin pulled thoughtfully at his cigar. 'The State is full of Singhs,' he said. 'Which?'

'I, Juggut Singh, of the household of the Maharajah.'

'H'm. Does the King want to see me?'

The figure advanced a pace nearer.

'No, Sahib; the Queen.'

'Which?' repeated Tarvin.

The figure was in the verandah at his side, almost whispering in his ear. 'There is only one who would dare to leave the palace. It is the Gipsy.'

Tarvin snapped his fingers blissfully and soundlessly in the dark, and made a little click of triumph with his tongue. 'Pleasant calling hours the lady keeps,' he said.

'This is no place for speaking, Sahib. I was to say, "Come, unless you are afraid of the dark."'

'Oh, were you? Well, now, look here, Juggut; let's talk this thing out. I'd like to see your friend

Sitabhai. Where are you keeping her? Where
do you want me to go?'

'I was to say, "Come with me." Are you
afraid?' The man spoke this time at his own
prompting.

'Oh, I'm *afraid* fast enough,' said Tarvin,
blowing a cloud of smoke from him. 'It isn't
that.'

'There are horses—very swift horses. It is the
Queen's order. Come with me.'

Tarvin smoked on, unhurrying; and when he
finally picked himself out of the chair it was
muscle by muscle. He drew his revolver from his
pocket, turned the chambers slowly one after
another to the vague light, under Juggut Singh's
watchful eye, and returned it to his pocket again,
giving his companion a wink as he did so.

'Well, come on, Juggut,' he said, and they
passed behind the rest-house to a spot where two
horses, their heads enveloped in cloaks to prevent
them from neighing, were waiting at their pickets.
The man mounted one, and Tarvin took the
other silently, satisfying himself before getting into
the saddle that the girths were not loose this time.
They left the city road at a walking pace by a
cart-track leading to the hills.

'Now,' said Juggut Singh, after they had gone
a quarter of a mile in this fashion, and were alone
under the stars, 'we can ride.'

He bowed forward, struck his stirrups home,
and began lashing his animal furiously. Nothing
short of the fear of death would have made the
pampered eunuch of the palace ride at this pace.

Tarvin watched him roll in the saddle, chuckled a little, and followed.

'You wouldn't make much of a cow-puncher, Juggut, would you?'

'Ride!' gasped Juggut Singh. 'For the cleft between the two hills—ride!'

The dry sand flew behind their horses' hoofs, and the hot winds whistled about their ears as they headed up the easy slope toward the hills, three miles from the palace. In the old days, before the introduction of telegraphs, the opium speculators of the desert were wont to telegraph the rise and fall in the price of the drug from little beacon-towers on the hills. It was toward one of these disused stations that Juggut Singh was straining. The horses fell into a walk as the slope grew steeper, and the outline of the squat-domed tower began to show clear against the sky. A few moments later Tarvin heard the hoofs of their horses ring on solid marble, and saw that he was riding near the edge of a great reservoir, full of water to the lip.

Eastward, a few twinkling lights in the open plain showed the position of Rhatore, and took him back to the night when he had said good-bye to Topaz from the rear platform of a Pullman. Night-fowl called to one another from the weeds at the far end of the tank, and a great fish leaped at the reflection of a star.

'The watch-tower is at the further end of the dam,' said Juggut Singh. 'The Gipsy is there.'

'Will they never have done with that name?' uttered an incomparably sweet voice out of the darkness. 'It is well that I am of a gentle temper, or the fish would know more of thee, Juggut Singh.'

Tarvin checked his horse with a jerk, for almost under his bridle stood a figure enveloped from head to foot in a mist of pale yellow gauze. It had started up from behind the red tomb of a once famous Rajput cavalier who was supposed by the country-side to gallop nightly round the dam he had built. This was one of the reasons why the Dungar Talao was not visited after nightfall.

'Come down, Tarvin Sahib,' said the voice mockingly in English. 'I, at least, am not a grey ape. Juggut Singh, go wait with the horses below the watch-tower.'

'Yes, Juggut ; and don't go to sleep,' enjoined Tarvin—'we might want you.' He alighted, and stood before the veiled form of Sitabhai.

'Shekand,' she said, after a little pause, putting out a hand that was smaller even than Kate's. 'Ah, Sahib, I knew that you would come. I knew that you were not afraid.'

She held his hand as she spoke, and pressed it tenderly. Tarvin buried the tiny hand deep in his engulfing paw, and, pressing it in a grip that made her give an involuntary cry, shook it with a hearty motion.

'Happy to make your acquaintance,' he said, as she murmured under her breath, 'By Indur, he has a hold !'

'And I am pleased to see you, too,' she answered aloud. Tarvin noted the music of the voice. He wondered what the face behind the veil might look like.

She sat down composedly on the slab of the tomb, motioning him to a seat beside her.

'All white men like straight talk,' she said, speaking slowly, and with uncertain mastery of English pronunciation. 'Tell me, Tarvin Sahib, how much you know.'

She withdrew her veil as she spoke, and turned her face toward him. Tarvin saw that she was beautiful. The perception thrust itself insensibly between him and his other perceptions about her.

'You don't want me to give myself away, do you, Queen?'

'I do not understand. But I know you do not talk like the other white men,' she said sweetly.

'Well, then, you don't expect me to tell you the truth?'

'No,' she replied. 'Else you would tell me why you are here. Why do you give me so much trouble?'

'*Do* I trouble you?'

Sitabhai laughed, throwing back her head, and clasping her hands behind her neck. Tarvin watched her curiously in the starlight. All his senses were alert; he was keenly on his guard, and he cast a wary eye about and behind him from time to time. But he could see nothing but the dull glimmer of the water that lapped at the foot of the marble steps, and hear nothing save the cry of the night-owls.

'O Tarvin Sahib,' she said. 'You know! After the first time I was sorry.'

'Which time was that?' inquired Tarvin vaguely.

'Of course it was when the saddle turned. And then when the timber fell from the archway I thought at least that I had maimed your horse. Was he hurt?'

'No,' said Tarvin, stupefied by her engaging frankness.

'Surely you knew,' she said almost reproachfully.

He shook his head. 'No, Sitabhai, my dear,' he said slowly and impressively. 'I wasn't on to you, and it's my eternal shame. But I'm beginning to sabe. You worked the little business at the dam, too, I suppose, and the bridge and the bullock-carts. And I thought it was their infernal clumsiness? Well, I'll be——' He whistled melodiously, and the sound was answered by the hoarse croak of a crane across the reeds.

The Queen leaped to her feet, thrusting her hand into her bosom. 'A signal!' Then sinking back upon the slab of the tomb, 'But you have brought no one with you. I know you are not afraid to go alone.'

'Oh, I'm not trying to do *you* up, young lady,' he answered. 'I'm too busy admiring your picturesque and systematic deviltry. So you're at the bottom of all my troubles? That quicksand trick was a pretty one. Do you often work it?'

'Oh, on the dam!' exclaimed the Queen, waving her hands lightly. 'I only gave them orders to do what they could. But they are very clumsy people—only coolie people. They told me what they had done, and I was angry.'

'Kill any one?'

'No; why should I?'

'Well, if it comes to that, why should you be so hot on killing me?' inquired Tarvin dryly.

'I do not like any white men to stay here, and I knew that you had come to stay.' Tarvin smiled at the unconscious Americanism. 'Besides,' she went on, 'the Maharajah was fond of you, and I had never killed a white man. Then, too, I like you.'

'Oh!' responded Tarvin expressively.

'By Malang Shah, and you never knew!' She was swearing by the god of her own clan—the god of the gipsies.

'Well, don't rub it in,' said Tarvin.

'And you killed my big pet ape,' she went on. 'He used to salaam to me in the mornings like Luchman Rao, the prime minister. Tarvin Sahib, I have known many Englishmen. I have danced on the slack-rope before the mess-tents of the officers on the line of march, and taken my little begging gourd up to the big bearded colonel when I was no higher than his knee.' She lowered her hand to within a foot of the ground. 'And when I grew older,' she continued, 'I thought that I knew the hearts of all men. But, by Malang Shah, Tarvin Sahib, I never saw a man like unto you! Nay,' she went on almost beseechingly, 'do not say that you did not know. There is a love song in my tongue, "I have not slept between moon and moon because of you"; and indeed for

me that song is quite true. Sometimes I think
that I did not quite wish to see you die. But it
would be better that you were dead. I, and I
alone, command this State. And now, after that
which you have told the King——'

'Yes? You heard, then?'

She nodded. 'After that I cannot see that
there is any other way—unless you go away.'

'I'm not going,' said Tarvin.

'That is good,' said the Queen, with a little
laugh. 'And so I shall not miss seeing you in
the courtyard day by day. I thought the sun
would have killed you when you waited for the
Maharajah. Be grateful to me, Tarvin Sahib, for
I made the Maharajah come out. And you did me
an ill turn.'

'My dear young lady,' said Tarvin earnestly,
'if you'd pull in your wicked little fangs, no one
wants to hurt you. But I can't let you beat me
about the Maharaj Kunwar. I'm here to see that
the young man stays with us. Keep off the grass,
and I'll drop it.'

'Again I do not understand,' said the Queen,
bewildered. 'But what is the life of a little child
to you who are a stranger here?'

'What is it to me? Why, it's fair-play; it's
the life of a little child. What more do you
want? Is nothing sacred to you?'

'I also have a son,' returned the Queen, 'and
he is not weak. Nay, Tarvin Sahib, the child
always was sickly from his birth. How can he
govern men? *My* son will be a Rajput; and in
the time to come—— But that is no concern of

the white men. Let this little one go back to the gods!'

'Not if I know it,' responded Tarvin decisively.

'Otherwise,' swept on the Queen, 'he will live infirm and miserable for ninety years. I know the bastard Kulu stock that he comes from. Yes; I have sung at the gate of his mother's palace when she and I were children—I in the dust, and she in her marriage-litter. To-day she is in the dust. Tarvin Sahib'—her voice melted appealingly—'I shall never bear another son; but I may at least mould the State from behind the curtain, as many queens have done. I am not a palace-bred woman. Those'—she pointed scornfully toward the lights of Rhatore—'have never seen the wheat wave, or heard the wind blow, or sat in a saddle, or talked face to face with men in the streets. They call me the gipsy, and they cower under their robes like fat slugs when I choose to lift my hand to the Maharajah's beard. Their bards sing of their ancestry for twelve hundred years. They are noble, forsooth! By Indur and Allah—yea, and the God of your missionaries too —their children and the British Government shall remember me for twice twelve hundred years. *Ahi*, Tarvin Sahib, you do not know how wise my little son is. I do not let him go to the missionary's. All that he shall need afterward—and indeed it is no little thing to govern this State— he shall learn from me; for I have seen the world, and I know. And until you came all was going so softly, so softly, to its end! The little one would have died—yes; and there would have been no more trouble. And never man nor woman in the palace would have breathed to the King one word of what you cried aloud before the sun in the courtyard. Now, suspicion will never cease in the King's mind, and I do not know—I do not know——' She bent forward earnestly. 'Tarvin Sahib, if I have spoken one word of truth this night, tell me how much is known to you.'

Tarvin preserved absolute silence. She stole one hand pleadingly on his knee. 'And none would have suspected. When the ladies of the Viceroy came last year, I gave out of my own treasures twenty-five thousand rupees to the nursing hospital, and the lady sahib kissed me on both cheeks, and I talked English, and showed them how I spent my time knitting—I who knit and unknit the hearts of men.'

This time Tarvin did not whistle; he merely smiled and murmured sympathetically. The large and masterly range of her wickedness, and the coolness with which she addressed herself to it, gave her a sort of distinction. More than this, he respected her for the personal achievement which of all feats most nearly appeals to the breast of the men of the West—she had done him up. It was true her plans had failed; but she had played them all on him without his knowledge. He almost revered her for it.

'Now you begin to understand,' said Sitabhai; 'there is something more to think of. Do you mean to go to Colonel Nolan, Sahib, with all your story about me?'

'Unless you keep your hands off the Maharaj

Kunwar—yes,' said Tarvin, not allowing his feel-
ings to interfere with business.

'That is very foolish,' said the Queen; 'because
Colonel Nolan will give much trouble to the
King, and the King will turn the palace into
confusion, and every one of my handmaids, except
a few, will give witness against me; and I perhaps
shall come to be much suspected. Then you
would think, Tarvin Sahib, that you had prevented
me. But you cannot stay here for ever. You
cannot stay here until I die. And so soon as you
are gone——' She snapped her fingers.

'You won't get the chance,' said Tarvin un-
shakenly. 'I'll fix that. What do you take me
for?'

The Queen bit the back of her forefinger
irresolutely. There was no saying what this man,
who strode unharmed through her machinations,
might or might not be able to do. Had she been
dealing with one of her own race she would have
played threat against threat. But the perfectly
composed and loose-knit figure by her side, watching every movement, chin in hand, ready, alert,
confident, was an unknown quantity that baffled
and distressed her.

There was a sound of a discreet cough, and
Juggut Singh waddled toward them, bowing
abjectly, to whisper something to the Queen.
She laughed scornfully, and motioned him back to
his post.

'He says the night is passing,' she explained,
'and it is death for him and for me to be without
the palace.'

'Don't let me keep you,' said Tarvin, rising.
'I think we understand each other.' He looked
into her eyes. 'Hands off!'

'Then I may not do what I please?' she said,
'and you will go to Colonel Nolan to-morrow?'

'That depends,' said Tarvin, shutting his lips.
He thrust his hands into his pockets as he stood
looking down at her.

'Seat yourself again a moment, Tarvin Sahib,'
said Sitabhai, patting the slab of the tomb invit-
ingly with her little palm. Tarvin obeyed. 'Now,
if I let no more timber fall, and keep the grey
apes tied fast——'

'And dry up the quicksands in the Amet
River,' pursued Tarvin grimly. 'I see. My dear
little spitfire, you are at liberty to do what you
like. Don't let me interfere with your amuse-
ments.'

'I was wrong. I should have known that
nothing would make you afraid,' said she, eyeing
him thoughtfully out of the corner of her eye;
'and, excepting you, Tarvin Sahib, there is no
man that I fear. If you were a king as I a queen,
we would hold Hindustan between our two hands.'

She clasped his locked fist as she spoke, and
Tarvin, remembering that sudden motion to her
bosom when he had whistled, laid his own hand
quickly above hers, and held them fast.

'Is there nothing, Tarvin Sahib, that would
make you leave me in peace? What is it you
care for? You did not come here to keep the
Maharaj Kunwar alive.'

'How do you know I didn't?'

'You are very wise,' she said, with a little laugh, 'but it is not good to pretend to be too wise. Shall I tell you why you came?'

'Well, why did I? Speak up.'

'You came here, as you came to the temple of Iswara, to find that which you will never find, unless'—she leaned toward him—'I help you. Was it very cold in the Cow's Mouth, Tarvin Sahib?'

Tarvin drew back, frowning, but not betraying himself further.

'I was afraid that the snakes would have killed you there?'

'*Were* you?'

'Yes,' she said softly. 'And I was afraid, too, that you might not have stepped swiftly enough for the turning stone in the temple.'

Tarvin glanced at her. 'No?'

'Yes. Ah! I knew what was in your mind, even before you spoke to the King—when the bodyguard charged.'

'See here, young woman, do you run a private inquiry agency?'

She laughed. 'There is a song in the palace now about your bravery. But the boldest thing was to speak to the King about the Naulahka. He told me all you said. But he—even he did not dream that any *feringhi* could dare to covet it. And I was so good—I did not tell him. But I knew men like you are not made for little things. Tarvin Sahib,' she said, leaning close, releasing her hand and laying it softly on his shoulder, 'you and I are kin indeed! For it is more easy to govern this State—ay, and from this State to recapture all Hindustan from these white dogs, the English— than to do what you have dreamed of. And yet a stout heart makes all things easy. Was it for yourself, Tarvin Sahib, that you wanted the Naulahka, or for another—even as I desire Gokral Seetarun for my son? We are not little people. It is for another, is it not?'

'Look here,' said Tarvin reverently, as he took her hand from his shoulder and held it firmly in his clutch again, 'are there many of you in India?'

'But one. I am like yourself—alone.' Her chin drooped against his shoulder, and she looked up at him out of her eyes as dark as the lake. The scarlet mouth and the quivering nostrils were so close to his own that the fragrant breath swept his cheek.

'Are you making states, Tarvin Sahib, like me? No; surely it is a woman. Your government is decreed for you, and you do what it orders. I turned the canal which the Government said should run through my orange-garden, even as I will bend the King to my will, even as I will kill the boy, even as I will myself rule in Gokral Seetarun through my child. But you, Tarvin Sahib—you wish only a woman! Is it not so? And she is too little to bear the weight of the Luck of the State. She grows paler day by day.' She felt the man quiver, but he said nothing.

From the tangle of scrub and brushwood at the far end of the lake broke forth a hoarse barking cough that filled the hills with desolation as water brims a cup. Tarvin leaped to his feet. For the first time he heard the angry complaint of the tiger going home to his lair after a fruitless night of ranging.

'It is nothing,' said the Queen, without stirring. 'It is only the tiger of the Dungar Talao. I have heard him howling many times when I was a gipsy, and even if he came you would shoot him, would you not, as you shot the ape?'

She nestled close to him, and, as he sank beside her on the stone again, his arm slipped unconsciously about her waist.

The shadow of the beast drifted across an open space by the lake-shore as noiselessly as thistledown draws through the air of summer, and Tarvin's arm tightened in its resting-place— tightened on a bossed girdle that struck cold on his palm through many folds of muslin.

'So little and so frail—how could she wear it?' resumed the Queen.

She turned a little in his embrace, and Tarvin's arm brushed against one, and another, and then another, strand of the girdle, studded like the first with irregular bosses, till under his elbow he felt a great square stone.

He started, and tightened his hold about her waist, with paling lips.

'But we two,' the Queen went on, in a low voice, regarding him dreamily, 'could make the kingdoms fight like the water-buffaloes in spring. Would you be my prime minister, Tarvin Sahib, and advise me through the curtain?'

'I don't know whether I could trust you,' said Tarvin briefly.

'I do not know whether I could trust myself,' responded the Queen; 'for after a time it might be that I should be servant who have always been queen. I have come near to casting my heart under the hoofs of your horse—not once, but many times.' She put her arms around his neck and joined them there, gazing into his eyes, and drawing his head down to hers. 'Is it a little thing,' she cooed, 'if I ask you to be my king? In the old days, before the English came, Englishmen of no birth stole the hearts of begums, and led their armies. They were kings in all but the name. We do not know when the old days may return, and we might lead our armies together.'

'All right. Keep the place open for me. I might come back and apply for it one of these days when I've worked a scheme or two at home.'

'Then you are going away—you will leave us soon?'

'I'll leave you when I've got what I want, my dear,' he answered, pressing her closer.

She bit her lip. 'I might have known,' she said softly. 'I, too, have never turned aside from anything I desired. Well, and what is it?'

The mouth drooped a little at the corners, as the head fell on his shoulder. Glancing down, he saw the ruby-jewelled jade handle of a little knife at her breast.

He disengaged himself from her arms with a quick movement, and rose to his feet. She was very lovely as she stretched her arms appealingly out to him in the half light; but he was there for other things.

Tarvin looked at her between the eyes, and her glance fell.

'I'll take what you have around your waist, please.'

'I might have known that the white man thinks only of money!' she cried scornfully.

She unclasped a silver belt from her waist and threw it from her, clinking, upon the marble.

Tarvin did not give it a glance.

'You know me better than that,' he said quietly. 'Come, hold up your hands. Your game is played.'

'I do not understand,' she said. 'Shall I give you some rupees?' she asked scornfully. 'Be quick, Juggut Singh is bringing the horses.'

'Oh, I'll be quick enough. Give me the Naulahka.'

'The Naulahka?'

'The same. I'm tired of tipsy bridges and ungirt horses and uneasy arches and dizzy quicksands. I want the necklace.'

'And I may have the boy?'

'No; neither boy nor necklace.'

'And will you go to Colonel Nolan in the morning?'

'The morning is here now. You'd better be quick.'

'Will you go to Colonel Nolan?' she repeated, rising and facing him.

'Yes; if you don't give me the necklace.'

'And if I do?'

'No. Is it a trade?' It was his question to Mrs. Mutrie.

The Queen looked desperately at the day-star that was beginning to pale in the East. Even her power over the King could not save her from death if the day discovered her beyond the palace walls.

The man spoke as one who held her life in the hollow of his hand ; and she knew he was right. If he had proof he would not scruple to bring it before the Maharajah ; and if the Maharajah believed—— Sitabhai could feel the sword at her throat. She would be no founder of a dynasty, but a nameless disappearance in the palace. Mercifully, the King had not been in a state to understand the charges Tarvin had brought against her in the courtyard. But she lay open now to anything this reckless and determined stranger might choose to do against her. At the least he could bring upon her the formless suspicion of an Indian court, worse than death to her plans, and set the removal of Maharaj Kunwar beyond her power, through the interposition of Colonel Nolan ; and at the worst—— But she did not pursue this train of thought.

She cursed the miserable weakness of liking for him which had prevented her from killing him just now as he lay in her arms. She had meant to kill him from the first moment of their interview ; she had let herself toy too long with the fascination of being dominated by a will stronger than her own, but there was still time.

'And if I do not give you the Naulahka ?' she asked.

'I guess you know best about that.'

As her eye wandered out on the plain she saw that the stars no longer had fire in them ; the black water of the reservoir paled and grew grey, and the wild-fowl were waking in the reeds. The dawn was upon her, as merciless as the man. Juggut Singh was leading up the horses, motioning to her in an agony of impatience and terror. The sky was against her ; and there was no help on earth.

She put her hands behind her. Tarvin heard the snap of a clasp, and the Naulahka lay about her feet in ripples of flame.

Without looking at him or the necklace, she moved toward the horses. Tarvin stooped swiftly and possessed himself of the treasure. Juggut Singh had released his horse. Tarvin strode forward and caught at the bridle, cramming the necklace into his breast-pocket.

He bent to make sure of his girth. The Queen, standing behind her horse, waited an instant to mount.

'Good-bye, Tarvin Sahib ; and remember the gipsy,' she said, flinging her arm out over the horse's withers. ' *Heh !* '

A flicker of light passed his eye. The jade handle of the Queen's knife quivered in the saddle-flap, half an inch above his right shoulder. His horse plunged forward at the Queen's stallion, with a snort of pain.

'Kill him, Juggut Singh ! ' gasped the Queen, pointing to Tarvin, as the eunuch scrambled into his saddle. ' Kill him ! '

Tarvin caught her tender wrist in his fast grip.

'Easy there, girl! Easy!' She returned his gaze, baffled. 'Let me put you up,' he said.

He put his arms about her and swung her into the saddle.

'Now give us a kiss,' he said, as she looked down at him.

She stooped. 'No, you don't! Give me your hands.' He prisoned both wrists, and kissed her full upon the mouth. Then he smote the horse resoundingly upon the flank, and the animal blundered down the path and leaped out into the plain.

He watched the Queen and Juggut Singh disappear in a cloud of dust and flying stones, and turned with a deep sigh of relief to the lake. Drawing the Naulahka from its resting-place, and laying it fondly out upon his hands, he fed his eyes upon it.

The stones kindled with the glow of the dawn, and mocked the shifting colours of the hills. The shining ropes of gems put to shame the red glare that shot up from behind the reeds, as they had dulled the glare of the torches on the night of the little Prince's wedding. The tender green of the reeds themselves, the intense blue of the lake, the beryl of the flashing kingfishers, and the blinding ripples spreading under the first rays of the sun, as a bevy of coots flapped the water from their wings—the necklace abashed them all. Only the black diamond took no joy from the joy of the morning, but lay among its glorious fellows as sombre and red-hearted as the troublous night out of which Tarvin had snatched it.

Tarvin ran the stones through his hands one by one, and there were forty-five of them—each stone perfect and flawless of its kind; nipped, lest any of its beauty should be hidden, by a tiny gold clasp, each stone swinging all but free from the strand of soft gold on which it was strung, and each stone worth a king's ransom or a queen's good name.

It was a good moment for Tarvin. His life gathered into it. Topaz was safe!

The wild duck were stringing to and fro across the lake, and the cranes called to one another, stalking through reeds almost as tall as their scarlet heads. From some temple hidden among the hills a lone priest chanted sonorously as he made the morning sacrifice to his god, and from the city in the plain came the boom of the first ward-drums, telling that the gates were open and the day was born.

Tarvin lifted his head from the necklace. The jade-handled knife was lying at his feet. He picked up the delicate weapon and threw it into the lake.

'And now for Kate,' he said.

XVIII

Now we are come to our Kingdom,
  And the State is thus and thus :
Our legions wait at the palace gate—
  Little it profits us,
    Now we are come to our Kingdom.

Now we are come to our Kingdom,
  The crown is ours to take—
With a naked sword at the council board,
  And under the throne the snake,
    Now we are come to our Kingdom.

Now we are come to our Kingdom,
  But my love's eyelids fall,
All that I wrought for, all that I fought for,
  Delight her nothing at all.
  My crown is withered leaves,
  For she sits in the dust and grieves,
    Now we are come to our Kingdom.
                              King Anthony.

THE palace on its red rock seemed to be still asleep
as he cantered across the empty plain. A man on
a camel rode out of one of the city gates at right
angles to his course, and Tarvin noted with interest
how swiftly a long-legged camel of the desert can
move. Familiar as he had now become with the
ostrich-necked beasts, he could not help associating

R

them with Barnum's Circus and boyhood memories. The man drew near and crossed in front of him. Then, in the stillness of the morning, Tarvin heard the dry click of a voice he understood. It was the sound made by bringing up the cartridge of a repeating rifle. Mechanically he slipped from the saddle, and was on the other side of the horse as the rifle spoke, and a puff of blue smoke drifted up and hung motionless above the camel.

'I might have known she'd get in her work early,' he muttered, peering over his horse's withers. 'I can't drop him at this distance with a revolver. What's the fool waiting for?'

Then he perceived that, with characteristic native inaptitude, the man had contrived to jam his lever, and was beating it furiously on the fore-part of the saddle. He remounted hastily, and galloped up, revolver in hand, to cover the blanched visage of Juggut Singh.

'*You!* Why, Juggut, old man, this isn't kind of you.'

'It was an order,' said Juggut, quivering with apprehension. 'It was no fault of mine. I—I do not understand these things.'

'I should smile. Let me show you.' He took the rifle from the trembling hand. 'The cartridge is jammed, my friend; it don't shoot as well that way. It only needs a little knack—so! You ought to learn it, Juggut.' He jerked the empty shell over his shoulder.

'What will you do to me?' cried the eunuch. 'She would have killed me if I had not come.'

'Don't you believe it, Juggut. She's a Jumbo

at theory, but weak in practice. Go on ahead, please.'

They started back toward the city, Juggut leading the way on his camel, looking back apprehensively every minute. Tarvin smiled at him dryly but reassuringly, balancing on his hip the captured rifle. He observed that it was a very good rifle if properly used.

At the entrance to Sitabhai's wing of the palace, Juggut Singh dismounted and slunk into the court-yard, the livid image of fear and shame. Tarvin clattered after him, and as the eunuch was about to disappear through a door, called him back.

'You have forgotten your gun, Juggut,' he said. 'Don't be afraid of it.' Juggut was putting up a doubtful hand to take it from him. 'It won't hurt anybody this trip. Take yourself back to the lady, and tell her you are returned, with thanks.'

No sound came to his ear from behind the green shutters as he rode away, leaving Juggut staring after him. Nothing fell upon him from out of the arch, and the apes were tied securely. Sitabhai's next move was evidently yet to be played.

His own next move he had already reckoned with. It was a case for bolting.

He rode to the mosque outside the city, routed out his old friend in dove-coloured satin, and made him send this message :—

'MRS. MUTRIE, DENVER.—*Necklace is yours. Get throat ready and lay that track into Topaz.* —TARVIN.'

Then he turned his horse's head toward Kate.

He buttoned his coat tightly across his chest, and patted the resting-place of the Naulahka fondly, as he strode up the path to the missionary's verandah, when he had tethered Fibby outside. His high good humour with himself and the world spoke through his eyes as he greeted Mrs. Estes at the door.

'You have been hearing something pleasant,' she said. 'Won't you come in ?'

'Well, either the pleasantest, or next to the pleasantest ; I'm not sure which,' he answered with a smile, as he followed her into the familiar sitting-room. 'I'd like to tell you all about it, Mrs. Estes. I feel almightily like telling somebody. But it isn't a healthy story for this neighbourhood.' He glanced about him. 'I'd hire the town crier and a few musical instruments and advertise it, if I had my way ; and we'd all have a little Fourth of July celebration and a bonfire, and I'd read the Declaration of Independence over the natives with a relish. But it won't do. There *is* a story I'd like to tell you, though,' he added, with a sudden thought. 'You know why I come here so much, don't you, Mrs. Estes—I mean outside of your kindness to me, and my liking you all so much, and our always having such good times together? You know, don't you ?'

Mrs. Estes smiled. 'I suppose I do,' she said.

'Well ; that's right ! That's right. I thought you did. Then I hope you're my friend !'

'If you mean that I wish you well, I do. But you can understand that I feel responsible for Miss Sheriff. I have sometimes thought I ought to let her mother know.'

'Oh, her mother knows! She's full of it. You might say she liked it. The trouble isn't there, you know, Mrs. Estes.'

'No. She's a singular girl; very strong, very sweet. I've grown to love her dearly. She has wonderful courage. But I should like it better for her if she would give it up, and all that goes with it. She would be better married,' she said meditatively.

Tarvin gazed at her admiringly. 'How wise you are, Mrs. Estes! How wise you are!' he murmured. 'If I've told her that once I've told her a dozen times. Don't you think, also, that it would be better if she were married at once—right away, without too much loss of time?'

His companion looked at him to see if he was in earnest. Tarvin was sometimes a little perplexing to her. 'I think if you are clever you will leave it to the course of events,' she replied, after a moment. 'I have watched her work here, hoping that she might succeed where every one else has failed. But I know in my heart that she won't. There's too much against her. She's working against thousands of years of traditions, and training, and habits of life. Sooner or later they are certain to defeat her; and then, whatever her courage, she must give in. I've thought sometimes lately that she might have trouble very soon. There's a good deal of dissatisfaction at the hospital. Lucien hears some stories that make me anxious.'

'Anxious! I should say so. That's the worst of it. It isn't only that she won't come to me,

Mrs. Estes—that you can understand—but she is
running her head meanwhile into all sorts of impossible dangers. I haven't time to wait until she
sees that point. I haven't time to wait until she
sees any point at all but that this present moment,
now and here, would be a good moment in which
to marry Nicholas Tarvin. I've got to get out of
Rhatore. That's the long and the short of it, Mrs.
Estes. Don't ask me why. It's necessary. And
I must take Kate with me. Help me if you love
her.'

To this appeal Mrs. Estes made the handsomest
response in her power, by saying that she would
go up and tell her that he wished to see her. This
seemed to take some time; and Tarvin waited
patiently, with a smile on his lips. He did not
doubt that Kate would yield. In the glow of
another success it was not possible to him to
suppose that she would not come around now.
Had he not the Naulahka? She went with it;
she was indissolubly connected with it. Yet he
was willing to impress into his service all the help
he could get, and he was glad to believe that Mrs.
Estes was talking to her.

It was an added prophecy of success when he
found from a copy of a recent issue of the *Topaz
Telegram*, which he picked up while he waited,
that the 'Lingering Lode' had justified his
expectations. The people he had left in charge
had struck a true fissure vein, and were taking out
$500 a week. He crushed the paper into his
pocket, restraining an inclination to dance; it was
perhaps safest, on reflection, to postpone that

exercise until he had seen Kate. The little congratulatory whistle that he struck up instead, he had to sober a moment later into a smile as Kate opened the door and came in to him. There could be no two ways about it with her now. His smile, do what he would, almost said as much.

A single glance at her face showed him, however, that the affair struck her less simply. He forgave her; she could not know the source of his inner certitude. He even took time to like the grey house-dress, trimmed with black velvet, that she was wearing in place of the white which had become habitual to her.

'I'm glad you've dropped white for a moment,' he said, as he rose to shake hands with her. 'It's a sign. It represents a general abandonment and desertion of this blessed country; and that's just the mood I want to find you in. I want you to drop it, chuck it, throw it up.' He held her brown little hand in the swarthy fist he pushed out from his own white sleeve, and looked down into her eyes attentively.

'What?'

'India—the whole business. I want you to come with me.' He spoke gently.

She looked up, and he saw in the quivering lines about her mouth signs of the contest on this theme she had passed through before coming down to him.

'You are going? I'm so glad.' She hesitated a moment. 'You know why!' she added, with what he saw was an intention of kindness.

Tarvin laughed as he seated himself. 'I like

that. Yes; I'm going,' he said. 'But I'm not going alone. You're in the plan,' he assured her, with a nod.

She shook her head.

'No; don't say that, Kate. You mustn't. It's serious this time.'

'Hasn't it always been?' she sank into a chair. 'It's always been serious enough for me — that I couldn't do what you wish, I mean. Not doing it—that is doing something else; the one thing I want to do—is the most serious thing in the world to me. Nothing has happened to change me, Nick. I would tell you in a moment if it had. How is it different for either of us?'

'Lots of ways. But that I've got to leave Rhatore for a sample. You don't think I'd leave you behind, I hope.'

She studied the hands she had folded in her lap for a moment. Then she looked up and faced him with her open gaze.

'Nick,' she said, 'let me try to explain as clearly as I can how all this seems to me. You can correct me if I'm wrong.'

'Oh, you're sure to be wrong!' he cried; but he leaned forward.

'Well, let me try. You ask me to marry you!'

'I do,' answered Tarvin solemnly. 'Give me a chance of saying that before a clergyman, and you'll see.'

'I am grateful, Nick. It's a gift—the highest, the best, and I'm grateful. But what is it you really want? Shall you mind my asking that,

Nick? You want me to round out your life ; you want me to complete your other ambitions. Isn't that so? Tell me honestly, Nick ; isn't that so?'

'No!' roared Tarvin.

'Ah, but it is! Marriage is that way. It is right. Marriage means that—to be absorbed into another's life : to live your own, not as your own but another's. It is a good life. It's a woman's life. I can like it ; I can believe in it. But I can't see myself in it. A woman gives the whole of herself in marriage—in all happy marriages. I haven't the whole of myself to give. It belongs to something else. And I couldn't offer you a part ; it is all the best men give to women, but from a woman it would do no man any good.'

'You mean that you have the choice between giving up your work and giving up me, and that the last is easiest.'

'I don't say that ; but suppose I did, would it be so strange? Be honest, Nick. Suppose I asked you to give up the centre and meaning of *your* life? Suppose I asked you to give up *your* work? And suppose I offered in exchange— marriage! No, no!' She shook her head. 'Marriage is good ; but what man would pay that price for it?'

'My dearest girl, isn't that just the opportunity of women?'

'The opportunity of the happy women—yes ; but it isn't given to every one to see marriage like that. Even for women there is more than one kind of devotion.'

'Oh, look here, Kate! A man isn't an Orphan

Asylum or a Home for the Friendless. You take him too seriously. You talk as if you had to make him your leading charity, and give up everything to the business. Of course you have to pretend something of the kind at the start, but in practice you only have to eat a few dinners, attend a semi-annual board meeting, and a strawberry festival or two to keep the thing going. It's just a general agreement to drink your coffee with a man in the morning, and be somewhere around, not too far from the fire, in not too ugly a dress, when he comes home in the evening. Come! It's an easy contract. Try me, Kate, and you'll see how simple I'll make it for you. I know about the other things. I understand well enough that you would never care for a life which didn't allow you to make a lot of people happy besides your husband. I recognise that. I begin with it. And I say that's just what I want. You have a talent for making folks happy. Well, I secure you on a special agreement to make me happy, and after you've attended to that, I want you to sail in and make the whole world bloom with your kindness. And you'll do it, too. Confound it, Kate, *we'll* do it! No one knows how good *two* people could be if they formed a syndicate and made a business of it. It hasn't been tried. Try it with me! O Kate, I love you, I need you, and if you'll let me, I'll make a life for you!'

'I know, Nick, you would be kind. You would do all that a man can do. But it isn't the man who makes marriages happy or possible; it's the woman, and it must be. I should either do my part and shirk the other, and then I should be miserable ; or I should shirk *you* and be more miserable. Either way such happiness is not for me.'

Tarvin's hand found the Naulahka within his breast, and clutched it tight. Strength seemed to go out of it into him—strength to restrain himself from losing all by a dozen savage words.

'Kate, my girl,' he said quietly, 'we haven't time to conjure dangers. We have to face a real one. You are not safe here. I can't leave you in this place, and I've got to go. That is why I ask you to marry me at once.'

'But I fear nothing. Who would harm me?'

'Sitabhai,' he answered grimly. 'But what difference does it make? I tell you, you are not safe. Be sure that I know.'

'And you?'

'Oh, I don't count.'

'The truth, Nick!' she demanded.

'Well, I always said that there was nothing like the climate of Topaz.'

'You mean you are in danger—great danger, perhaps.'

'Sitabhai isn't going round hunting for ways to save my precious life, that's a fact.' He smiled at her.

'Then you must go away at once ; you mustn't lose an hour. O Nick, you won't wait!'

'That's what I say. I can do without Rhatore ; but I can't do without you. You must come.'

'Do you mean that if I don't you will stay?' she asked desperately.

'No; that would be a threat. I mean I'll wait for you.' His eyes laughed at her.

'Nick, is this because of what I asked you to do?' she demanded suddenly.

'You didn't ask me,' he defended.

'Then it is, and I am much to blame.'

'What, because I spoke to the King? My dear girl, that isn't more than the introductory walk-around of this circus. Don't run away with any question of responsibility. The only thing you are responsible for at this moment is to run with me—flee, vamoose, get out! Your life isn't worth an hour's purchase here. I'm convinced of that. And mine isn't worth a minute's.'

'You see what a situation you put me in,' she said accusingly.

'I don't put you in it; but I offer you a simple solution.'

'Yourself!'

'Well, yes; I said it was simple. I don't claim it's brilliant. Almost any one could do more for you; and there are millions of better men, but there isn't one who could love you better. O Kate, Kate,' he cried, rising, 'trust yourself to my love, and I'll back myself against the world to make you happy.'

'No, no,' she exclaimed eagerly; 'you must go away.'

He shook his head. 'I can't leave you. Ask that of some one else. Do you suppose a man who loves you can abandon you in this desert wilderness to take your chances? Do you suppose any man could do that? Kate, my darling, come with me. You torment me, you kill me, by forcing me to allow you a single moment out of my sight. I tell you, you are in imminent, deadly peril. You won't stay, knowing that. Surely you won't sacrifice your life for these creatures.'

'Yes,' she cried, rising, with the uplifted look on her face. 'Yes! If it is good to live for them, it is good to die for them. I do not believe my life is necessary; but if it is necessary, that too!'

Tarvin gazed at her, baffled, disheartened, at a loss. 'And you won't come?'

'I can't. Good-bye, Nick. It's the end.'

He took her hand. 'Good afternoon,' he responded. 'It's end enough for to-day.'

She pursued him anxiously with her eye as he turned away; suddenly she started after him. 'But you will go?'

'Go! No! No!' he shouted. 'I'll stay now if I have to organise a standing army, declare myself king, and hold the rest-house as the seat of government. *Go!*'

She put forth a detaining, despairing hand, but he was gone.

Kate returned to the little Maharaj Kunwar, who had been allowed to lighten his convalescence by bringing down from the palace a number of his toys and pets. She sat down by the side of the bed, and cried for a long time silently.

'What is it, Miss Kate?' asked the Prince, after he had watched her for some minutes, wondering. 'Indeed, I am quite well now, so there is nothing to cry for. When I go back to

the palace I will tell my father all that you have
done for me, and he will give you a village. We
Rajputs do not forget.'

'It's not that, Lalji,' she said, stooping over
him, drying her tear-stained eyes.

'Then my father will give you *two* villages.
No one must cry when I am getting well, for I
am a king's son. Where is Moti? I want him
to sit upon a chair.'

Kate rose obediently, and began to call for the
Maharaj Kunwar's latest pet—a little grey monkey,
with a gold collar, who wandered at liberty through
the house and garden, and at night did his best to
win a place for himself by the young Prince's side.
He answered the call from the boughs of a tree in
the garden, where he was arguing with the wild
parrots, and entered the room, crooning softly in
the monkey tongue.

'Come here, little Hanuman,' said the Prince,
raising one hand. The monkey bounded to his
side. 'I have heard of a king,' said the Prince,
playing with his golden collar, 'who spent three
lakhs in marrying two monkeys. Moti, wouldst
thou like a wife? No, no—a gold collar is enough
for thee. We will spend our three lakhs in marrying Miss Kate to Tarvin Sahib, when we get well,
and thou shalt dance at the wedding.' He was
speaking in the vernacular, but Kate understood
too well the coupling of her name with Tarvin's.

'Don't, Lalji, don't!'

'Why not, Kate? Why, even I am married.'

'Yes, yes. But it is different. Kate would
rather you didn't, Lalji.'

'Very well,' answered the Maharaj, with a pout.
'Now I am only a little child. When I am well
I will be a king again, and no one can refuse my
gifts. Listen. Those are my father's trumpets.
He is coming to see me.'

A bugle call sounded in the distance. There
was a clattering of horses' feet, and a little later
the Maharajah's carriage and escort thundered up
to the door of the missionary's house. Kate
looked anxiously to see if the noise irritated her
young charge ; but his eyes brightened, his nostrils
quivered, and he whispered, as his hand tightened
on the hilt of the sword always by his side—

'That is very good ! My father has brought
all his sowars.'

Before Kate could rise, Mr. Estes had ushered
the Maharajah into the room, which was dwarfed
by his bulk and by the bravery of his presence.
He had been assisting at a review of his body-
guard, and came therefore in his full uniform as
commander-in-chief of the army of the State,
which was no mean affair. The Maharaj Kunwar
ran his eyes delightedly up and down the august
figure of his father, beginning with the polished
gold-spurred jack-boots, and ascending to the
snowy-white doeskin breeches, the tunic blazing
with gold, and the diamonds of the Order of the
Star of India, ending with the saffron turban and
its nodding emerald aigrette. The King drew off
his gauntlets and shook hands cordially with Kate.
After an orgy it was noticeable that his Highness
became more civilised.

'And is the child well ?' he asked. 'They

told me that it was a little fever, and I, too, have had some fever.'

'The Prince's trouble was much worse than that, I am afraid, Maharajah Sahib,' said Kate.

'Ah, little one,' said the King, bending over his son very tenderly, and speaking in the vernacular, 'this is the fault of eating too much.'

'Nay, father, I did not eat, and I am quite well.'

Kate stood at the head of the bed stroking the boy's hair.

'How many troops paraded this morning?'

'Both squadrons, my General,' answered the father, his eye lighting with pride. 'Thou art all a Rajput, my son.'

'And my escort—where were they?'

'With Pertab Singh's troop. They led the charge at the end of the fight.'

'By the Sacred Horse,' said the Maharaj Kunwar, 'they shall lead in true fight one day. Shall they not, my father? Thou on the right flank, and I on the left.'

'Even so. But to do these things, a prince must not be ill, and he must learn many things.'

'I know,' returned the Prince reflectively. 'My father, I have lain here some nights, thinking. Am I a little child?' He looked at Kate a minute, and whispered, 'I would speak to my father. Let no one come in.'

Kate left the room quickly, with a backward smile at the boy, and the King seated himself by the bed.

'No, I am not a little child,' said the Prince.

'In five years I shall be a man, and many men will obey me. But how shall I know the right or the wrong in giving an order?'

'It is necessary to learn many things,' repeated the Maharajah vaguely.

'Yes, I have thought of that lying here in the dark,' said the Prince. 'And it is in my mind that these things are not all learned within the walls of the palace, or from women. My father, let me go away to learn how to be a prince!'

'But whither wouldst thou go? Surely my kingdom is thy home, beloved.'

'I know, I know,' returned the boy. 'And I will come back again, but do not let me be a laughing-stock to the other princes. At the wedding the Rawut of Bunnaul mocked me because my school-books were not as many as his. And *he* is only the son of an ennobled lord. He is without ancestry. But he has been up and down Rajputana as far as Delhi and Agra, ay, and Abu; and he is in the upper class of the Princes' School at Ajmir. Father, all the sons of the kings go there. They do not play with the women; they ride with men. And the air and the water are good at Ajmir. And I should like to go!'

The face of the Maharajah grew troubled, for the boy was very dear to him.

'But an evil might befall thee, Lalji. Think again.'

'I *have* thought,' responded the Prince. 'What evil can come to me under the charge of the Englishmen there? The Rawut of Bunnaul
s

told me that I should have my own rooms, my own servants, and my own stables, like the other princes—and that I should be much considered there.'

'Yes,' said the King soothingly. 'We be children of the sun—thou and I, my Prince.'

'Then it concerns me to be as learned and as strong and as valiant as the best of my race. Father, I am sick of running about the rooms of the women, of listening to my mother, and to the singing of the dance girls; and they are always pressing their kisses on me. Let me go to Ajmir. Let me go to the Princes' School. And in a year, even in a year—so says the Rawut of Bunnaul— I shall be fit to lead my escort, as a King should lead them. Is it a promise, my father?'

'When thou art well,' answered the Maharajah, 'we will speak of it again—not as a father to a child, but as a man to a man.'

The Maharaj Kunwar's eyes grew bright with pleasure. 'That is good,' he said—'as a man to a man.'

The Maharajah fondled him in his arms for a few minutes, and told him the small news of the palace—such things as would interest a little boy. Then he said laughing, 'Have I your leave to go?'

'Oh! my father!' The Prince buried his head in his father's beard and threw his arms around him. The Maharajah disengaged himself gently, and as gently went out into the verandah. Before Kate returned he had disappeared in a cloud of dust and a flourish of trumpets. As he was going, a messenger came to the house bearing a grass-woven basket, piled high with shaddock, banana, and pomegranate—emerald, gold, and copper, which he laid at Kate's feet, saying, ' It is a present from the Queen.'

The little Prince within heard the voice, and cried joyfully, ' Kate, my mother has sent you those. Are they big fruits ? Oh, give me a pomegranate,' he begged as she came back into his room. ' I have tasted none since last winter.'

Kate set the basket on the table, and the Prince's mood changed. He wanted pomegranate sherbet, and Kate must mix the sugar and the milk and the syrup and the plump red seeds. Kate left the room for an instant to get a glass, and it occurred to Moti, who had been foiled in an attempt to appropriate the Prince's emeralds, and had hidden under the bed, to steal forth and seize upon a ripe banana. Knowing well that the Maharaj Kunwar could not move, Moti paid no attention to his voice, but settled himself deliberately on his haunches, chose his banana, stripped off the skin with his little black fingers, grinned at the Prince, and began to eat.

' Very well, Moti,' said the Maharaj Kunwar, in the vernacular ; ' Kate says you are not a god, but only a little grey monkey, and I think so too. When she comes back you will be beaten, Hanu-man.'

Moti had half eaten the banana when Kate returned, but he did not try to escape. She cuffed the marauder lightly, and he fell over on his side.

'Why, Lalji, what's the matter with Moti?'
she asked, regarding the monkey curiously.

'He has been stealing, and now I suppose he
is playing dead man. Hit him!'

Kate bent over the limp little body ; but there
was no need to chastise Moti. He was dead.

She turned pale, and, rising, took the basket of
fruit quickly to her nostrils, and sniffed delicately
at it. A faint, sweet, cloying odour rose from
the brilliant pile. It was overpowering. She set
the basket down, putting her hand to her head.
The odour dizzied her.

'Well?' said the Prince, who could not see his
dead pet. 'I want my sherbet.'

'The fruit is not quite good, I'm afraid, Lalji,'
she said, with an effort. As she spoke she tossed
into the garden, through the open window, the
uneaten fragment of the banana that Moti had
clasped so closely to his wicked little breast.

A parrot swooped down on the morsel instantly
from the trees, and took it back to his perch in
the branches. It was done before Kate, still un-
steadied, could make a motion to stop it, and a
moment later a little ball of green feathers fell
from the covert of leaves, and the parrot also lay
dead on the ground.

'No, the fruit is not good,' she said mechanically, her eyes wide with terror, and her face
blanched. Her thoughts leaped to Tarvin. Ah,
the warnings and the entreaties that she had put
from her! He had said she was not safe. Was
he not right? The awful subtlety of the danger
in which she stood was a thing to shake a stronger

woman than she. From where would it come
next? Out of what covert might it not leap?
The very air might be poisoned. She scarcely
dared to breathe.

The audacity of the attack daunted her as much
as its design. If this might be done in open day,
under cover of friendship, immediately after the
visit of the King, what might not the gipsy in the
palace dare next? She and the Maharaj Kunwar
were under the same roof; if Tarvin was right in
supposing that Sitabhai could wish her harm, the
fruit was evidently intended for them both. She
shuddered to think how she herself might have
given the fruit to the Maharaj innocently.

The Prince turned in his bed and regarded
Kate. 'You are not well?' he asked, with grave
politeness. 'Then do not trouble about the
sherbet. Give me Moti to play with.'

'O Lalji! Lalji!' cried Kate, tottering to the
bed. She dropped beside the boy, cast her arms
defendingly about him, and burst into tears.

'You have cried twice,' said the Prince, watching her heaving shoulders curiously. 'I shall tell
Tarvin Sahib.'

The word smote Kate's heart, and filled her
with a bitter and fruitless longing. Oh, for a
moment of the sure and saving strength she had
just rejected! Where was he? she asked herself
reproachfully. What had happened to the man
she had sent from her to take the chances of life
and death in this awful land?

At that hour Tarvin was sitting in his room at
the rest-house, with both doors open to the stifling

wind of the desert, that he might command all
approaches clearly, his revolver on the table in
front of him, and the Naulahka in his pocket,
yearning to be gone, and loathing this conquest
that did not include Kate.

XIX

We be the Gods of the East—
   Older than all—
Masters of mourning and feast,
   How shall we fall ?

Will they gape to the husks that ye proffer,
   Or yearn to your song ?
And we, have we nothing to offer
   Who ruled them so long
In the fume of the incense, the clash of the cymbal, the blare
   of the conch and the gong ?

Over the strife of the schools,
   Low the day burns—
Back with the kine from the pools,
   Each one returns,
To the life that he knows where the altar-flame glows
   And the *tulsi* is trimmed in the urns.

                                   In Seeonee.

THE evening and the long night gave Kate ample
time for self-examination after she had locked up
the treacherous fruit, and consoled the Maharaj,
through her tears, for the mysterious death of
Moti. One thing only seemed absolutely clear to
her, when she rose red-eyed and unrefreshed the
next morning: her work was with the women so
long as life remained, and the sole refuge for her

present trouble was in the portion of that work which lay nearest to her hand. Meanwhile the man who loved her remained in Gokral Seetarun, in deadly peril of his life, that he might be within call of her; and she could not call him, for to summon him was to yield, and she dared not.

She took her way to the hospital. The dread for him that had assailed her yesterday had become a horror that would not let her think.

The woman of the desert was waiting as usual at the foot of the steps, her hands clasped over her knee, and her face veiled. Behind her was Dhunpat Rai, who should have been among the wards; and she could see that the courtyard was filled with people—strangers and visitors, who, by her new regulations, were allowed to come only once a week. This was not their visiting day, and Kate, strained and worn by all that she had passed through since the day before, felt an angry impulse in her heart go out against them, and spoke wrathfully.

'What is the meaning of this, Dhunpat Rai?' she demanded, alighting.

'There is commotion of popular bigotry within,' said Dhunpat Rai. 'It is nothing. I have seen it before. Only do not go in.'

She put him aside without a word, and was about to enter when she met one of her patients, a man in the last stage of typhoid fever, being borne out by half a dozen clamouring friends, who shouted at her menacingly. The woman of the desert was at her side in an instant, raising her hand, in the brown hollow of which lay a long, broad-bladed knife.

'Be still, dogs!' she shouted, in their own tongue. 'Dare not to lay hands on this *peri*, who has done all for you!'

'She is killing our people,' shouted a villager.

'Maybe,' said the woman, with a flashing smile; 'but I know who will be lying here dead if you do not suffer her to pass. Are you Rajputs, or Bhils from the hills, hunters of fish, and diggers after grubs, that you run like cattle because a lying priest from nowhere troubles your heads of mud? Is she killing your people? How long can *you* keep that man alive with your charms and your *mantras*?' she demanded, pointing to the stricken form on the stretcher. 'Out—go out! Is this hospital your own village to defile? Have you paid one penny for the roof above you or the drugs in your bellies? Get hence before I spit upon you!' She brushed them aside with a regal gesture.

'It is best not to go in,' said Dhunpat Rai in Kate's ear. 'There is local holy man in the courtyard, and he is agitating their minds. Also, I myself feel much indisposed.'

'But what does all this mean?' demanded Kate again.

For the hospital was in the hands of a hurrying crowd, who were strapping up bedding and cooking-pots, lamps and linen, calling to one another up and down the staircases in subdued voices, and bringing the sick from the upper wards as ants bring eggs out of a broken hill, six or eight to each man—some holding bunches of marigold flowers in their hands, and pausing to mutter prayers at each step, others peering fearfully into the dispensary, and yet others drawing water from the well and pouring it out around the beds.

In the centre of the courtyard, as naked as the lunatic who had once lived there, sat an ash-smeared, long-haired, eagle-taloned, half-mad, wandering native priest, and waved above his head his buckhorn staff, sharp as a lance at one end, while he chanted in a loud monotonous voice some song that drove the men and women to work more quickly.

As Kate faced him, white with wrath, her eyes blazing, the song turned to a yelp of fierce hatred.

She dashed among the women swiftly—her own women, who she thought had grown to love her. But their relatives were about them, and Kate was thrust back by a bare-shouldered, loud-voiced dweller of the out-villages in the heart of the desert.

The man had no intention of doing her harm, but the woman of the desert slashed him across the face with her knife, and he withdrew howling.

'Let me speak to them,' said Kate, and the woman beside her quelled the clamour of the crowd with uplifted hands. Only the priest continued his song. Kate strode toward him, her little figure erect and quivering, crying in the vernacular, 'Be silent, thou, or I will find means to close thy mouth!'

The man was hushed, and Kate, returning to

her women, stood amongst them, and began to speak impassionedly.

'Oh, my women, what have I done?' she cried, still in the vernacular. 'If there is any fault here, who should right it but your friend? Surely you can speak to me day or night.' She threw out her arms. 'Listen, my sisters! Have you gone mad, that you wish to go abroad now, half-cured, sick, or dying? You are free to go at any hour. Only, for your own sake, and for the sake of your children, do not go before I have cured you, if God so please. It is summer in the desert now, and many of you have come from many *koss* distant.'

'She speaks truth! She speaks truth,' said a voice in the crowd.

'Ay, I do speak truth. And I have dealt fairly by ye. Surely it is upon your heads to tell me the cause of this flight, and not to run away like mice. My sisters, ye are weak and ill, and your friends do not know what is best for you. But I know.'

'*Arre!* But what can we do?' cried a feeble voice. 'It is no fault of ours. I, at least, would fain die in peace, but the priest says——'

Then the clamour broke out afresh. 'There are charms written upon the plasters——'

'Why should we become Christians against our will? The wise woman that was sent away asks it.'

'What are the meanings of the red marks on the plasters?'

'Why should we have strange devil-marks stamped upon our bodies? And they burn, too, like the fires of hell.'

'The priest came yesterday—that holy man

yonder—and he said it had been revealed to him,
sitting among the hills, that this devil's plan was
on foot to make us lose our religion——'

'And to send us out of the hospital with marks
upon our bodies—ay, and all the babies we should
bear in the hospital should have tails like camels,
and ears like mules. The wise woman says so;
the priest says so.'

'Hush! hush!' cried Kate, in the face of these
various words. 'What plasters? What child's
talk is this of plasters and devils? Not one child,
but many have been born here, and all were
comely. Ye know it! This is the word of the
worthless woman, whom I sent away because she
was torturing you.'

'Nay, but the priest said——'

'What care I for the priest? Has he nursed
you? Has he watched by you of nights? Has
he sat by your bedside, and smoothed your pillow,
and held your hand in pain? Has he taken your
children from you and put them to sleep, when ye
needed an hour's rest?'

'He is a holy man. He has worked miracles.
We dare not face the anger of the gods.'

One woman, bolder than the rest, shouted,
'Look at this'; and held before Kate's face one
of the prepared mustard-leaves lately ordered from
Calcutta, which bore upon the back, in red ink, the
maker's name and trade-mark.

'What is this devil's thing?' demanded the
woman fiercely.

The woman of the desert caught her by the
shoulder, and forced her to her knees.

'Be still, woman without a nose!' she cried, her voice vibrating with passion. 'She is not of thy clay, and thy touch would defile her. Remember thine own dunghill, and speak softly.'

Kate picked up the plaster, smiling.

'And who says there is devil's work in this?' she demanded.

'The holy man, the priest. Surely he should know!'

'Nay, *ye* should know,' said Kate patiently. She understood now, and could pity. 'Ye have worn it. Did it work thee any harm, Pithira?' She pointed directly toward her. 'Thou hast thanked me not once but many times for giving thee relief through this charm. If it was the devil's work, why did it not consume thee?'

'Indeed it burnt very much indeed,' responded the woman, with a nervous laugh.

Kate could not help laughing. 'That is true. I cannot make my drugs pleasant. But ye know that they do good. What do these people, your friends—villagers, camel-drivers, goat-herds—know of English drugs? Are they so wise among their hills, or is the priest so wise, that they can judge for thee here, fifty miles away from them? Do not listen. Oh, do not listen! Tell them that ye will stay with me, and I will make you well. I can do no more. It was for that I came. I heard of your misery ten thousand miles away, and it burnt into my heart. Would I have come so far to work you harm? Go back to your beds, my sisters, and bid these foolish people depart.'

There was a murmur among the women, as if

of assent and doubt. For a moment the decision swayed one way and the other.

Then the man whose face had been slashed shouted, 'What is the use of talking? Let us take our wives and sisters away! We do not wish to have sons like devils. Give us your voice, O father!' he cried to the priest.

The holy man drew himself up, and swept away Kate's appeal with a torrent of abuse, imprecation, and threats of damnation; and the crowd began to slip past Kate by twos and threes, half carrying and half forcing their kinsfolk with them.

Kate called on the women by name, beseeching them to stay — reasoning, arguing, expostulating. But to no purpose. Many of them were in tears; but the answer from all was the same. They were sorry, but they were only poor women, and they feared the wrath of their husbands.

Minute after minute the wards were depopulated of their occupants, as the priest resumed his song, and began to dance frenziedly in the courtyard. The stream of colours broke out down the steps into the street, and Kate saw the last of her carefully swathed women borne out into the pitiless sun-glare—only the woman of the desert remaining by her side.

Kate looked on with stony eyes. Her hospital was empty.

XX

Our sister sayeth such and such,
  And we must bow to her behests;
Our sister toileth overmuch,
  Our little maid that hath no breasts.

A field untilled, a web unwove,
  A bud withheld from sun or bee,
An alien in the courts of Love,
  And priestess of his shrine is she.

We love her, but we laugh the while;
  We laugh, but sobs are mixed with laughter;
Our sister hath no time to smile,
  She knows not what must follow after.

Wind of the South, arise and blow,
  From beds of spice thy locks shake free;
Breathe on her heart that she may know,
  Breathe on her eyes that she may see.

Alas! we vex her with our mirth,
  And maze her with most tender scorn,
Who stands beside the gates of Birth,
  Herself a child—a child unborn!

Our sister sayeth such and such,
  And we must bow to her behests;
Our sister toileth overmuch,
  Our little maid that hath no breasts.
                    From Libretto of Naulahka.

'HAS the miss sahib any orders?' asked Dhunpat

Rai, with Oriental calmness, as Kate turned toward the woman of the desert, staying herself against her massive shoulder.

Kate simply shook her head with closed lips.

'It is very sad,' said Dhunpat Rai thoughtfully, as though the matter were one in which he had no interest ; 'but it is on account of religious bigotry and intolerance which is prevalent mania in these parts. Once — twice before I have seen the same thing. About powders, sometimes ; and once they said that the graduated glasses were holy vessels, and zinc ointment was cow-fat. But I have never seen all the hospital disembark simultaneously. I do not think they will come back ; but my appointment is State appointment,' he said, with a bland smile, 'and so I shall draw my offeeshal income as before.'

Kate stared at him. 'Do you mean that they will never come back?' she asked falteringly.

'Oh yes—in time—one or two ; two or three of the men when they are hurt by tigers, or have ophthalmia ; but the women—no. Their husbands will never allow. Ask that woman!'

Kate bent a piteous look of inquiry upon the woman of the desert, who, stooping down, took up a little sand, let it trickle through her fingers, brushed her palms together, and shook her head. Kate watched these movements despairingly.

'You see it is all up—no good,' said Dhunpat Rai, not unkindly, but unable to conceal a certain expression of satisfaction in a defeat which the wise had already predicted. 'And now what will your honour do? Shall I lock up dispensary, or will you audit drug accounts now?'

Kate waved him off feebly. 'No, no! Not now. I must think. I must have time. I will send you word. Come, dear one,' she added in the vernacular to the woman of the desert, and hand in hand they went out from the hospital together.

The sturdy Rajput woman caught her up like a child when they were outside, and set her upon her horse, and tramped doggedly alongside, as they set off together toward the house of the missionary.

'And whither wilt thou go?' asked Kate, in the woman's own tongue.

'I was the first of them all,' answered the patient being at her side; 'it is fitting therefore that I should be the last. Where thou goest I will go—and afterward what will fall will fall.'

Kate leaned down and took the woman's hand in hers with a grateful pressure.

At the missionary's gate she had to call up her courage not to break down. She had told Mrs. Estes so much of her hopes for the future, had dwelt so lovingly on all that she meant to teach these helpless creatures, had so constantly conferred with her about the help she had fancied herself to be daily bringing to them, that to own that her work had fallen to this ruin was unspeakably bitter. The thought of Tarvin she fought back. It went too deep.

T

But, fortunately, Mrs. Estes seemed not to be at home, and a messenger from the Queen Mother awaited Kate to demand her presence at the palace with the Maharaj Kunwar.

The woman of the desert laid a restraining hand on her arm, but Kate shook it off.

'No, no, no! I must go. I must do something,' she exclaimed almost fiercely, 'since there is still some one who will let me. I must have work. It is my only refuge, kind one. Go you on to the palace.'

The woman yielded silently, and trudged on up the dusty road, while Kate sped into the house and to the room where the young Prince lay.

'Lalji,' she said, bending over him, 'do you feel well enough to be lifted into the carriage and taken over to see your mother?'

'I would rather see my father,' responded the boy from the sofa, to which he had been transferred as a reward for the improvement he had made since yesterday. 'I wish to speak to my father upon a most important thing.'

'But your mother hasn't seen you for so long, dear.'

'Very well; I will go.'

'Then I will tell them to get the carriage ready.'

Kate turned to leave the room.

'No, please; I will have my own. Who is without there?'

'Heaven-born, it is I,' answered the deep voice of a trooper.

'*Achcha!* Ride swiftly, and tell them to send down my barouche and escort. If it is not here in ten minutes, tell Saroop Singh that I will cut his pay and blacken his face before all my men. This day I go abroad again.'

'May the mercy of God be upon the heaven-born for ten thousand years,' responded the voice from without, as the trooper heaved himself into the saddle and clattered away.

By the time that the Prince was ready, a lumbering equipage, stuffed with many cushions, waited at the door. Kate and Mrs. Estes half-helped and half-carried the child into it, though he strove to stand on his feet in the verandah and acknowledge the salute of his escort as befitted a man.

'*Ahi!* I am very weak,' he said, with a little laugh, as they drove to the palace. 'Certainly it seems to myself that I shall never get well in Rhatore.'

Kate put her arm about him and drew him closer to her.

'Kate,' he continued, 'if I ask anything of my father, will you say that that thing is good for me?'

Kate, whose thoughts were still bitter and far away, patted his shoulder vaguely as she lifted her tear-stained eyes toward the red height on which the palace stood. 'How can I tell, Lalji?' She smiled down into his upturned face.

'But it is a most wise thing.'

'Is it?' asked she fondly.

'Yes; I have thought it out by myself. I am

myself a Raj Kumar, and I would go to the Raj Kumar College, where they train the sons of princes to become kings. That is only at Ajmir; but I must go and learn, and fight, and ride with the other princes of Rajputana, and then I shall be altogether a man. I am going to the Raj Kumar College at Ajmir, that I may learn about the world. But you shall see how it is wise. The world looks very big since I have been ill. Kate, how big is the world which you have seen across the Black Water? Where is Tarvin Sahib? I have wished to see him too. Is Tarvin Sahib angry with me or with you?'

He plied her with a hundred questions till they halted before one of the gates in the flank of the palace that led to his mother's wing. The woman of the desert rose from the ground beside it, and held out her arms.

'I heard the message come,' she said to Kate, 'and I knew what was required. Give me the child to carry in. Nay, my Prince, there is no cause for fear. I am of good blood.'

'Women of good blood walk veiled, and do not speak in the streets,' said the child doubtfully.

'One law for thee and thine, and another for me and mine,' the woman answered, with a laugh. 'We who earn our bread by toil cannot go veiled, but our fathers lived before us for many hundred years, even as did thine, heaven-born. Come then, the white fairy cannot carry thee so tenderly as I can.'

She put her arms about him, and held him to

her breast as easily as though he had been a three year-old child. He leaned back luxuriously, and waved a wasted hand ; the grim gate grated on its hinges as it swung back, and they entered together—the woman, the child, and the girl.

There was no lavish display of ornament in that part of the palace. The gaudy tilework on the walls had flaked and crumbled away in many places, the shutters lacked paint and hung awry, and there was litter and refuse in the courtyard behind the gates. A queen who has lost the King's favour loses much else as well in material comforts.

A door opened and a voice called. The three plunged into half darkness, and traversed a long, upward-sloping passage, floored with shining white stucco as smooth as marble, which communicated with the Queen's apartments. The Maharaj Kunwar's mother lived by preference in one long, low room that faced to the north-east, that she might press her face against the marble tracery and dream of her home across the sands, eight hundred miles away, among the Kulu hills. The hum of the crowded palace could not be heard there, and the footsteps of her few waiting-women alone broke the silence.

The woman of the desert, with the Prince hugged more closely to her breast, moved through the labyrinth of empty rooms, narrow staircases, and roofed courtyards with the air of a caged panther. Kate and the Prince were familiar with the dark and the tortuousness, the silence and the sullen mystery. To the one it was part and parcel of the horrors amid which she had elected to move ; to the other it was his daily life.

At last the journey ended. Kate lifted a heavy curtain, as the Prince called for his mother ; and the Queen, rising from a pile of white cushions by the window, cried passionately—

'Is it well with the child?'

The Prince struggled to the floor from the woman's arms, and the Queen hung sobbing over him, calling him a thousand endearing names, and fondling him from head to foot. The child's reserve melted—he had striven for a moment to carry himself as a man of the Rajput race : that is to say, as one shocked beyond expression at any public display of emotion—and he laughed and wept in his mother's arms. The woman of the desert drew her hand across her eyes, muttering to herself, and Kate turned to look out of the window.

'How shall I give you thanks?' said the Queen at last. 'Oh, my son—my little son—child of my heart, the gods and she have made thee well again. But who is that yonder?'

Her eyes fell for the first time on the woman of the desert, where the latter stood by the door-way draped in dull-red.

'She carried me here from the carriage,' said the Prince, 'saying that she was a Rajput of good blood.'

'I am of Chohan blood—a Rajput and a mother of Rajputs,' said the woman simply, still standing. 'The white fairy worked a miracle upon my man. He was sick in the head and did not know me. It is true that he died, but before the passing of the breath he knew me and called me by my name.'

'And *she* carried thee!' said the Queen, with a shiver, drawing the Prince closer to her, for, like all Indian women, she counted the touch and glance of a widow things of evil omen.

The woman fell at the Queen's feet. 'Forgive me, forgive me,' she cried. 'I had borne three little ones, and the gods took them all and my man at the last. It was good—it was so good— to hold a child in my arms again. Thou canst forgive,' she wailed ; 'thou art so rich in thy son, and I am only a widow.'

'And I a widow in life,' said the Queen, under her breath. 'Of a truth, I should forgive. Rise thou.'

The woman lay still where she had fallen, clutching at the Queen's naked feet.

'Rise, then, my sister,' the Queen whispered.

'We of the fields,' murmured the woman of the desert, 'we do not know how to speak to the great people. If my words are rough, does the Queen forgive me?'

'Indeed I forgive. Thy speech is softer than that of the hill-women of Kulu, but some of the words are new.'

'I am of the desert—a herder of camels, a milker of goats. What should I know of the speech of courts? Let the white fairy speak for me.'

Kate listened with an alien ear. Now that she had discharged her duty, her freed mind went back to Tarvin's danger and the shame and overthrow of an hour ago. She saw the women in her hospital slipping away one by one, her work unravelled, and all hope of good brought to wreck; and she saw Tarvin dying atrocious deaths, and, as she felt, by her hand.

'What is it?' she asked wearily, as the woman plucked at her skirt. Then to the Queen, 'This is a woman who alone of all those whom I tried to benefit remained at my side to-day, Queen.'

'There has been a talk in the palace,' said the Queen, her arm round the Prince's neck, 'a talk that trouble had come to your hospital, sahiba.'

'There is no hospital now,' Kate answered grimly.

'You promised to take me there, Kate, some day,' the Prince said in English.

'The women were fools,' said the woman of the desert quietly, from her place on the ground. 'A mad priest told them a lie—that there was a charm among the drugs——'

'Deliver us from all evil spirits and exorcisms,' the Queen murmured.

'A charm among her drugs that she handles with her own hands, and so forsooth, sahiba, they must run out shrieking that their children will be misborn apes and their chicken-souls given to the devils. *Aho!* They will know in a week, not one or two, but many, whither their souls go : for they will die—the corn and the corn in the ear together.'

Kate shivered. She knew too well that the woman spoke the truth.

'But the drugs!' began the Queen. 'Who

knows what powers there may be in the drugs?'
she laughed nervously, glancing at Kate.

'*Dekko!* Look at her,' said the woman, with
quiet scorn. 'She is a girl and naught else. What
could she do to the Gates of Life?'

'She has made my son whole, therefore she is
my sister,' said the Queen.

'She caused my man to speak to me before the
death hour; therefore I am her servant as well as
thine, sahiba,' said the other.

The Prince looked up in his mother's face
curiously. 'She calls thee "thou,"' he said, as
though the woman did not exist. 'That is not
seemly between a villager and a queen, thee and
thou!'

'We be both women, little son. Stay still in
my arms. Oh, it is good to feel thee here again,
worthless one.'

'The heaven-born looks as frail as dried maize,'
said the woman quickly.

'A dried monkey, rather,' returned the Queen,
dropping her lips on the child's head. Both
mothers spoke aloud and with emphasis, that the
gods, jealous of human happiness, might hear and
take for truth the disparagement that veils deepest
love.

'*Aho*, my little monkey is dead,' said the
Prince, moving restlessly. 'I need another one.
Let me go into the palace and find another
monkey.'

'He must not wander into the palace from this
chamber,' said the Queen passionately, turning to
Kate. 'Thou art all too weak, beloved. O miss

sahib, he must not go.' She knew by experience
that it was fruitless to cross her son's will.

'It is my order,' said the Prince, without turning his head. 'I will go.'

'Stay with us, beloved,' said Kate. She was
wondering whether the hospital could be dragged
together again, after three months, and whether it
was possible she might have overrated the danger
to Nick.

'I go,' said the Prince, breaking from his
mother's arms. 'I am tired of this talk.'

'Does the Queen give leave?' asked the woman
of the desert under her breath. The Queen
nodded, and the Prince found himself caught
between two brown arms, against whose strength
it was impossible to struggle.

'Let me go, *widow!*' he shouted furiously.

'It is not good for a Rajput to make light of a
mother of Rajputs, my king,' was the unmoved
answer. 'If the young calf does not obey the
cow, he learns obedience from the yoke. The
heaven-born is not strong. He will fall among
those passages and stairs. He will stay here.
When the rage has left his body he will be weaker
than before. Even now'—the large bright eyes
bent themselves on the face of the child—'even
now,' the calm voice continued, 'the rage is
going. One moment more, heaven-born, and
thou wilt be a prince no longer, but only a little,
little child, such as I have borne. *Ahi*, such as I
shall never bear again.'

With the last words the Prince's head nodded
forward on her shoulder. The gust of passion

had spent itself, leaving him, as she had foreseen, weak to sleep.

'Shame — oh, shame!' he muttered thickly. 'Indeed I do not wish to go. Let me sleep.'

She began to pat him on the shoulder, till the Queen put forward hungry arms, and took back her own again, and laying the child on a cushion at her side, spread the skirt of her long muslin robe over him, and looked long at her treasure. The woman crouched down on the floor. Kate sat on a cushion, and listened to the ticking of the cheap American clock in a niche in the wall. The voice of a woman singing a song came muffled and faint through many walls. The dry wind of noon sighed through the fretted screens of the window, and she could hear the horses of the escort swishing their tails and champing their bits in the courtyard a hundred feet below. She listened, thinking ever of Tarvin in growing terror. The Queen leaned over her son more closely, her eyes humid with mother love.

'He is asleep,' she said at last. 'What was the talk about his monkey, miss sahib?'

'It died,' Kate said, and spurred herself to the lie. 'I think it had eaten bad fruit in the garden.'

'In the garden?' said the Queen quickly.

'Yes, in the garden.'

The woman of the desert turned her eyes from one woman to the other. These were matters too high for her, and she began timidly to rub the Queen's feet.

'Monkeys often die,' she observed. 'I have

seen as it were a pestilence among the monkey folk over there at Banswarra.'

'In what fashion did it die?' insisted the Queen.

'I—I do not know,' Kate stammered, and there was another long silence as the hot afternoon wore on.

'Miss Kate, what do you think about my son?' whispered the Queen. 'Is he well, or is he not well?'

'He is not very well. In time he will grow stronger, but it would be better if he could go away for a while.'

The Queen bowed her head quietly. 'I have thought of that also many times sitting here alone; and it was the tearing out of my own heart from my breast. Yes, it would be well if he were to go away. But'—she stretched out her hands despairingly towards the sunshine—'what do I know of the world where he will go, and how can I be sure that he will be safe? Here—even here' . . . She checked herself suddenly. 'Since you have come, Miss Kate, my heart has known a little comfort, but I do not know when you will go away again.'

'I cannot guard the child against every evil,' Kate replied, covering her face with her hands; 'but send him away from this place as swiftly as may be. In God's name let him go away.'

'*Such hai! Such hai!* It is the truth, the truth!' The Queen turned from Kate to the woman at her feet.

'Thou hast borne three?' she said.

'Yea, three, and one other that never drew breath. They were all men - children,' said the woman of the desert.

'And the gods took them?'

'Of smallpox one, and fever the two others.'

'Art thou certain that it was the gods?'

'I was with them always till the end.'

'Thy man, then, was all thine own?'

'We were only two, he and I. Among our villages the men are poor, and one wife suffices.'

'*Arré!* They are rich among the villages. Listen now. If a co-wife had sought the lives of those three of thine——'

'I would have killed her. What else?' The woman's nostrils dilated and her hand went swiftly to her bosom.

'And if in place of three there had been one only, the delight of thy eyes, and thou hadst known that thou shouldst never bear another, and the co-wife working in darkness had sought for that life? What then?'

'I would have slain her—but with no easy death. At her man's side and in his arms I would have slain her. If she died before my vengeance arrived I would seek for her in hell.'

'Thou canst go out in the sunshine and walk in the streets and no man turns his head,' said the Queen bitterly. 'Thy hands are free and thy face is uncovered. What if thou wert a slave among slaves, a stranger among stranger people, and '— the voice dropped—'dispossessed of the favour of thy lord?'

The woman, stooping, kissed the pale feet under her hands.

'Then I would not wear myself with strife, but, remembering that a man-child may grow into a king, would send that child away beyond the power of the co-wife.'

'Is it so easy to cut away the hand?' said the Queen, sobbing.

'Better the hand than the heart, sahiba. Who could guard such a child in this place?'

The Queen pointed to Kate. 'She came from far off, and she has once already brought him back from death.'

'Her drugs are good and her skill is great, but —thou knowest she is but a maiden, who has known neither gain nor loss. It may be that I am luckless, and that my eyes are evil—thus did not my man say last autumn—but it may be. Yet I know the pain at the breast and the yearning over the child new-born—as thou hast known it.'

'As I have known it.'

'My house is empty and I am a widow and childless, and never again shall a man call me to wed.'

'As I am—as I am.'

'Nay, the little one is left, whatever else may go; and the little one must be well guarded. If there is any jealousy against the child it were not well to keep him in this hotbed. Let him go out.'

'But whither? Miss Kate, dost thou know? The world is all dark to us who sit behind the curtain.'

'I know that the child of his own motion
desires to go to the Princes' School in Ajmir.
He has told me that much,' said Kate, who had
lost no word of the conversation from her place
on the cushion, bowed forward with her chin
supported in her hands. 'It will be only for a
year or two.'

The Queen laughed a little through her tears.
'Only a year or two, Miss Kate. Dost thou know
how long is one night when he is not here?'

'And he can return at call; but no cry will
bring back mine own. Only a year or two. The
world is dark also to those who do not sit behind
the curtain, sahiba. It is no fault of hers. How
should she know?' said the woman of the desert
under her breath to the Queen.

Against her will, Kate began to feel annoyed
at this persistent exclusion of herself from the talk,
and the assumption that she, with her own great
trouble upon her, whose work was pre-eminently
to deal with sorrow, must have no place in this
double grief.

'How should I *not* know?' said Kate impetu-
ously. 'Do I not know pain? Is it not my
life?'

'Not yet,' said the Queen quietly. 'Neither
pain nor joy. Miss Kate, thou art very wise,
and I am only a woman who has never stirred
beyond the palace walls. But I am wiser than
thou, for I know that which thou dost not know,
though thou hast given back my son to me, and
to this woman her husband's speech. How shall
I repay thee all I owe?'

'Let her hear truth,' said the woman under her breath. 'We be all three women here, sahiba —dead leaf, flowering tree, and the blossom un-opened.'

The Queen caught Kate's hands and gently pulled her forward till her head fell on the Queen's knees. Wearied with the emotions of the morning, unutterably tired in body and spirit, the girl had no desire to lift it. The small hands put her hair back from her forehead, and the full dark eyes, worn with much weeping, looked into her own. The woman of the desert flung an arm round her waist.

'Listen, my sister,' began the Queen, with an infinite tenderness. 'There is a proverb among my own people, in the mountains of the north, that a rat found a piece of turmeric, and opened a druggist's shop. Even so with the pain that thou dost know and heal, beloved. Thou art not angry? Nay, thou must not take offence. Forget that thou art white, and I black, and remember only that we three be sisters. Little sister, with us women 'tis thus, and no other way. From all, except such as have borne a child, the world is hid. I make my prayers trembling to such and such a god, who thou sayest is black stone, and I tremble at the gusts of the night because I believe that the devils ride by my windows at such hours ; and I sit here in the dark knitting wool and preparing sweetmeats that come back untasted from my lord's table. And thou coming from ten thousand leagues away, very wise and fearing nothing, hast taught me, oh, ten

thousand things. Yet thou art the child, and I am
still the mother, and what I know thou canst not
know, and the wells of my happiness thou canst
not fathom, nor the bitter waters of my sorrow
till thou hast tasted happiness and grief alike.
I have told thee of the child—all and more than
all, thou sayest? Little sister, I have told thee less
than the beginning of my love for him, because I
knew that thou couldst not understand. I have
told thee my sorrows—all and more than all, thou
sayest, when I laid my head against thy breast?
How could I tell thee all? Thou art a maiden,
and the heart in thy bosom, beneath my heart,
betrayed in its very beat that it did not understand.
Nay, that woman there, coming from without,
knows more of me than thou? And they taught
thee in a school, thou hast told me, all manner of
healing, and there is no disease in life that thou
dost not understand? Little sister, how couldst
thou understand life that hast never given it?
Hast thou ever felt the tug of the child at the
breast? Nay, what need to blush? Hast thou?
I know thou hast not. Though I heard thy
speech for the first time, and looking from the
window saw thee walking, I should know. And
the others—my sisters in the world—know also.
But they do not all speak to thee as I do. When
the life quickens under the breast, they, waking
in the night, hear all the earth walking to that
measure. Why should they tell thee? To-day
the hospital has broken from under thee. Is it
not so? And the women went out one by one?
And what didst thou say to them?'

U

The woman of the desert, answering for her, spoke. 'She said, "Come back, and I will make ye well."'

'And by what oath did she affirm her words?'

'There was no oath,' said the woman of the desert; 'she stood in the gate and called.'

'And upon what should a maiden call to bring wavering women back again? The toil that she has borne for their sake? They cannot see it. But of the pains that a woman has shared with them, a woman knows. There was no child in thy arms. The mother look was not in thy eyes. By what magic, then, wouldst thou speak to women? There was a charm among the drugs, they said, and their children would be misshapen. What didst thou know of the springs of life and death to teach them otherwise? It is written in the books of thy school, I know, that such things cannot be. But we women do not read books. It is not from them that we learn of life. How should such an one prevail, unless the gods help her—and the gods are very far away. Thou hast given thy life to the helping of women. Little sister, when wilt thou also be a woman?'

The voice ceased. Kate's head was buried deep in the Queen's lap. She let it lie there without stirring.

'Ay!' said the woman of the desert. 'The mark of coverture has been taken from my head, my glass bangles are broken on my arm, and I am unlucky to meet when a man sets forth on a journey. Till I die I must be alone, earning my bread alone, and thinking of the dead. But though I knew that it was to come again, at the end of one year instead of ten, I would still thank the gods that have given me love and a child. Will the miss sahib take this in payment for all she did for my man ? " A wandering priest, a childless woman, and a stone in the water are of one blood." So says the talk of our people. What will the miss sahib do now ? The Queen has spoken the truth. The gods and thy own wisdom, which is past the wisdom of a maid, have helped thee so far, as I, who was with thee always, have seen. The gods have warned thee that their help is at an end. What remains? Is this work for such as thou ? Is it not as the Queen says? She, sitting here alone, and seeing nothing, has seen that which I, moving with thee among the sick day by day, have seen and known. Little sister, is it not so ? '

Kate lifted her head slowly from the Queen's knee, and rose.

' Take the child, and let us go,' she said hoarsely.

The merciful darkness of the room hid her face.

' Nay,' said the Queen, ' this woman shall take him. Go thou back alone.'

Kate vanished.

XXI

The Law whereby my lady moves
    Was never Law to me,
But 'tis enough that she approves
    Whatever Law it be.

For in that Law, and by that Law,
    My constant course I'll steer ;
Not that I heed or deem it dread,
    But that she holds it dear.

Tho' Asia sent for my content
    Her richest argosies,
Those would I spurn, and bid return,
    If that should give her ease.

With equal heart I'd watch depart
    Each spicèd sail from sight,
Sans bitterness, desiring less
    Great gear than her delight.

Yet such am I, yea such am I—
    Sore bond and freest free,—
The Law that sways my lady's ways
    Is mystery to me !

To sit still, and to keep sitting still, is the first
lesson that the young jockey must learn. Tarvin
was learning it in bitterness of spirit. For the
sake of his town, for the sake of his love, and,
above all, for the sake of his love's life, he must

go.   The town was waiting, his horse was saddled at the door, but his love would not come.   He must sit still.

The burning desert wind blew through the open verandah as remorselessly as Sitabhai's hate. Looking out, he saw nothing but the city asleep in the sunshine and the wheeling kites above it. Yet when evening fell, and a man might be able by bold riding to escape to the railway, certain shrouded figures would creep from the walls and take up their position within easy gunshot of the rest-house.   One squatted at each point of the compass, and between them, all night long, came and went a man on horseback.   Tarvin could hear the steady beat of the hoofs as he went his rounds, and the sound did not give him fresh hope.   But for Kate—but for Kate, he repeated to himself, he would have been long since beyond reach of horse or bullet.   The hours were very slow, and as he sat and watched the shadows grow and shorten it seemed to him, as it had seemed so often before, that this and no other was the moment that Topaz would choose to throw her chances from her.

He had lost already, he counted, eight-and-forty precious hours, and, so far as he could see, the remainder of the year might be spent in an equally unprofitable fashion.

Meantime Kate lay exposed to every imaginable danger.   Sitabhai was sure to assume that he had wrested the necklace from her for the sake of the 'frail white girl'; she had said as much on the dam.   It *was* for Kate's sake, in a measure; but

Tarvin reflected bitterly that an Oriental had no sense of proportion, and, like the snake, strikes first at that which is nearest. And Kate? How in the world was he to explain the case to her? He had told her of danger about her path as well as his own, and she had decided to face that danger. For her courage and devotion he loved her; but her obstinacy made him grit his teeth. There was but one grimly comical element in the terrible jumble. What would the King say to Sitabhai when he discovered that she had lost the Luck of the State? In what manner would she veil that loss; and, above all, into what sort of royal rage would she fall? Tarvin shook his head meditatively. 'It's quite bad enough for me,' he said, 'just about as bad as it can possibly be made; but I have a wandering suspicion that it may be unwholesome for Juggut. Yes! I can spare time to be very sorry for Juggut. My fat friend, you should have held straight that first time, outside the city walls!'

He rose and looked out into the sunlight, wondering which of the scattered vagrants by the roadside might be an emissary from the palace. A man lay apparently asleep by the side of his camel near the road that ran to the city. Tarvin stepped out casually from the verandah, and saw, as soon as he was fairly in the open, that the sleeper rolled round to the other side of his beast. He strolled forward a few paces. The sunlight glinted above the back of the camel on something that shone like silver. Tarvin marched straight toward the glitter, his pistol in his hand. The

man, when he came up to him, was buried in
innocent slumber. Under the fold of his garment peered the muzzle of a new and very clean
rifle.

' Looks as if Sitabhai was calling out the militia,
and supplying them with outfits from her private
armoury. Juggut's gun was new, too,' said Tarvin,
standing over the sleeper. ' But this man knows
more about guns than Juggut. Hi!' He stooped
down and stirred the man up with the muzzle of
his revolver. ' I'm afraid I must trouble you for
that gun. And tell the lady to drop it, will you?
It won't pay.'

The man understood the unspoken eloquence
of the pistol, and nothing more. He gave up his
gun sullenly enough, and moved away, lashing his
camel spitefully.

' Now, I wonder how many more of her army
I shall have to disarm,' said Tarvin, retracing his
steps, the captured gun over his shoulder. ' I
wonder—no, I won't believe that she would dare
to do anything to Kate! She knows enough of
me to be sure that I'd blow her and her old palace
into to-morrow. If she's half the woman she
pretends to be, she'll reckon with me before she
goes much further.'

In vain he attempted to force himself into this
belief. Sitabhai had shown him what sort of thing
her mercy might be, and Kate might have tasted
it ere this. To go to her now—to be maimed or
crippled at the least if he went to her now—was
impossible. Yet, he decided that he would go.
He returned hastily to Fibby, whom he had left

not three minutes before flicking flies off in the sunshine at the back of the rest-house. But Fibby lay on his side groaning piteously, hamstrung and dying.

Tarvin could hear his groom industriously polishing a bit round the corner, and when the man came up in response to his call he flung himself down by the side of the horse, howling with grief.

'An enemy hath done this, an enemy hath done this!' he clamoured. 'My beautiful brown horse that never did harm except when he kicked through fulness of meat! Where shall I find a new service if I let my charge die thus?'

'I wish I knew! I wish I knew!' said Tarvin, puzzled, and almost despairing. 'There'd be a bullet through one black head, if I were just a little surer. Get up, you! Fibby, old man, I forgive you all your sins. You were a good old boy, and—here's luck.'

The blue smoke enveloped Fibby's head for an instant, the head fell like a hammer, and the good horse was out of his pain. The groom, rising, rent the air with grief, till Tarvin kicked him out of the pickets and bade him begone. Then it was noticeable that his cries ceased suddenly, and, as he retreated into his mud-house to tie up his effects, he smiled and dug up some silver from a hole under his bedstead.

Tarvin, dismounted, looked east, west, north, south for help, as Sitabhai had looked on the dam. A wandering gang of gipsies with their lean bullocks and yelping dogs turned an angle of the

city wall, and rested like a flock of unclean
birds by the city gate. The sight in itself was
not unusual, but city regulations forbade camping
within a quarter of a mile of the walls.

'Some of the lady's poor relatives, I suppose.
They have blocked the way through the gate pretty
well. Now, if I were to make a bolt of it to
the missionary's they'd have me, wouldn't they?'
muttered Tarvin to himself. 'On the whole, I've
seen prettier professions than trading with Eastern
queens. They don't seem to understand the rules
of the game.'

At that moment a cloud of dust whirled through
the gipsy camp, as the escort of the Maharaj
Kunwar, clearing the way for the barouche,
scattered the dark band to the left and right.
Tarvin wondered what this might portend. The
escort halted with the customary rattle of accoutre-
ments at the rest-house door, the barouche behind
them. A single trooper, two hundred yards or
more in the rear, lifted his voice in a deferential
shout as he pursued the carriage. He was answered
by a chuckle from the escort, and two shrill
screams of delight from the occupants of the
barouche.

A child whom Tarvin had never before seen
stood upright in the back of the carriage, and hurled
a torrent of abuse in the vernacular at the outpaced
trooper. Again the escort laughed.

'Tarvin Sahib! Tarvin Sahib!' piped the
Maharaj Kunwar. 'Come and look at us.'

For a moment Tarvin fancied this a fresh device
of the enemy; but reassured by the sight of his

old and trusted ally, the Maharaj, he stepped
forward

'Prince,' he said, as he took his hand, 'you
ought not to be out.'

'Oh, it is all right,' said the young man hastily,
though his little pale face belied it. 'I gave the
order and we came. Miss Kate gives me orders;
but she took me over to the palace, and there I
give orders. This is Umr Singh—my brother, the
little Prince; but *I* shall be King.'

The second child raised his eyes slowly and
looked full at Tarvin. The eyes and the low
broad forehead were those of Sitabhai, and the
mouth closed firmly over the little pearl-like teeth,
as his mother's mouth had closed in the conflict
on the Dungar Talao.

'He is from the other side of the palace,'
continued the Maharaj, still in English. 'From
the other side, where I must not go. But when I
was in the palace I went to him—ha, ha, Tarvin
Sahib—and he was killing a goat. Look! His
hands are all red now.'

Umr Singh opened a tiny palm at a word from
the Maharaj in the vernacular, and flung it outward at Tarvin. It was dark with dried blood,
and a bearded whisper ran among the escort. The
commandant turned in his saddle, and, nodding at
Tarvin, muttered, '*Sitabhai.*' Tarvin caught the
word, and it was sufficient for him. Providence
had sent him help out of a clear sky. He framed
a plan instantly.

'But how did you come here, you young imps?'
he demanded.

'Oh, there are only women in the palace yonder, and I am a Rajput and a man. He cannot speak any English at all,' he added, pointing to his companion ; 'but when we have played together I have told him about you, Tarvin Sahib, and about the day you picked me out of my saddle, and he wished to come too, to see all the things you show me, so I gave the order very quietly, and we came out of the little door together. And so we are here ! *Salaam, baba,*' he said patronisingly to the child at his side, and the child, slowly and gravely, raised his hand to his forehead, still gazing with fixed, incurious eyes on the stranger. Then he whispered something that made the Maharaj Kunwar laugh. 'He says,' said the Maharaj Kunwar, 'that you are not so big as he thought. His mother told him that you were stronger than any man, but some of these troopers are bigger than you.'

'Well, what do you want me to do?' asked Tarvin.

'Show him your gun, and how you shoot rupees, and what you do that makes horses quiet when they kick, and all those things.'

'All right,' said Tarvin. 'But I can't show them here. Come over to Mr. Estes with me.'

'I do not like to go there. My monkey is dead. And I do not think Kate would like to see us. She is always crying now. She took me up to the palace yesterday, and this morning I went to her again ; but she would not see me.'

Tarvin could have hugged the child for the blessed assurance that Kate at least still lived.

'Isn't she at the hospital, then?' he asked thickly.

'Oh, the hospital has all gone *phut*. There are no women now. They all ran away.'

'No!' cried Tarvin. 'Say that again, little man. What for?'

'Devils,' said the Maharaj Kunwar briefly. 'What do I know? It was some women's talk. Show him how you ride, Tarvin Sahib.'

Again Umr Singh whispered to his companion, and put one leg over the side of the barouche. 'He says he will ride in front of you, as I told him I did,' interpreted the Prince. 'Gurdit Singh, dismount!'

A trooper flung himself out of the saddle on the word, and stood to attention at the horse's head. Tarvin, smiling to himself at the perfection of his opportunity, said nothing, but leapt into the saddle, picked Umr Singh out of his barouche, and placed him carefully before him.

'Sitabhai would be rather restless if she could see me,' he murmured to himself, as he tucked his arm round the lithe little figure. 'I don't think there will be any Juggutting while I carry this young man in front of me.'

As the escort opened to allow Tarvin to take his place at their head, a wandering priest, who had been watching the episode from a little distance, turned and shouted with all the strength of his lungs across the plain, in the direction of the city. The cry was taken up by unseen voices, passed on to the city walls, and died away on the sands beyond.

Umr Singh smiled, as the horse began to trot, and urged Tarvin to go faster. This the Maharaj forbade. He wished to see the sight comfortably from his seat in the barouche. As he passed the gipsy camp, men and women threw themselves down on the sands, crying, '*Jai! Jungle da Badshah jai!*' and the faces of the troopers darkened.

'That means,' cried the Maharaj Kunwar, 'Victory to the King of the Desert. I have no money to give them. Have you, Tarvin Sahib?'

In his joy at being now safely on his way to Kate, Tarvin could have flung everything he possessed to the crowd — almost the Naulahka itself. He emptied a handful of copper and small silver among them, and the cry rose again, but bitter laughter was mingled with it, and the gipsy folk called to each other, mocking. The Maharaj Kunwar's face turned scarlet. He leaned forward listening for an instant, and then shouted, 'By Indur, it is for *him!* Scatter their tents!' At a wave of his hand the escort, wheeling, plunged through the camp in line, driving the light ash of the fires up in clouds, slashing the donkeys with the flat of their swords until they stampeded, and carrying away the frail brown tents on the butts of their reversed lances.

Tarvin looked on contentedly at the dispersal of the group, which he knew would have stopped him if he had been alone.

Umr Singh bit his lip. Then, turning to the Maharaj Kunwar, he smiled, and put forward from his belt the hilt of his sword in sign of fealty.

'It is just, my brother,' he said in the vernacular. 'But I '—here he raised his voice a little—'would not drive the gipsy folk too far. They always return.'

'Ay,' cried a voice from the huddled crowd, watching the wreck of the camp, significantly, 'gipsies always return, my King.'

'So does a dog,' said the Maharaj, between his teeth. 'Both are kicked. Drive on.'

And a pillar of dust came to Estes's house, Tarvin riding in safety in the midst of it.

Telling the boys to play until he came out, he swept into the house, taking the steps two at a time, and discovered Kate in a dark corner of the parlour with a bit of sewing in her hand. As she looked up he saw that she was crying.

'Nick!' she exclaimed voicelessly. '*Nick!*' He had stopped, hesitating on the threshold; she dropped her work, and rose breathless. 'You have come back! It is you! You are alive!'

Tarvin smiled, and held out his arms. 'Come and see!' She took a step forward.

'Oh, I was afraid——'

'Come!'

She went doubtfully toward him. He caught her fast, and held her in his arms.

For a long minute she let her head lie on his breast. Then she looked up. 'This isn't what I meant,' she protested.

'Oh, don't try to improve on it!' Tarvin said hastily.

'She tried to poison me. I was sure when I heard nothing that she must have killed you. I fancied horrible things.'

'Poor child! And your hospital has gone wrong! You have been having a hard time. But we will change all that. We must leave as soon as you can get ready. I've nipped her claws for a moment; I'm holding a hostage. But we can't keep that up for ever. We must get away.'

'We!' she repeated feebly.

'Well, do you want to go alone?'

She smiled as she released herself. 'I want you to.'

'And you?'

'I'm not worth thinking of. I have failed. Everything I meant to do has fallen about me in a heap. I feel burnt out, Nick—burnt out!'

'All right! We'll put in new works and launch you on a fresh system. That's what I want. There shall be nothing to remind you that you ever saw Rhatore, dear.'

'It was a mistake,' she said.

'What?'

'Everything. My coming. My thinking I could do it. It's not a girl's work. It's my work, perhaps; but it's not for me. I have given it up, Nick. Take me home.'

Tarvin gave an unbecoming shout of joy, and folded her in his arms again. He told her that they must be married at once, and start that night, if she could manage it; and Kate, dreading what might befall him, assented doubtfully. She spoke of preparations; but Tarvin said that they would

prepare after they had done it. They could buy
things at Bombay — stacks of things. He was
sweeping her forward with the onrush of his ex-
tempore plans, when she said suddenly, ' But what
of the dam, Nick ? You can't leave that.'

'Shucks !' exclaimed Tarvin heartily. ' You
don't suppose there's any gold in the old river, do
you ?'

She recoiled quickly from his arms, staring at
him in accusation and reproach.

'Do you mean that you have always known
that there was no gold there ?' she asked.

Tarvin pulled himself together quickly; but
not so quickly that she did not catch the confession
in his eye.

'I see you have,' she said coldly.

Tarvin measured the crisis which had suddenly
descended on him out of the clouds ; he achieved
an instantaneous change of front, and met her
smiling.

'Certainly,' he said ; ' I have been working it as
a blind.'

'A blind ?' she repeated. 'To cover what ?'
'You.'

'What do you mean ?' she inquired, with a
look in her eyes which made him uncomfortable.

'The Indian Government allows no one to
remain in the State without a definite purpose.
I couldn't tell Colonel Nolan that I had come
courting you, could I ?'

'I don't know. But you could have avoided
taking the Maharajah's money to carry out this—
this plan. An honest man would have avoided that.'

'Oh, look here!' exclaimed Tarvin.

'How could you cheat the King into thinking that there was a reason for your work, how could you let him give you the labour of a thousand men, how could you take his money? O Nick!'

He gazed at her for a vacant and hopeless minute. 'Why, Kate,' he exclaimed, 'do you know you are talking of the most stupendous joke the Indian empire has witnessed since the birth of time?'

This was pretty good, but it was not good enough. He plunged for a stronger hold as she answered, with a perilous little note of breakdown in her voice, 'You make it worse.'

'Well, your sense of humour never was your strongest point, you know, Kate.' He took the seat next her, leaned over and took her hand, as he went on. 'Doesn't it strike you as rather amusing, though, after all, to rip up half a state to be near a very small little girl—a very sweet, very extra lovely little girl, but still a rather tiny little girl in proportion to the size of the Amet valley? Come—doesn't it?'

'Is that all you have to say?' asked she. Tarvin turned pale. He knew the tone of finality he heard in her voice; it went with a certain look of scorn when she spoke of any form of moral baseness that moved her. He recognised his condemnation in it and shuddered. In the moment that passed, while he still kept silence, he recognised this for the crisis of his life. Then he took strong hold of himself, and said quietly, easily, unscrupulously—

x

'Why, you don't suppose that I'm not going to ask the Maharajah for his bill, do you?'

She gasped a little. Her acquaintance with Tarvin did not help her to follow his dizzying changes of front. His bird's skill to make his level flight, his reeling dips and circling returns upon himself, all seem part of a single impulse, must ever remain confusing to her. But she rightly believed in his central intention to do the square thing, if he could find out what it was; and her belief in his general strength helped her not to see at this moment that he was deriving his sense of the square thing from herself. She could not know, and probably could not have imagined, how little his own sense of the square thing had to do with any system of morality, and how entirely he must always define morality as what pleased Kate. Other women liked confections; she preferred morality, and he meant she should have it, if he had to turn pirate to get it for her.

'You didn't think I wasn't paying for the show?' he pursued bravely; but in his heart he was saying, 'She loathes it. She hates it. Why didn't I think; why didn't I think?' He added aloud, 'I had my fun, and now I've got you. You're both cheap at the price, and I'm going to step up and pay it like a little man. You must know that.'

His smile met no answering smile. He mopped his forehead and stared anxiously at her. All the easiness in the world couldn't make him sure what she would say next. She said nothing, and he had to go on desperately, with a cold fear gathering about his heart. ' Why, it's just like me, isn't it, Kate, to work a scheme on the old Maharajah? It's like a man who owns a mine that's turning out $2000 a month, to rig a game out in this desert country to do a confiding Indian Prince out of a few thousand rupees?' He advanced this recently inspired conception of his conduct with an air of immemorial familiarity, born of desperation.

' What mine?' she asked, with dry lips.

' The "Lingering Lode," of course. You've heard me speak of it?'

' Yes, but I didn't know——'

' That it was doing that? Well, it is—right along. Want to see the assay?'

' No,' she answered. ' No. But that makes you——Why, but, Nick, that makes you——'

' A rich man? Moderately, while the lead holds out. Too rich for petty larceny, I guess.'

He was joking for his life. The heart-sickening seriousness of his unseriousness was making a hole in his head; the tension was too much for him. In the mad fear of that moment his perceptions doubled their fineness. Something went through him as he said ' larceny.' Then his heart stopped. A sure, awful, luminous perception leaped upon him, and he knew himself for lost.

If she hated this, what would she say to the other? Innocent, successful, triumphant, even gay it seemed to him; but what to her? He turned sick.

Kate or the Naulahka. He must choose. The Naulahka or Kate?

' Don't make light of it,' she was saying.

'You would be just as honest if you couldn't afford it, Nick. Ah,' she went on, laying her hand on his lightly, in mute petition for having even seemed to doubt him, 'I know you, Nick! You like to make the better seem the worse reason; you like to pretend to be wicked. But who is so honest? O Nick! I knew you had to be true. If you weren't, everything else would be wrong.'

He took her in his arms. 'Would it, little girl?' he asked, looking down at her. 'We must keep the other things right, then, at any expense.'

He heaved a deep sigh as he stooped and kissed her.

'Have you such a thing as a box?' he asked, after a long pause.

'Any sort of box?' asked Kate bewilderedly.

'No—well, it ought to be the finest box in the world, but I suppose one of those big grape boxes will do. It isn't every day that one sends presents to a queen.'

Kate handed him a large chip box in which long green grapes from Kabul had been packed. Discoloured cotton wool lay at the bottom.

'That was sold at the door the other day,' she said. 'Is it big enough?'

Tarvin turned away without answering, emptied something that clicked like a shower of pebbles upon the wool, and sighed deeply. Topaz was in that box. The voice of the Maharaj Kunwar lifted itself from the next room.

'Tarvin Sahib—Kate, we have eaten all the fruit, and now we want to do something else.'

'One moment, little man,' said Tarvin.   With
his back still toward Kate, he drew his hand
caressingly, for the last time, over the blazing heap
at the bottom of the box, fondling the stones one
by one.   The great green emerald pierced him, he
thought, with a reproachful gaze.   A mist crept
into his eyes : the diamond was too bright.   He
shut the lid down upon the box hastily, and put it
into Kate's hands with a decisive gesture ; he made
her hold it while he tied it in silence.   Then, in a
voice not his, he asked her to take the box to
Sitabhai with his compliments.   'No,' he continued, seeing the alarm in her eyes.   'She won't
—she daren't hurt you now.   Her child's coming
along with us ; and I'll go with you, of course, as
far as I can.   Glory be, it's the last journey that
you'll ever undertake in this infernal land.   The
last but one, that's to say.   We live at high
pressure in Rhatore—too high pressure for me.
Be quick, if you love me.'

Kate hastened to put on her helmet, while
Tarvin amused the two princes by allowing them
to inspect his revolver, and promising at some
more fitting season to shoot as many coins as
they should demand.   The lounging escort at
the door was suddenly scattered by a trooper
from without, who flung his horse desperately
through their ranks, shouting, 'A letter for
Tarvin Sahib !'

Tarvin stepped into the verandah, took a
crumpled half-sheet of paper from the outstretched
hand, and read these words, traced painfully and
laboriously in an unformed round hand :—

'DEAR MR. TARVIN—Give me the boy and keep the other thing. Your affectionate

FRIEND.'

Tarvin chuckled and thrust the note into his waistcoat pocket. 'There is no answer,' he said —and to himself: 'You're a thoughtful girl, Sitabhai, but I'm afraid you're just a little too thoughtful. That boy's wanted for the next half-hour. Are you ready, Kate?'

The princes lamented loudly when they were told that Tarvin was riding over to the palace at once, and that, if they hoped for further entertainment, they must both go with him. 'We will go into the great Durbar Hall,' said the Maharaj Kunwar consolingly to his companion at last, 'and make all the music-boxes play together.'

'I want to see that man shoot,' said Umr Singh. 'I want to see him shoot something dead. I do not wish to go to the palace.'

'You'll ride on my horse,' said Tarvin, when the answer had been interpreted, 'and I'll make him gallop all the way. Say, Prince, how fast do you think your carriage can go?'

'As fast as Miss Kate dares.'

Kate stepped in, and the cavalcade galloped to the palace, Tarvin riding always a little in front with Umr Singh clapping his hands on the saddle-bow.

'We must pull up at Sitabhai's wing, dear,' Tarvin cried. 'You won't be afraid to walk in under the arch with me?'

'I trust you, Nick,' she answered simply, getting out of the carriage.

'Then go in to the women's wing. Give the box into Sitabhai's hands, and tell her that I sent it back. You'll find she knows my name.'

The horse trampled under the archway, Kate at its side, and Tarvin holding Umr Singh very much in evidence. The courtyard was empty, but as they came out into the sunshine by the central fountain the rustle and whisper behind the shutters rose, as the tiger-grass rustles when the wind blows through it.

'One minute, dear,' said Tarvin, halting, 'if you can bear this sun on your head.'

A door opened and a eunuch came out, beckoning silently to Kate. She followed him and disappeared, the door closing behind her. Tarvin's heart rose into his mouth, and unconsciously he clasped Umr Singh so closely to his breast that the child cried out.

The whisper rose, and it seemed to Tarvin as if some one were sobbing behind the shutters. Then followed a peal of low, soft laughter, and the muscles at the corner of Tarvin's mouth relaxed. Umr Singh began to struggle in his arms.

'Not yet, young man. You must wait until— ah! thank God.'

Kate reappeared, her little figure framed against the darkness of the doorway. Behind her came the eunuch, crawling fearfully to Tarvin's side. Tarvin smiled affably, and dropped the amazed young prince into his arms. Umr Singh was borne away kicking, and ere they left the courtyard Tarvin heard the dry roar of an angry child, followed by an unmistakable yelp of pain. Tarvin smiled.

'They spank young princes in Rajputana.
That's one step on the path to progress. What
did she say, Kate?'

'She said I was to be sure and tell you that she
knew you were not afraid. "Tell Tarvin Sahib
that I knew he was not afraid."'

'Where's Umr Singh?' asked the Maharaj
Kunwar from the barouche.

'He's gone to his mother. I'm afraid I can't
amuse you just now, little man. I've forty thousand things to do, and no time to do them in.
Tell me where your father is.'

'I do not know. There has been trouble and
crying in the palace. The women are always
crying, and that makes my father angry. I shall
stay at Mr. Estes', and play with Kate.'

'Yes. Let him stay,' said Kate quickly.
'Nick, do you think I ought to leave him?'

'That's another of the things I must fix,' said
Tarvin. 'But first I must find the Maharajah, if
I have to dig up Rhatore for him. What's that,
little one?'

A trooper whispered to the young Prince.

'This man says that he is there,' said the
Maharaj Kunwar. 'He has been there since two
days. I also have wished to see him.'

'Very good. Drive home, Kate. I'll wait
here.'

He re-entered the archway, and reined up.
Again the whisper behind the shutter rose; and a
man from a doorway demanded his business.

'I must see the Maharajah,' said Tarvin.

'Wait,' said the man. And Tarvin waited for

a full five minutes, using his time for concentrated thought.

Then the Maharajah emerged, and amiability sat on every hair of his newly-oiled moustache.

For some mysterious reason Sitabhai had withdrawn the light of her countenance from him for two days, and had sat raging in her own apartments. Now the mood had passed, and the gipsy would see him again. Therefore the Maharajah's heart was glad within him ; and wisely, as befitted the husband of many wives, he did not inquire too closely into the reasons that had led to the change.

'Ah, Tarvin Sahib,' said he, 'I have not seen you for long. What is the news from the dam ? Is there anything to see ?'

'Maharajah Sahib, that's what I've come to talk about. There is nothing to see, and I think that there is no gold to be got at.'

'That is bad,' said the King lightly.

'But there is a good deal to be seen, if you care to come along. I don't want to waste your money any more, now I'm sure of the fact ; but I don't see the use of saving all the powder on the dam. There must be five hundred pounds of it.'

'I do not understand,' said the Maharajah, whose mind was occupied with other things.

'Do you want to see the biggest explosion that you've ever seen in your life? Do you want to hear the earth shake, and see the rocks fly ?'

The Maharajah's face brightened.

'Will it be seen from the palace ?' he said ; 'from the top of the palace ?'

'Oh yes. But the best place to watch it will

be from the side of the river. I shall put the
river back at five o'clock. It's three o'clock now.
Will you be there, Maharajah Sahib?'

'I will be there. It will be a big *tamasha*.
Five hundred pounds of powder! The earth will
be rent in two.'

'I should remark. And after that, Maharajah
Sahib, I am going to be married; and then I am
going away. Will you come to the wedding?'

The Maharajah shaded his eyes from the sun-
glare, and peered up at Tarvin under his turban.

'By God, Tarvin Sahib,' said he, 'you are a
quick man. So you will marry the doctor-lady,
and then you will go away? I will come to the
wedding. I and Pertab Singh.'

The next two hours in the life of Nicholas
Tarvin will never be adequately chronicled. There
was a fierce need upon him to move mountains
and shift the poles of the earth; there was a strong
horse beneath him, and in his heart the knowledge
that he had lost the Naulahka and gained Kate.
When he appeared, a meteor amid the coolies on
the dam, they understood, and a word was spoken
that great things were toward. The gang foreman
turned to his shouts, and learned that the order
of the day was destruction—the one thing that the
Oriental fully comprehends.

They dismantled the powder-shed with outcries
and fierce yells, hauled the bullock-carts from the
crown of the dam, and dropped the derrick after
them, and tore down the mat and grass coolie-
lines. Then, Tarvin urging them always, they

buried the powder-casks in the crown of the half-built dam, piled the wrapped charges upon them, and shovelled fresh sand atop of all.

It was a hasty onslaught, but the powder was at least all in one place ; and it should be none of Tarvin's fault if the noise and smoke at least did not delight the Maharajah.

A little before five he came with his escort, and Tarvin, touching fire to a many-times-lengthened fuse, bade all men run back. The fire ate slowly the crown of the dam. Then with a dull roar the dam opened out its heart in a sheet of white flame, and the masses of flying earth darkened the smoke above.

The ruin closed on itself for an instant ere the waters of the Amet plunged forward into the gap, made a boiling rapid, and then spread themselves lazily along their accustomed levels.

The rain of things descending pitted the earth of the banks and threw the water in sheets and spurts. Then only the smoke and the blackened flanks of the dam, crumbling each minute as the river sucked them down, remained to tell of the work that had been.

' And now, Maharajah Sahib, what do I owe you ?' said Tarvin, after he had satisfied himself that none of the more reckless coolies had been killed.

' That was very fine,' said the Maharajah. ' I never saw that before. It is a pity that it cannot come again.'

' What do I owe you ?' repeated Tarvin.

' For that ? Oh, they were my people. They ate a little grain, and many were from my jails.

The powder was from the arsenal. What is the use to talk of paying? Am I a *bunnia* that I can tell what there is to pay? It was a fine *tamasha*. By God, there is no dam left at all.'

'You might let me put it right.'

'Tarvin Sahib, if you waited one year, or perhaps two years, you would get a bill; and besides, if anything was paid, the men who pay the convicts would take it all, and I should not be richer. They were my people, and the grain was cheap, and they have seen the *tamasha*. Enough. It is not good to talk of payment. Let us return to the city. By God, Tarvin Sahib, you are a quick man. Now there will be no one to play pachisi with me or to make me laugh. And the Maharaj Kunwar will be sorry also. But it is good that a man should marry. Yes, it is good. Why do you go, Tarvin Sahib? Is it an order of the Government?'

'Yes; the American Government. I am wanted there to help govern my State.'

'No telegram has come for you,' said the King simply. 'But you are so quick.'

Tarvin laughed lightly, wheeled his horse, and was gone, leaving the King interested but unmoved. He had finally learned to accept Tarvin and his ways as a natural phenomenon beyond control. As he drew rein instinctively opposite the missionary's door and looked for an instant at the city, the sense of the otherness of things daily seen that heralds swift coming change smote the mind of the American, and he shivered. 'It was a bad dream—a very bad dream,' he muttered, 'and the

worst of it is not one of the boys in Topaz would
ever believe half of it.' Then the eyes that swept the
arid landscape twinkled with many reminiscences.
'Tarvin, my boy, you've played with a kingdom,
and for results it lays over monkeying with the
buzz-saw. You were left when you sized this State
up for a played-out hole in the ground; badly left.
If you have been romping around six months after
something you hadn't the sabe to hold when you'd
got it you've learned that much. . . . Topaz!
Poor old Topaz!' Again his eyes ran round the
tawny horizon, and he laughed aloud. The little
town under the shadow of Big Chief, ten thousand miles away and all ignorant of the mighty
machinery that had moved on its behalf, would
have resented that laugh; for Tarvin, fresh from
events that had shaken Rhatore to its heart, was
almost patronising the child of his ambition.

He brought his hand down on his thigh with
a smack, and turned his horse toward the telegraph-
office. 'How in the name of all that's good and
holy,' said he, 'am I to clear up this business with
the Mutrie? Even a copy of the Naulahka in glass
would make her mouth water.' The horse cantered
on steadily, and Tarvin dismissed the matter with
a generous sweep of his free hand. 'If I can stand
it she can. But I'll prepare her by electricity.'

The dove-coloured telegraph-operator and Postmaster-General of the State remembers even to-day
how the Englishman who was not an Englishman,
and, therefore, doubly incomprehensible, climbed
for the last time up the narrow stairs, sat down
in the broken chair, and demanded absolute silence;

how, at the end of fifteen minutes' portentous meditation and fingering of a thin moustache, he sighed heavily as is the custom of Englishmen when they have eaten that which disagrees with them, waved the operator aside, called up the next office, and clicked off a message with a haughty and high-stepping action of the hands. How he lingered long and lovingly over the last click, applied his ear to the instrument as though it could answer, and turning with a large sweet smile said—
'Finis, Babu. Make a note of that,' and swept forth chanting the war-cry of his State :

> It is not wealth nor rank nor state,
> But get-up-and-git that makes men great.

.   .   .   .   .   .

The bullock-cart creaked down the road to Rawut Junction in the first flush of a purple evening, and the low ranges of the Aravallis showed as many coloured cloud banks against the turquoise sky-line. Behind it the red rock of Rhatore burned angrily on the yellow floors of the desert, speckled with the shadows of the browsing camels. Overhead the crane and the wild duck were flocking back to their beds in the reeds, and grey monkeys, family by family, sat on the roadside, their arms round one another's necks. The evening star came up from behind a jagged peak of rock and brushwood, so that its reflection might swim undisturbed at the bottom of an almost dried reservoir, buttressed with time-yellowed marble and flanked with silver plume-grass. Between the star and the earth wheeled huge fox-headed bats and night-jars hawking for the feather-winged moths. The buffaloes had left their water-holes, and the cattle were lying down for the night. Then villagers in far-away huts began to sing, and the hillsides were studded with home lights. The bullocks grunted as the driver twisted their tails, and the high grass by the roadside brushed with the wash of a wave of the open beach against the slow-turning tyres.

The first breath of a cold-weather night made Kate wrap her rugs about her more closely. Tarvin was sitting at the back of the cart, swinging his legs and staring at Rhatore before the bends of the roads should hide it. The realisation of defeat, remorse, and the torture of an over well-trained conscience were yet to come to Kate. In that hour, luxuriously disposed upon many cushions, she realised nothing more than a woman's complete contentment with the fact that there was a man in the world to do things for her, though she had not yet learned to lose her interest in how they were done.

The reiterated and passionate farewells of the women in the palace, and the cyclonic sweep of a wedding at which Nick had refused to efface himself as a bridegroom should, but had flung all their world forward on the torrent of his own vitality, had worn her out. The yearning of homesickness —she had seen it in Mrs. Estes' wet eyes at the missionary's house an hour before—lay strong upon her, and she would fain have remembered her plunge into the world's evil as a dream of the night, but—

'Nick,' she said, softly.

'What is it, little woman?'

'Oh, nothing : I was thinking. Nick, what *did* you do about the Maharaj Kunwar?'

'He's fixed, or I'm mistaken. Don't worry your head about that. After I'd explained a thing or two to old man Nolan he seemed to think well of inviting that young man to board with him until he starts for the Mayo College. Tumble?'

'His poor mother! If only I could have——'

'But you couldn't, little woman. Hi! Look quick, Kate! There she goes! The last of Rhatore.'

A string of coloured lights, high up on the hanging gardens of the palace, was being blotted out behind the velvet blackness of a hill shoulder. Tarvin leaped to his feet, caught the side of the cart, and bowed profoundly after the Oriental manner.

The lights disappeared one by one, even as the glories of a necklace had slidden into a Kabuli grape-box, till there remained only the flare from a window on a topmost bastion—a point of light as red and as remote as the blaze of the Black Diamond. That passed too, and the soft darkness rose out of the earth fold upon fold wrapping the man and the woman.

'After all,' said Tarvin, addressing the new-lighted firmament, 'that was distinctly a side issue.'

THE END